Alexander Lyman Holley

Memorial of Alexander Lyman Holley, C. E., LL. D.

Alexander Lyman Holley

Memorial of Alexander Lyman Holley, C. E., LL. D.

ISBN/EAN: 9783744714884

Printed in Europe, USA, Canada, Australia, Japan

Cover: Foto ©Raphael Reischuk / pixelio.de

More available books at **www.hansebooks.com**

MEMORIAL

OF

ALEXANDER LYMAN HOLLEY, C.E. LL.D.

PRESIDENT OF THE AMERICAN INSTITUTE OF MINING ENGINEERS, VICE-
PRESIDENT OF THE AMERICAN SOCIETY OF CIVIL ENGINEERS, VICE-
PRESIDENT OF THE AMERICAN SOCIETY OF MECHANICAL ENGI-
NEERS, MEMBER OF THE INSTITUTION OF CIVIL ENGINEERS,
AND OF THE IRON AND STEEL INSTITUTE OF GREAT
BRITAIN, ETC., ETC.

BORN JULY 20, 1832. DIED JANUARY 29, 1882.

———————

PUBLISHED BY THE AMERICAN INSTITUTE OF MINING ENGINEERS,

AT THE OFFICE OF THE SECRETARY,

13 BURLING SLIP, NEW YORK CITY.

1884.

CONTENTS.

PREFACE.

THE Chairman of the Memorial Session of the American Institute of Mining Engineers, held at Washington in February, 1882, was charged with the duty of preparing an address, in commemoration of the life and life-work of ALEXANDER LYMAN HOLLEY, and the Council of the Institute was at the same time requested to take into consideration the publication of a Memorial Volume, to contain the above-mentioned address, the proceedings of that meeting, and such other matters as it might be deemed expedient to include in it.

In accordance with that request, the Council now issues the present volume, concerning the contents and scope of which a few words may fitly be said in this place.

It was evidently proper that the proceedings of other societies, as well as our own, in honor of Mr. Holley, should be published in this connection. Upon that head no explanation is needed, beyond the expression of regret that the record is incomplete—the action of various societies and the eulogies pronounced by many admirers not having been communicated to the secretary of the Institute. The testimony of the press, technical and non-technical, was overwhelmingly abundant; but, upon due consideration, it was decided that the obituary notices and articles published in American and foreign journals should be omitted, because to publish them would be to occupy many pages with but slightly varied repetitions of the leading facts of Mr. Holley's career.

It was the general desire of members of the Institute that Mr. Holley's professional papers and addresses, and also, if possible, some or all of his brilliant speeches should be included in the volume.

With regard to the former, a reference to the catalogue, beginning on page 143, will show that their number was so great as to preclude all idea of comprehending them in a single book. More-over, most of them were accompanied with plates, which could not well be reproduced or included in a work of the present character. A few papers and addresses, not illustrated with drawings, and adapted to display the versatile ability of their author, have, therefore, been selected; and it is believed that the choice thus made will be generally approved.

Concerning his humorous and eloquent speeches on special occa-sions, difficulty of another sort has been encountered. It is, per-haps, not just to the memory of any man to make public after his death what he deliberately and intentionally withheld from publi-cation during his lifetime. In this case, the notes for many occa-sional speeches, found among Mr. Holley's papers by his biographer, would give, if published, no adequate notion of the speeches them-selves. They do not even accurately convey what he said—still less, the personal charm of his presence and manner. As the editor of *London Engineering* has justly said : " We think that American engineers cordially acceded to him the place of orator *par excellence* of the profession. . . . Holley was both orator and poet in his speech ; his voice was beautiful and under perfect training ; his power of language as remarkable as his readiness at all times to em-ploy it to good and emphatic purpose."

It is notoriously impossible to preserve in printed words the power and the effect of such gifts. Some hint of them may be obtained from his speeches, in reception of the Pittsburgh testimonial, and at the De Lesseps banquet, which are given in full in the following pages, and from several extracts contained in the Memorial Address. As an example of his wit and ready command of language, the " Metallurgist's Ode to Spring," read at the Baltimore banquet of the Institute, has been selected.

To complete the record contained in this book, it is necessary to add a brief statement of the circumstances of Mr. Holley's death, January 29th, 1882. He had already once recovered, in the sum-mer of 1881, from a supposed bilious attack, which was universally expected to prove fatal, and had enjoyed another year of sufficient health and strength to permit the resumption of professional work. But his malady (subsequently proved to be an internal tumor, obstructing the gall-duct, and producing many apparent symptoms of liver-disease) was, in its nature, incurable. Early in the autumn of 1881 he was attacked, during a professional journey in Belgium, with what he deemed to be a malarial ague. Unable to throw it off, he went forward, nevertheless, with desperate resolution until he had completed, in England and Scotland, the programme of his work. To his wife and daughters, then travelling in Europe, he made light of his illness, lest they should abandon their tour to rejoin him; and when at last the family was reunited in London, the anxiety of all was concentrated upon the terrible fever which had seized the elder daughter, rather than the slow disease which was gradually stealing upon the father. Relieved at last from the worst pressure of this anxiety, Mr. Holley could give some attention to his own condition, and, soon concluding that in London, at least, he could not get well, he returned to this country, leaving his family to follow, a few weeks later, with the convalescent invalid. Up to the time of their sailing from England, he seemed to maintain a cheerful hope of recovery, and dictated frequent encouraging dispatches to them, rapidly arranging, at the same time, his business affairs, with, perhaps, unconscious prescience of the end. Five days before his death, the certainty of a fatal termination was recognized by all, and the only question left was, whether he would live to greet once more those who, comforted by his last, cheerful message, were on their way to him across the sea. It was not to be; they reached the house a few moments after he had passed away.

The portrait of Mr. Holley, which constitutes the frontispiece of this volume, shows him, as all who knew him will delight to remember him, in the healthful vigor of his prime. Strength and beauty, courage and gentleness, enthusiasm and judgment, earnest purpose and happy humor, were blended in his face, as they were, in overflowing power yet exquisite balance, united in his character and illustrated in his life.

MEMORIAL

OF

ALEXANDER LYMAN HOLLEY.

I.

FUNERAL SERVICES.

FEBRUARY 1, 1882.

Private Service held at the House, Brooklyn, N. Y.

HYMN.—"Nearer, my God, to Thee."
SCRIPTURE.—Psalm XXIII.
REMARKS.—By Rev. Joseph Twichell, of Hartford, Conn.

It is left for me to say a word—the last in his own dwelling—by the side of the remains of our dear friend; and since, lacking a few words from me, no words will be spoken, I may be permitted to say that while in my thoughts and in my heart I can compass, so far as ever we can, the theme of this event of his departure from our midst, I feel wholly unable to compass it in words. It seems the strangest thing in the world, the most impossible thing in the world, that he is dead. They seem incredible words, when they are taken upon the lips, that Alexander Holley is dead, and that we shall see him no more in this world. For a good many years, to me, as to many of us here, he stood as the image of vitality, physically, mentally, and in his affections. He was full of ripe fruit. How active he was! What a vivacity he had! What a spring! What an overflow of animal spirits! What a pleasure it was to meet him! How cordial his greeting was! He was one of those friends whose countenance made your face to shine. It was a joy to come in contact with him. What a sweet and sudden surprise at meeting he would always testify! Is it possible that that great pleasure of life for many of us has been tasted for the last time? Shall we never see

2

that dancing eye again? Shall we never again hear with joy that cordial greeting? I can hardly believe that he lies helpless in the coffin here before us.

Then, as to his mental activity, we never saw him, in all these many past years, that his mind was not in full movement—in full play; that he was not engaged in a tough, sturdy, mental struggle with some matter on hand, or reaching out in plans which were always for the benefit of mankind—for selfishness had a very small part in his composition. There was a live, a bright prospectus always within him, which he had a cheerful confidence, and with good ground that he could realize; and how many anticipations of his he did realize! I think he could say, as few men can, to God, who endowed him as few men have been endowed, "I have done what I could." God gave him great powers, extraordinary capacities; He gave him a genius for work; and throughout all his working years (indeed they. *were* working years), he put forth those powers to the utmost; and that he did with them the best that could be done, stands to his record. It is a glorious record for any man. Is it possible that all this activity of mind is forever stayed, arrested at its very height and prime, and in its mid-career? I do not believe it for a moment; it is impossible to believe it.

Now, as to his life in its affections. Only those (and they are not few) to whom God gave it for a good gift to be in close personal relations with him, can know what an ocean of love his heart was out-pouring—*always* outpouring. It was more blessed to give than to receive with him, always. When you met him it was evident that it was he that gave and you that received, liberally. It was perfectly evident that his ruling idea always was to make his meeting with you a pleasure to you as well as to himself. He went through these years of his labor, I believe, with a great interest, in the first place, in the public to which he belonged, and, in the second place, with a deep and tender interest in all those in the private circles to which he belonged, dominant in him; and God has given him to confer unusual benefit and pleasure upon us. He has been a maker of happiness in this world—this beloved man. A great many of us feel that we never can enjoy such a friendship again; our hearts are in his coffin; and a large part of our hearts are going into the grave, never again to live in this world. Oh, that God might make all our hearts and our lives as rich as his has been!

May God comfort those (He alone can do it) who stand most bereaved in this desolate time. May the Lord approach them as He knows how. May the Lord draw near to them, and by those immortal intimations which He can give, lead them into the region of serene, triumphant rest in Jesus Christ.

HYMN.—" Friend after friend departs."

PRAYER.—By Rev. H. W. Beecher.

HYMN.—" There's a land that is fairer than day."

Public Service held at Plymouth Church, Brooklyn, N. Y.

PROCESSIONAL ANTHEM.—" Fair are these houses, fairer far the dwelling built by the Master."

HYMN.—" Tranquil and peaceful is the path to heaven."

SCRIPTURE.—Psalm XC.

HYMN.—Solo, " O heart, that, sad and weary, dost count thy load too great."

SCRIPTURE.—II. Cor. IV., 12–18; II. Cor. V., 1–8.

REMARKS.—By Rev. H. W. Beecher.

There has come down to us from the ages the yearning and the sorrowing cry that life is so short; that its scenes are so interrupted; that its outcome, often, is so small; and especially when life has been abundant in its offerings and blessings, that death, like an untimely frost, falls upon the garden of our expectations and blights everything. There is a longing in nature itself that the seed should not perish with the blossom, but should sow itself again somewhere in a fairer clime and in a longer summer. Talk as we will in regard to these subjects (and I am not saying that that is true which we want to be true, and that there is a heaven of hope and immortality merely because we long for it; I am not entrapped in any such thought as that), we must own that this hope, which has sprung up even in the barbaric soul and rudely pictured to itself another life out of the material with which the yet unopened thought of man could best furnish itself, has grown brighter, stronger, deeper, as men have emerged from ignorance and have advanced in civilization. It meets rebuffs, resistance or a calm endurance of unbelief in only here and there a pioneering soul that goes into the realm of the uncertain future, seeking by the analogies of inferior matter to determine what shall be the estate of superior matter. And whatever men may say in regard to the organization of the soul, whether it be regarded as an immutable spirit, or whether it be regarded as the most exquisitely organized matter, one thing is certain—that if it be spirit, it does not necessarily perish with the body; and if it be matter, it does not necessarily perish with the body; for, as rude and inchoately organized matter is subject to its own laws, as compared with the highest forms of organization, so it may be that this asserted last development of matter has laws occult and unknown to us, and is neither to be measured by our measure nor weighed by our scales, but weighed and measured by laws of its own. On either hand, therefore, I do not feel that we are driven into unbelief, or into a hopeless yearning or longing that amounts to unbelief in the continued ongoing of our personal existence organized in this life.

And why should we wish to doubt it? Why should we, who are faring through this troubled life, so often becalmed or bestormed, so often over-weighted, so continually helpless in the presence of those great movements which are going on in the visible and in the invisible world, wish to blot out almost the only hope left to wretchedness, to weakness and to despondency.

There is not a cradle which empties its contents into the grave, that does not cry out to us to believe that there is something beyond the grave. There is not an anchored love which finds itself driven from its moorings that does not beseech us to believe that there is a haven beyond. There is not one single experience of wasting strength, whether it be by sickness or by age, that does not lament in the thought that we shall have accomplished all that is given us to accomplish, and that we shall have no other chance. Whether we look to superior wisdom, to affection, or to sentiment, they all point alike in the one direction of the beyond, the greater, the nobler—in the direction of that sphere where human life, comprehensively, shall evolve and take on its next and grandest stage.

But there is another view of this subject which has its standpoint in pride and the better sense of pride. It is an emanation of that royalty which every man feels in himself; for there is not a man worthy of the name who, at some hour, does not know that he is crowned and that he is a king; and by as much as we feel the sweep of intellect, and survey our knowledge, and the power of knowledge; by as much as we feel heroic impulses and are driven to noble and generous deeds thereby; by as much as we have those flashes and intimations, obscure though they may be, but of endless power; by so much we refuse to die and to be dead eternally; by so much we demand that there shall be to us something beyond (even in their best estate) those miserable experiences of life which are rebuked day by day by our ideality, and which day by day are put under foot and measured at their true value by our imagination.

When, therefore, there comes to us, clear as the unspotted heaven washed after storms, and associated with all that is most venerable and useful, a faith that brings with it all the most noble minds that ever lived on the face of the earth—when such a hope hangs over the future, why should we forge missiles to destroy it? Why should we smash the bells that are ringing out this hope, and bearing us on waves of music over the rude difficulties of life, into the blessed conception of another life?

And where shall we find expressions more simple, more manly, and more sublime, than those that were uttered by the apostle Paul, in these fourth and fifth chapters of the Second Corinthians? Where is there a thought of death that so rebukes the ineffable weakness of a poor, defrauding materialism?

Is death, then, the running down of the clock? and is that the end? Is death that which makes a man only the same as an animal or a vegetable—a decaying root, a wasted seed—that and nothing more? No; the apostle, looking down into the grave, says, "The man is not buried there. Death is buried there. Life is there testified to. Death is swallowed up in life."

We are united, then, in that grand hope which has been the best legacy of days gone by, inspired by our best feelings when we are in our most noble state, inspired by all the hopes that we have, inspired by all our pride, and inspired by the faith of immortality.

As to reasoning, when I require reasoning to make me admire the grandeur of the Transfiguration of Raphael, or of the figures which Michel Angelo painted; when I call mathematics and logic to teach me that these are sublime and beautiful; then I will need reasoning to keep my soul from belief in the degrading abomination of annihilation. Nay, I hold with ineffable faith to my very soul the bright vision of a world to come, where the glory of the Lord is revealed, and where we are lifted without hindrance or obstruction into the full sphere and dignity of sons of God.

We are gathered, this morning, my friends, at this unaccustomed hour, and in this unaccustomed place, not alone to express our profound sympathy with a beloved household whose door has been opened from the earthly into the heavenly sphere, but also to speak of one who, as a citizen and as a professional laborer in the great fields of knowledge and of attainment, has done well by the commonwealth, and by mankind. Without stopping to rank men, as to which is highest or lowest, all men are honorable who keep time to the great march of humanity and of benevolence. Some may be

leaders, and some may be subalterns. The honor of the lowest is
greater than any other honor bestowed upon mankind; but as they
go up and their sphere and privilege of usefulness is widened, so also
is our intelligent admiration of them, and so, likewise, is our desire
to express, in some worthy way, our esteem for them, and our honor-
ing thought of them.

Our friend who has gone from us, richly endowed, holding in
himself the legacy of the past, springing from a parentage that had
in it a gathered excellence of the best New England sort (there may
be better, but not on this soil), born under propitious influences, with
the luminous door of education thrown wide open, following the
bent of his genius, turned aside from one path of scholarship, from
classical lore, to that scientific walk which had in it not alone a wide
range of intelligence and invention, but also a wide range of instruction.

Now, there has come to be a better understanding in our days—
an understanding that men who build in matter, or distribute it, or
change its forms to better uses, are almoners of God's great benevolence. If one were so rich that he could give to men a thousand
tons of grain, that certainly would be a great gift of benevolence;
but if one should, by his invention, so alter the machinery of agriculture that the poorest man could earn a thousand tons of grain for
himself, that would be a greater benevolence, and a greater gift. If
one were to supply all the implements of a refined industry, himself
paying the cost, that would certainly be a very noble benefaction;
but if one may take hold, as a master-spirit, of all the metals, and
command them into forms, and at such rates that they shall become
the common property of the whole community, is not that a greater
benefaction? He who supplies the lack of men gives a great deal;
but he who teaches men to supply their own lack gives even more.
And the whole pursuit of the life of him who has left us and gone
singing to a higher bough of the Tree of Life, was a beneficence; it
was an organized bounty. Consciously and unconsciously, he served
his day and generation in this field; and with such fruitfulness and
such success that it is the testimony of all his compeers and associates
that he stood easily among the first.

But quite aside from this, his spirit, his manliness, his exquisite
modesty and diffidence have plucked all the nettles of envy; and
he is crowned with no thorns among the bay leaves, and stands
honored because he was beloved by all those who were most intimate

with him, and associated with him in the great undertakings which have been so much to this nation and generation.

He was a man of boundless industry; a man of fruitful invention; a successful man in the execution of untried schemes largely developed through him, and through those who were associated with him, never failing to give them due praise, and only taking the least portion to himself, even if he took any. Such buoyancy, such sweetness of temper, such unaffected modesty, such genuine affection, such generous sincerity, and such a luminous manhood had he, that you who were among the representatives of that great, growing and honored class to which he belonged, desire to express in this public way your estimation of him, and to raise, if not a monument to the outer eye, yet a monument in thoughts, to the man who has gone higher.

To my thought he stands unspeakably higher, now that he has buried himself as to outward form. All that is mortal is swallowed up of life. He rests, that gave himself no rest. He shines in full, that was inclosed but in a lantern while on earth. He sought and searched, but now he knows. He tried and experimented, but now all things lie open and plain to his easy soul. He looks down from no tombstone; he looks up from no grave; but in his Father's home, where many have stood waiting for him to come, I believe in my very soul that he rests from his earthly labors, and looking back, sees that they do follow him—that the good he did upon earth is marching on, and that multitudes, unknowing who blessed them, will go to meet him in that heavenly land.

Is there any greater honor that can be bestowed on a man than to say that he took loyally all the gifts that God gave him, to use them not for himself, but in genuine modesty and simplicity for others? He lived in the atmosphere of benefaction, and was surrounded by another atmosphere of respect and of love.

His end was given to him soon. He was permitted earlier than many of us to fly away and be at rest. Not those that live longest are most fortunate, but those who live best and are soonest dismissed to their higher manhood—to the reward of divine glory.

I do not desire to pass by what perhaps in confidential conversation many of you already know—that in that transition state into which the inquiries of science have brought us, where many of the exterior forms of Christian truth hitherto given have been modified, and where some substantial truths are struggling now for a new birth of expression, he did not accept all the views and truths of the fathers. Yet he never scornfully rejected them. He held his spirit in equipoise, waiting for more light—not light for rejection, but light by which he could reconcile the old and the new, and bring into unity the revelations of God made in days gone by, and the revelations of God which we are exploring and trying to understand and harmonize to-day.

While in the process of education it may be necessary that we should have catechetical and theological dogmas, one thing stands revealed in the testimony of the Divine Word, that all ordinances, and all technical philosophy, and all instruction, are for the purpose of producing godliness; and if godliness is the result of concurrent external influences as well as of intellectual conviction, the end is gained. Holiness of life and disposition is all that makes any religion good for anything. If you look at the sweetness of his temper; if you look at the spotlessness of his honor; if you look at the whole drift and upward tendency of his life; if you look at the fruits of the Spirit as they are delineated in the word of God, and say, " Did he not possess a larger share of these than is usually seen in those who are professedly religious? Did we not see in him the fruits of Christian thought and Christian faith?" I think there can be no doubt as to the answer. He is with God.

Not doubting myself, I speak of him with confidence as one that could not know any other place but heaven, and could not find a place of darkness which he would not illuminate and make light; and in the large faith that Christ and God are revealed to us not alone by the letter and in the printed book, but in the greater book that existed long before the experience of mankind found it out and registered it—in that faith I greet him, and bid him farewell, until the day shall come when we shall arise to see our Father as He is—not as through dim glasses we imagine him to be, but in the fulness and the glory of that which He is. There we shall find our friend, and there we shall rejoice with him.

HYMN.—(Written for the occasion.)

> Weary hands, O weary hands!
> Resting now from life's endeavor,
> From the conflict, from the fever,
> Lying peaceful where ye fell:
> O folded hands, farewell, farewell!

Gentle heart, O gentle heart!
Faithful service thou didst render,
Beating ever true and tender;
On thee lies the silent spell:
O loving heart, farewell, farewell!

Parted soul, O parted soul!
Passed beyond this earthly portal,
Entered through the gate immortal
Into life no tongue can tell:
O brother-soul, farewell, farewell!

II.

MEMORIAL SESSION OF THE AMERICAN INSTITUTE OF MINING ENGINEERS.

WASHINGTON, February 22d, 1882.

PRESIDENT WILLIAM METCALF, of Pittsburgh, Pa., called the meeting to order, and spoke as follows:

When the sad news of the event we to-day commemorate came to me over the wires, my first thought was that at our annual meeting we must have a memorial service. I instantly sat down and wrote to the secretary, suggesting this meeting. By the same mail, Dr. Raymond wrote to the secretary making the same suggestion; and by the next return mail the secretary wrote to me indorsing the suggestion. I feel that, owing to the very intimate connection of Dr. Raymond with the Institute, and the more than intimate relations that existed between him and our departed friend, it is only fitting and due to him that I should retire from the chair, and make this not exactly an Institute meeting, but a Holley memorial meeting in truth and reality, and to call Dr. Raymond to the chair, as the one who properly and fittingly ought to preside, and I have arranged the meeting accordingly.

Gentlemen of the Institute, we are met to-day to pay the highest honor to our friend that earth can give. We are to lay bare our hearts, open the storehouse of memory, and bring to view, each in his own way, the pictures treasured there, of the rare merits of him who painted them. From the day when, in a little dingy pattern-room of a Pittsburgh foundry, I first met Mr. Holley, till the last day I spent with him in June last, the impression left is one of almost uninterrupted sunshine. Though never his client, I always found him to pour out his knowledge without stint, and if he ever asked anything in return, he did it in such a way that it was felt that a great favor had been granted, only to find later that he had left behind more than he had taken away. He was a charged receiver. His mind was full; and when anything was dropped into it, it spilled always what at the time was of greater value. He was a gatherer and a scatterer. He gathered items and gave whole systems in return. He gathered flowers from every place, but handed to his friends bouquets of knowledge and artistic plants of rare beauty. He gathered for himself a few thousands, and scattered to his clients and friends throughout the world untold millions. He gathered all hearts into his own large heart, which shed its overflowing love on every one he met. He had a rare insight, and saw use and good where others only tried to avoid the dust and smoke which their eyes could not penetrate. Perhaps the noblest phase of his character was shown in his full knowledge and steady use of the greatest force known to man; the only force authorized by the Saviour of mankind, and left by him to conquer all the world. I mean the enduring, all-powerful, irresistible force of love. Beyond all his science, his wit, or his skill, his love for us is what makes us hold his memory so dear. His winning smile, sunny face and cordial greeting we all remember well; but how entirely they are all put into the shade by the memory of his quiet talks when the sweetness of his heart poured itself out as from a ceaseless spring! He was modest and did not seek his own preferment. He was content to let others precede him. I wish I dared tell how he once averted a great estrangement of friends in the Institute by going to each, and humbly making himself out the greater sinner; and how nicely his friends fell into the trap. We shall miss him indeed the next time the waters of strife arise. I have known him in some severe trials, and some of his disappointments as well as triumphs. I feel it a true thing to record of him: "His ways were ways of pleasantness and all his paths were peace."

I now call upon Dr. RAYMOND to take the chair.

DR. R. W. RAYMOND, of Brooklyn, N. Y., Ex-President of the Institute: My friends—for friends indeed we are, and drawn more closely together at this moment in the sympathy of mutual grief—what can I say, what can any one say, in these first days of the paralysis of bereavement, except to ring the changes on the two themes, love and loss? He was so much to us; we miss him so sorely! A meeting, and no paper from Holley; a banquet, and no speech from Holley; a cordial reunion of fraternal joy, and no smile or hand-clasp from Holley; it is more than sad, it is bewildering. We stand as those before whom the earth, suddenly opening, has swallowed up the place where their affections and their occupations alike centred, and who know not whither to turn. Our sense of loss is almost greater than our sense of pain. We loved him deeply, dearly; but a man is not necessarily missed in proportion as he is loved. He is missed in proportion to the number of points at which he entered into our lives, and the emphasis with which he impressed his being upon ours at each point.

Mr. Holley entered the Institute in November, 1871, the first year of it existence. He brought to it a reputation already assured, a wide acquaintance and an intense enthusiasm. He devoted to it from that hour his unexampled gifts, in a spirit of absolute self-abnegation. After serving as vice-president, he accepted with joy and pride the unsought nomination and election to the presidency, because he felt that it was in his power to increase the sphere of the influence of the Institute, and enlarge its sources of power. At the end of a year he declined a re-election, resisting all solicitations to continue what had unquestionably been a most brilliant and success-ful administration, because he felt—what no one else felt—that in the Centennial year, we should be represented by some one better prepared to receive and entertain foreign guests. He worked harder to get out of the presidency than many men would work to obtain public honors. Who among us can remember any movement for the advancement of the interest and profit of our members, in which he was not active? Who is not personally indebted to him for some-thing that will be a precious memory hereafter? These debts we cannot pay; but we can at least acknowledge them. For my part, among all the services which I have attempted to render to the In-stitute, the one upon which I look with the greatest satisfaction is, that it was my good fortune to overcome the modest reluctance of Mr. Holley, and induce him to enter upon that prominent activity in our affairs for which he was so brilliantly qualified, and which he so fruitfully pursued. It seems strange to recall that when I knew him first, fourteen or fifteen years ago, he was afraid to speak in public —he, by whose eloquence and humor we have been charmed so many times since!

He was not wont to parade his accomplishments. I remember how, in 1873, I first discovered, after years of acquaintance with him, his knowledge of architecture and his skill as an artist. It was after one of the sessions of our Easton meeting in 1873, and he was wait-ing for some of us who were detained in a committee-meeting. It was in my lecture-room at Lafayette College; and the blackboard stood invitingly empty. Seizing the chalk, Holley employed the

five minutes of idleness in an incredibly rapid and apparently care-
less scratching upon the board, and when we came from the committee-meeting, lo! there stood before us a magnificent Gothic
cathedral, arch, buttress and spire complete, recalling, though not
precisely repeating, the white glory of Milan, or the stately splendor
of York. In all that hasty work, not a line had been thrown away;
not an essential detail had been omitted. I love to think of the incident as a type of all his work—the clear creative conception, the
trained skill of execution, the art become a second nature, the intuitive use of means to ends, that shone through it all.

It is by reason of his many-sided activity that it has seemed best
to make this meeting a many-voiced testimony to him. No single
minstrel—only a great chorus—can fitly chant his praise.

DR. T. STERRY HUNT, of Montreal, Canada, Ex-President of the
Institute: I know that all the friends around me will agree with
me when I say how weak and inadequate I feel any language of
mine to express my appreciation of the many virtues of our friend,
and my sense of grief and desolation at his loss. I cannot, however,
forbear to recall on this occasion some few incidents which are to me
as landmarks in the course of my long friendship with Alexander
Holley, and which now rise before me with peculiar force as grateful
memories of one whose absence we all mourn to-day.

My acquaintance with him began fourteen years since, in 1868,
when he was at Troy, as a member of the firm of Griswold, Winslow
& Holley, and engaged in the beginnings of an industry with which
his name was hereafter to be so conspicuously identified. It was as a
student interested in the Bessemer process that I first met Holley, and
then and there began an intercourse which ripened into friendship. I
soon learned to recognize in him that eager spirit of scientific inquiry,
and that patience and courage under difficulties which were to lead
him to the eminence in this, which he had already achieved in other
branches of his profession.

Afterwards, in 1870, I was with him in a journey for metallurgical observation and study during a week. Through parts of Pennsylvania and Ohio, visiting steel-works, rolling-mills and other
establishments, in all of which his special knowledge was shown,
and was freely given for the instruction of myself and his other companions, one of whom is with us here to-day to join his testimony to
my own of the great pleasure and profit which we then found in the
society and friendship of Holley.

Next, it was my good fortune to find myself associated with our friend as one of the Judges at the Centennial Exhibition at Philadelphia, in 1876, when we met daily in the same class, and week after week prosecuted our examination in the department of metallurgy, or encountered in social intercourse the distinguished representatives of various foreign nations, who, as our colleagues, then learned to know and to honor him.

Again. I shall never forget the pleasure which I felt when, in 1878, I found myself with our friend in Paris at the meeting of the British Iron and Steel Institute. There were present three Americans, Holley, John Fritz, and myself. At the grand dinner, at which we were all invited guests, Holley was chosen to speak for the American nation and for our own Institute. I have often listened to him, and we all remember his wit, his wisdom and his eloquence, but those who were not there present have never, it seems to me, heard him at his greatest and his best, as inspired by the occasion, he addressed that brilliant assembly. How well I recall the emotion of pride which filled my heart when Holley rose and, in a glowing speech, replied to the toast of "The American Institute of Mining Engineers." As a member of this Institute, and moreover, as being like him, a son of Connecticut, I was proud to claim Alexander Holley as my friend and countryman, and as a representative American in the best and highest sense of the term, representing American science, American technical skill, American manhood, and American eloquence, grace and genius as well.

One more memory of Holley and the last. Soon after arriving in England from the Continent, I chanced, on the 10th of last November, to hear that our friend was lying sick at Morley's hotel in London. I hastened thither at once, but was met by the glad intelligence that Mr. Holley was much better and had gone out. A moment afterwards, as I was leaving the hotel, I met him coming up the stair. His joyous countenance beaming with the bright expression which we see depicted in the portrait now before us, his delighted surprise at the unexpected meeting, and the hearty grasp of welcome greeting which he gave me, I shall never forget, nor the interest with which he listened to an account of my recent travels in various European countries, and to my plans for the future. He then believed his health restored, and was to leave in a day or two for the north of England, and to join his family in Paris in a few weeks. I spoke with regret of my enforced absence from the late gatherings of our Institute, and we then promised to meet each other at this February meeting. And so we parted for the last time. He, on his death-bed, told with evident delight to a dear friend the story of our brief interview in London, and I am here alone to repeat it to you. For the rest, you all know the sad sequel, and I feel that I cannot add another word. My heart is full, but in the words of another:

> "I may not unlock my heart;
> The key is gone with him.
> The silent organ loudest chants
> The Master's requiem."

A. S. HEWITT, of New York City, Ex-President of the Institute: I come with no set phrases to speak of our departed friend. In fact, I did not know that I was expected to speak on this occasion; but to be silent in the presence of such a loss, knowing Holley as I knew him, would be more than the heart could tolerate. I do not know who in this audience first had the pleasure of his acquaintance; my own knowledge of him goes back somewhere between twenty-five and thirty years. He came into my office; I do not know whether he brought me a letter, or whether he introduced himself to my notice, but I never shall forget, and I never *have* forgotten, the wonderful impression which that boyish face made upon me. The look of intelligence, of honesty, of calm consciousness of power was more marked in his case than in any young man who had ever come under my eye. At that time I think he was engaged in some literary work with Mr. Colburn. It was my privilege to introduce him to my old friend, Mr. Edwin A. Stevens, of Hoboken, one of those born mechanical engineers who understood the laws of nature and the laws of character—of personal character—alike, and made no mistakes among the men whom he chose to aid him in his work. Under his patronage Mr. Holley made one of his first visits to Europe; and in all his subsequent career he enjoyed the confidence and the friendship of Mr. Stevens and of the great engineers with whom he was thus put in connection. I think that I first called his attention to the Bessemer process, I mean to the subject of its introduction into this country. My firm had made a feeble effort within six weeks after the famous Cheltenham paper was read in 1856, to see whether pig iron could be thus converted into steel. It was three or four years, perhaps, after that, that Mr. Holley's attention was called to the matter, and he went to Europe and brought back for his friends the control of that patent. I am not going to pursue the story of his contributions—you know them better than I do—to the successful introduction of this wonderful civilizing agent.

Men are to be measured by two standards. One is the standard of personal character, as we judge of it in each other by personal conduct. Those of you who enjoyed his friendship need no words from any one else to elevate the standard of judgment which you will apply to Holley. There is another standard by which we measure men when they have passed away, and that is by the influence they have exerted upon the progress of civilization and the advancement of humanity. Of all the men at this day, in this line, I know of none surviving him who has contributed as much to the growth of material wealth and the advancement of industrial progress in this country, as Holley did. I look upon the invention of Mr. Bessemer as almost the greatest invention of the ages. I do not mean measured by its chemical or its mechanical attributes, I mean by virtue of its great results upon the structure of society, and of government. It is the great enemy of privilege, it is the great destroyer of monopoly, it will be the great equalizer of wealth. I have no time to pursue that line of thought longer, but those who have studied its effect upon transportation, the cheapening of food, the lowering of rents of land, the obliteration of aristocratic privilege upon the other side of the Atlantic, will readily comprehend what I mean by calling your attention to this view of the subject. To these results, second only to that of Bessemer himself, the contribution of Holley is greater than that of any other man, who has lived, or who can possibly live. It is said that the world knows little of its great men; and this is true. The man who, in his closet, in the recesses of his own workshop, discovers a new law of nature or makes a new application of hidden forces by which the structure of society is changed, modified, revolutionized, is often little known in his own day, even in his own country. It may require the historian of future ages to find out what his contribution has been to the progress of humanity. But happily, in this day of rapid communication, we know better the work which is done by such men as Holley; and I think that even now, so soon after his departure, we can assign him to the place which he will hereafter occupy in the history of mechanical industry,—a mechanical engineer of unerring judgment, an inventor of the true means for great results, a lover of his race who subjected his science, his talents and his labor to the good of his fellow-men; and he will live in the memory of those who knew him, and in the grateful recollections of those who will come after him, for many a generation.

I would not say more; but I shall be condemned by all of you, if I do not relate an incident that happened in London, at the time Holley was sick, with reference to the movable shell, his patent, which, as I understand, is necessary to the success of the basic process in America. While in Europe in 1880, in the fall of the year, I was astonished and pained to hear that Holley was dying in London. I immediately went to Clapham, where he was said to be, to see whether he could speak to me. I was shown into his room, but, before I went up, the attending physician, who had just left him, met me at the foot of the stairs, and said his death was a question only of hours, or at most only of three or four days. Three consulting physicians had arrived at the same conclusion; and I was so sure that his death was imminent that I afterward wrote home to advise a friend to prepare his family for the sad result. I went into his room and found him the very picture of dissolution. He smiled his old smile, and, after a few words had passed and, I suppose, seeing upon my face the expression of profound sympathy, he said : " Well, I suppose that they have told you that I am going to die, and I suppose I am, although I mean to get home first if I can ; but," said he, " I have been trying to amuse myself while I am dying by inventing something that will enable me to die with credit. I want to make the basic process practicable, and I have just perfected here upon my bed the details of the movable shell; and if I don't live long enough myself to introduce it, I have explained it in full to my assistant, so that this invention shall be known to my countrymen." His recovering as he did, rising, as by a miracle, from that deathbed, only adds to this remarkable evidence of the extraordinary vitality and energy which characterized him, and which surpassed that of any man I ever knew.

W. P. SHINN, of Pittsburgh, Pa., Ex-President of the Institute: It is fitting that I should bear my tribute to the memory of our departed friend on this occasion, not only because of my having been a president of this Institute, but because it was through. Mr. Holley that I became a member of it. It was at his suggestion that I made application; it was upon his recommendation that the council approved my application, and I more than suspect that it was through his kind offices that I was nominated to the position of president of the Institute.

3

It is now more than twenty years since I first came in contact with the professional labors of the late Alexander L. Holley in his publication, with the late Zerah Colburn, of their report on European railroads. Engaged as I was at that time actively in railway management, the report was of great practical importance to me, and had almost the character of a revelation. Then "permanent way," as it was known in Europe, was without an example in this country. Many of the appliances which are now so familiar to us were unheard of. The fish-joint had not yet been adopted, and many experienced railroad officials first learned of it in Holley and Colburn's report.

My personal acquaintance with Mr. Holley began with the discussion of the ground-plans for the Edgar Thomson Steel Works in 1873; and what surprised me most was to find that the Holley of the European railway report was still a young man, and that since making that report, which involved the mastery of an art, he had become the acknowledged authority on Bessemer steel machinery and manufacture, and had meanwhile published a report on ordnance, also accepted as a standard work.

My personal relations with him were intimate for about seven years, during which I never knew which to admire most, the versatility of his genius, the depth of his professional knowledge, or that geniality of disposition and quickness of perception which made personal intercourse with him a pleasure, whether the object to be attained was strictly of a business nature, or merely social pastime. He appropriated and imparted valuable information with equal facility and apparent gratification, and in the amenities of private and social life he was as happy as in his professional knowledge he was thorough. Not only to those who knew him best will he remain an ever-present memory, but to all who frequently met him, particularly at the meetings of the Engineering societies with which he was so prominently connected, and of which he was the life. His death has left a void which time will efface but slowly. Those who heard the ineffable tenderness with which he responded to the presentation address which, by the partiality of his friends, I was deputed to make at the Pittsburgh convention in 1879, will never forget his beautiful apostrophe to that final "conversion" of this world's life which he, of all those then present, has been the first to experience.

MR. ASHBEL WELCH, of Lambertville, N. J., President of the American Society of Civil Engineers: About a quarter of a cen-

tury ago there was a young man who had already attained eminence as an author. He was highly educated and highly accomplished in every way, but with a red shirt with sleeves rolled up,
and hands all smirched, ran a locomotive on the Camden and Amboy
Railroad. Such a prodigy attracted my attention. I found that
he was studying to be an expert in steam-engineering; that he was
not content to take his knowledge from books, but that he wanted
to see everything, and on the railroad he took the best way of
getting at it by going into it. That man, as you will all recognize,
was the man whose portrait you see yonder. Now I want to say,
if there are any educators here, and I am sure there are, I want
you to say to your students, do not be afraid of smirching your
hands; do not be afraid of dirtying your fingers; if you want to
learn mechanical engineering or steam-engineering, do as Holley
did.

Twenty years ago there was lying at Hoboken what was called
the Stevens battery. It had been made many years before for the
purpose of defending the harbor of New York. It was adapted to
that purpose, and to no other purpose. The designer of it never
thought of any other purpose, but the changes in events had made
it unnecessary for that purpose. The Stevens battery, as you all
know, was the father of ironclads, or rather of proposed ironclads.
The then proprietor of the ship was desirous of adapting it to sea-
going purposes. He had had years previously a good deal of experience in firing large shots, a thing never brought to this country
in armored ordnance. I was called in, and Mr. Holley was called
in, and we worked together for some months to see what we could
do there. It was my good fortune to inform Mr. Holley of a great
many of the experiments that had been previously made, and he
saw some of those made at the time. And that was the seed sown
in his mind which afterward grew up into his great book on armor
and ordnance. I can indorse all that has been said, or all that can
be said, of his genial, lovely disposition. I am tempted to mention
one incident, yet I cannot describe it. We were here together, at
Washington, when he got word from home that his oldest daughter
was born; and I remember the beams of parental love then dis-
closed. Mr. Holley was one of the most wonderful men that I
have ever known, in character and capacity. A single word dropped
in his ear, a single little seed sown, was sure to grow up into a
powerful plant, a great tree, just as the little suggestion at Hoboken
grew up into his book on armor and ordnance. I am sorry that I

did not know I was to be called upon, or I might have said something more fitting to the subject.

E. D. LEAVITT, JR., of Cambridgeport, Mass.: I first met Mr. Holley in 1859. He was then a young man, who seemed to me the finest looking I had ever seen. He impressed me, as Mr. Hewitt said he did him, with his force of character as a man who would carry through anything that he undertook, and I claim that he was such a man. I had been connected for several years previously with the establishment to which Mr. Holley went first on leaving Brown University, and the traditions of his ability, of what might be called his budding genius, are still there. I remember what an impression it made upon us, notwithstanding the feeling that working mechanics had for a man who was just out of college. We all know that such men are not generally regarded with much favor, and it was then more so than now. But Holley had impressed these men as an honest worker for truth—ready to roll up his sleeves and do anything that any of them would do. He would never shirk any duty, however menial. I again met him in 1876, when he invited me to join this Institute. Through his kind offices it was, I merely granting permission for the use of my name, that I became a member; and I have been more or less intimate with him ever since. When the Society of Mechanical Engineers was formed, Holley was the moving spirit. He presided at our first meeting. I was a member of the nominating committee for the first board of officers, and to illustrate his extreme modesty, which impressed me very strongly at the time, I remember with what great difficulty we persuaded him to resign from our committee, in order that we might make him an officer of the society. We found it was absolutely indispensable to have him in a prominent capacity if the society was to succeed. He was the most enthusiastic and energetic member, doing more for us than any other two or half-dozen men, from the fact that he was so well acquainted with the leading engineers throughout the country. When the wire flashed to me the information of his death, I felt at once an overpowering sense of loss. I was about leaving home, and it seemed like going away from a death-bed in my own household. All through the night it came to me—what a loss! And I cannot express fitly and fully the feeling which dwells within me at this time, at the loss we have met with in the decease of our dear friend.

CAPTAIN C. E. DUTTON, U. S. A., Washington, D. C.: It is a gratification to me to be able to unite with yours my testimony of love and affection. It was my great privilege to be very intimate with Mr. Holley at a period of his career which was, perhaps, the most interesting. We all know how broad a man he was, how wide a field of mechanical art his attainments covered, how splendid was his culture in all respects. But we know him best, perhaps, through his relations to the Bessemer process—that great epic or drama of the modern arts. And in that epic we will all concede that he played the part of Achilles or Æneas. When I knew him most intimately and was most closely associated with him, the Bessemer process was in its dark days. Those who are familiar with the history of the early development of that process cannot fail to recall the vast multiplicity of difficulties which stood in the way of the development of its details—how they rose up on every hand, how they met the engineer at every step. The art had no precedents whatever. Everything connected with it had to be created anew. It was in this stage of the process that it seemed to me that Holley showed the noblest and strongest traits of his character, both intellectual and moral. I think that Holley was undoubtedly the first to take a broad view of the policy of a Bessemer establishment, which subsequent experience has proved to be a correct one. He knew at that time, although he was perhaps unable to demonstrate it—still he knew, and constantly asserted, that it was necessary for all purposes to take a wider range and involve larger amounts of capital than anybody at that time thought necessary. Men persisted in dependence upon the converter. They said that if they could only manufacture ingots, they could sell them; that it was a patented process, and on that everything rested. But from the very start Holley was convinced that the Bessemer process always meant blast-furnaces, blooming-mills, and rolling-mills. He was unable for a long time to engage in any Bessemer enterprise in which he could carry out his own ideas to his satisfaction. Perhaps it was not in the long run unfortunate that it was so, for there were matters of detail to be overcome which even he could not have foreseen. It was from the period of 1866 to 1869 that those great difficulties presented themselves most numerously, and were battled with most successfully. There was many and many a time when Holley became almost discouraged; his whole soul was wrapped up in that great enterprise, for which he seemed to live. Everything else for the time being was thrown away, and as disappointment after disappointment came over him, he would frequently break out to me, in moments of confidence, in a feeling almost bordering upon despair. Probably very few of those who knew Holley can associate him with any such frame of mind. To almost all of us the recollection presented to us is that of a man of extremely cheerful, warm, genial disposition—a man whose temper would more probably lack sufficient hardness of edge to stand the blows of severe trial and adversity. But it was not so. No man ever showed truer temper under trials and difficulties than he. No man was ever more fully persuaded of the difficulty of his task than he was, or ever brought to bear more expedients and struggled with more courage and more vigilance. It was in this stage of his career that I knew him best and was associated with him most closely. I felt his troubles as if they were my own, for I think I was at that time almost the only person with whom he associated upon terms of extreme intimacy outside of his own family. But when his success came, no person ever rejoiced with him more heartily than I did. I am very glad to speak of this portion of his life and career, because I presume that very few people knew of it as well as I did ; and if anything could add to the strong love and affection we bear for him, it is perhaps the conviction that he, too, had trials which were bitter to suffer, and that he surmounted them and conquered like a true hero.

ROBERT W. HUNT, of Troy, N. Y.: Had our dear friend and brother been asked to select the tribute most grateful to him, I feel certain he would have desired it to be paid by the American Institute of Mining Engineers. Feeling this, I am glad to add my mite to the expression of grief and respect which you propose to pay his memory to-day, and which will be but an echo of that already gone up from all over our own country, and will have been re-echoed from abroad when we receive tidings of the reception there of this sad news.

I first met Holley in the fall of 1865. He was then a member of the firm of Winslow, Griswold & Holley, and manager of their Bessemer Works at Troy. Those works then consisted of the $2\frac{1}{2}$ ton experimental plant, which he built on his return from England in 1864, after having purchased for his firm Bessemer's American patents.

In the light of the present Bessemer practice it seems like a dream to look back to this time, and a full realization of the diffi-

culties encountered and overcome can only be realized by the men
who came through those early days. An imperfect knowledge of
the chemical requirements of the process, an utter absence of tested
and approved refractory materials, and, above all, imperfect machinery, were the conditions of the problem which, in 1864, Holley
set himself to solve. With his own hands he had to make his first
tuyeres; mould his first stoppers; line his converter and ladles.
When meeting with failure after failure, through the imperfection
of some of the materials employed or the breaking down of some
of the machinery, he not only maintained his own high courage and
confidence in ultimate success, but kept up as well the doubting
faith of those associated with him.

Encountering these troubles, his ever active mind and wonderful
inventive genius at once grasped the mechanical difficulties, and as
a result gave us the present American Bessemer plant. These
mechanical departures he patented, and in the final settlement of
his firm relations these patents became the property of his partners,
and subsequently of the Bessemer Steel Co. Moreover, Mushet's,
Kelley's, and Bessemer's patents having expired, they are now the
only ones on which this company can collect royalties.

One of the finest monuments to his ability as an engineer exists
in the only Bessemer plant yet built in this country outside of his
patents. I think my fellow Bessemer managers will unite with me
in deciding it far below the standard of a Holley plant. It is very
good, indeed; but, compelled to avoid him, they also avoided much
that was good. But in the criticism of these very works, his
lovable nature was shown. I am certain to no one sooner than
myself would he have freely expressed himself, but never did I
hear him utter an unkind or slighting word about this, if I may so
call it, rival plant. So many of its owners were his friends (as
who were not?), I suspect many a hint was given by him of dangers
to be avoided.

After leaving Troy, upon the dissolution of the firm of Winslow,
Griswold & Holley, he assumed charge of the completion of the
Harrisburgh works. At this time began our closer acquaintance,
ripening into warmest friendship. We at Cambria rolled the steel
made by him at Harrisburgh. This brought George Fritz and
Holley together, and a most intimate relation it became. I regard
these two men as having been among the most brilliant metallurgical
engineers the world has yet seen. Entirely unlike in all save
genius and heart, they became mutual-helping, utterly trusting

friends. George Fritz was a rugged, self-educated, self-made man, naturally jealous and distrustful of assumed scientific knowledge. But Holley, with all his science, his culture, and polish, won to him this man of iron. I know George Fritz loved him as with the love of a woman. A few short years ago we buried him, his labor over—his enduring monument left in his works; and over his grave stood no sincerer mourner, no more stricken heart, than Alexander Holley. And he also is at rest, with a monument of imperishable work even greater than his friend's. Their country, the world, gainers by their lives; but, alas! their reward attained all too soon.

During those Harrisburgh days, Holley encountered many difficulties, many trials. Even his brave spirit was often almost daunted; and having made the works a success for that period, I think he was glad to accept the offer of John A. Griswold, for whom he entertained the greatest affection, to again assume control of the Troy works. Mr. Griswold, himself a most captivating man, fully appreciated Holley, and their intercourse was entirely satisfactory. But the field of one works was too small for his restless genius; so, in 1871, he relinquished the management, and became the consulting engineer to several of the works then built, or in course of construction. Hence it came that he was connected with the construction of all the eleven works forming the Bessemer Association save two.

While ever loyal to the Bessemer process, Holley early became interested in the Siemens-Martin method, and devoted much time to its study, and in working out the details of the plant. Here, as in the Bessemer, he at once cut loose from the accepted practice, and at least partially as a result of his professional advice the first open-hearth works, built with him as consulting engineer, are the finest in this country, if not, for their size, in the world. He was a firm believer in the Pernot furnace, and the results now being attained in the plants built under his advice certainly point toward his belief having been well founded.

After full investigation in Europe he became fully impressed with the merits of the Basic Process, and mainly through his exertions were the Thomas-Gilchrist patents purchased by the Bessemer Steel Co. In this connection came his last triumph as an engineer. While there is not a doubt about the chemical success of the Basic Process, still from an American steel-maker's standpoint it would not pay without some such invention as Holley gave us in his removable shell. We must have speed. Slow work may answer abroad, and even pay better than fast; but not so here. Of America, Holley was most American; and I regard his last invention, in its boldness, in its simplicity of detail, in its entire practicability, as a fitting crown to his illustrious career.

We have spoken of Holley the engineer. As such the world mourns his loss; but we weep for Holley, the genial companion, the brilliant wit, the sympathizing friend, the noble man. His sympathy was always ready. His heart was for his fellow-man. His friendship, once given, never faltered. Probably no one had his good offices worse abused; but he never soured, and ever had an excuse for the delinquent. Some eighteen months ago his friends waited with fear the tidings from his dangerous illness while abroad, and, as you will remember, at our last Philadelphia meeting one of our members so beautifully referred to our then late fears, and expressed our thankfulness for his safe return. Alas! even then, while we were toasting his safety, the hand of death was upon him, the grim monster smiling mockingly at our human hopes. But when this presence was known to him, he met it, as he had lived, with quiet self-possession, thoughtfulness for others, with a brave, undaunted spirit.

Shall I, while thinking of greater, speak of my personal loss? Associated with him as I was for fifteen years, he had become part of my professional life. Alexander Holley was my closest, dearest friend. I loved him as an own brother. The void is unrealizable. But the world rolls on. Our daily duties, difficulties, trials, present themselves. Can we not better meet them, can we not be better men, from having known and loved that spirit, who did more than his duty; who surmounted all difficulties; who shrunk from no trial? Our hearts are stricken, but in our grief we rejoice that we loved the bright one who has so early left us for his rest.

DR. THOMAS EGLESTON, Columbia College School of Mines, New York city: There are some men who impress themselves so thoroughly upon our lives that it is impossible to tell when we first became acquainted with them. I have been trying ever since the Monday morning when I saw his death announced to tell when it was that I first met Holley. I do not know. It seems as if I must have known him always. I have looked forward month after month, week after week, for so many years, to meeting him, waiting to hear his cheerful greeting, to learn something of the progress of his

work, or to have some word of encouragement when I was discouraged in my own, that it is almost impossible to say when I
first met him. There is a side of his character that I knew perhaps better than any of you. Probably some of you may remember
the stand that Holley took in the Philadelphia meeting of 1876,
during the discussion upon technical education. He said those of
us who were engineers, who design and who build works, are in
duty bound, when called upon, to teach those who come after us
upon what principles it is done. The work of teaching should be
one of just as much conscientious endeavor as is the prosecution of
the professional work we are doing. It did not strike me at the
time as being a thought so pregnant as it really is, but I learned
its meaning when I heard him lecture a few months after this
speech was made. Holley was called by the trustees of the Columbia College to lecture at the School of Mines on the manufacture of iron and steel; I took it for granted that on account of his
professional engagements he would refuse. The reply he made to
me was, "It is my duty, if I am called upon to lecture upon iron
and steel, to do so. I cannot make my arrangements to do it this
year, but I will do it next;" and he did so for several years, as a
matter of principle and at great personal inconvenience. There are
some here who have heard Holley lecture to young men. It was
my privilege to attend nearly all of his lectures. How earnestly
he talked to young men about how scientific and engineering work
should be done! I don't think I ever heard such lectures. They
were full of the practice and experience of a great engineer. He
criticised freely the work of others, and did not forget to blame
himself when any of his own practice had been wrong. I have
heard him speak in the meetings of the Institute and say brilliant
things, but I do not think I have ever heard him surpass his own
lectures upon metallurgical engineering. I used to remonstrate
with him about his excessive, and what I thought his unnecessary,
labor. "Yes," he would reply, "I know I am burning the candle
at both ends, but I must be here to-day, and be in Pittsburgh,
Chicago, or St. Louis to meet engagements, and back here again to
lecture. I cannot do otherwise." I said to him: "Holley, in justice
to yourself, in justice to your friends, in justice to your profession,
you ought to stop." He said, "I am going to stop. I shall not
always work so hard, but I cannot stop now." He wrote every
word of every lecture he delivered. I urged upon him: "You are
doing for the young men what young men do not appreciate." His

lectures were worthy of an audience of engineers, and I expostulated with him for doing for young men what they did not and could not appreciate. His reply to me was the reply of a man who was thoroughly satisfied that he was right, and who was fully convinced that it was due to his profession that he should magnify his position as a teacher. "I cannot," said he, "afford not to write what I am to say, for I am in duty bound not to be too profuse when I am teaching young men the science of metallurgical engineering." I told him that I thought that young men would understand his own work better when presented to them in the more familiar form of an extempore lecture, and just as he used to talk to us when every one felt it a privilege to listen. "But," said he, "I am enunciating principles to be remembered. It is my business, my duty, my pleasure to put them down, with my best thoughts, in the best language, and in the fewest words that I possibly can." After hearing these same lectures twice, I urged him to write a book. "Some time," he said, "I am going to write a book on Bessemer practice. I cannot now, for I have too much work to do, and am burning the candle at both ends already; but some time I am going to write a book." The book is nearly written. The lectures were a book, and I hope some day some one will have the privilege of editing those lectures that he delivered at the School of Mines, and add to it the plans of the works he built and the practice he adopted, as the best tribute to his memory, because I do not think that any such discussion of steel metallurgical practice exists in print. Perhaps, if there is any satisfaction at all in thinking of·Holley as a man that has gone from us forever, it is in thinking of the fact that not one stroke of his overwork hastened his departure. We feel almost called upon to regret that he did not do more work, for he was bound to die; death struck him months before, and of all the brilliant work that he ever did, the most brilliant was what he accomplished in the last two or three years of his life, when, no matter what he had done, he could not have been saved.

G. W. MAYNARD, of New York city: I made the acquaintance of Mr. Holley in 1869, at Troy, while he was rebuilding the Bessemer works of John A. Griswold & Co. The introduction was at the table of our mutual friend, Captain Dutton. The charm of that first meeting can never be effaced. From that evening dates a friendship which intensified as the years rolled on. The magnetic influence of the man has been experienced by many, and I believe you will agree with me that the friendship he inspired ripened into affection. It would be difficult to say in what quality Holley especially excelled, for he was excellent in all; there was one, however, which he possessed in a marked degree, and that was always doing whatever he promised to do, particularly if the doing meant the granting of a favor. Perhaps this is not to be wondered at, for the substratum of his character was truth, and this was undoubtedly the mainspring of his influence with his fellow-men. Another trait was his good nature and the wonderful pluck which never deserted him in the most trying times, whether the trial was a lot of bad steel or personal physical suffering.

On one occasion, when he was looking into a cupola-tuyere, an explosion of gas blew hot coals and cinders into his eyes, and for a time it was thought that he had lost his sight. On learning of the accident I rushed over to his room. I found him in great pain; still the joke was uppermost, when he said: "I'm glad you have come, for I wanted a mining engineer to work this newly-discovered coal bed." As an illustration of the absolute reliance reposed in him, I hope I shall not at this late day betray confidence when I cite the words of his friend, Mr. Griswold, who sent for Mr. Holley one evening for the purpose of discussing the chances of success of the Bessemer process. The gist of the conference, which extended into the small hours of the night, was; "Aleck, how much more do you want to pull us through?" "About $100,000." "Go ahead, my boy; my faith in you is unshaken; I'll find the money." There were many characteristics which these two men possessed in common, and it may be said of our dear brother, as it was said by a prominent citizen of Troy of Mr. Griswold at the time of his death—he was always a *gentle* man.

From 1873–79 I made several trips with him to steel-works in England and on the Continent. The doors of works were thrown open to him as to no other man. His suavity, and the fact that he always gave more information than he received, accounted for the exceptional facilities afforded him. His capacity for work was something remarkable, and, as you all know, he had a world-wide reputation at an age when the majority of engineers have not yet got through with their preliminary training. Up to the time of the Philadelphia Exhibition he still appeared very youthful. On one occasion in London, in 1874, we casually met a prominent engineer, to whom I introduced Mr. Holley. "Ah! any relation to Mr. Holley the engineer?" "He ,is the engineer." "But not the great Holley who wrote that very thick book on ordnance and armor?" "Yes; he's the man!" "Ah, but that can't be, you know, for the man I mean must be about sixty years old." I am glad of the opportunity of paying this poor tribute to the memory of my friend, and the friend and brother of us all.

T. C. CLARKE, of New York city: Holley was such a many-sided character that it is difficult to know which to speak of. What one omits to say of him the next one can say. I will, therefore, be very brief. Some thirty years ago certain worthy gentlemen, realizing the horrors of impending war, took it upon themselves to call upon the Czar of all the Russias and ask him to aid in averting it. What was the success of their mission? The war broke out the next year in the Crimea. Now, I think everybody will admit that to the labors of Holley in perfecting the Bessemer steel process we owe the fact that the transportation of grain has been cheapened, so that it can be carried from the interior of this continent and across the sea at a less cost than it can be grown there, and if ever there is anything done to abolish the present military burdens of Europe, it will be through the competition so established. It is to the labors of Alexander L. Holley that this grand result will be due. So much for one side. As to his private character, I can say no better words than those of the poet:

> "He leaves behind him, freed from griefs and cares,
> Far worthier things than tears :
> The love of friends, without a single foe,
> Unequalled lot below !"

MARTIN CORYELL, of Lambertville, N. J., ex-Secretary of the Institute: The tribute of respect I would offer to the memory of Mr. Holley originates in the talent displayed in the publication made by Colburn and Holley several years ago, from which I received great advantage. It was a very able book, and came out at a time when it did great good to the whole country. Since then I have been connected with him in this society as well as in business, and in every emergency he has been kind, conciliatory, and obliging, adding greatly not only to my comfort, but to the comfort of all those about him. I can only say that I regard his death with the same feeling as I would that of a brother.

JOHN H. RICKETSON, of Pittsburgh, Pa.: My acquaintance with
Mr. Holley began some ten years ago, when this society held its
first meeting in Pittsburgh. I had, therefore, not known him as
long or as intimately as some of you, and yet when I heard that
he was dead I felt the keenest sense of personal bereavement; for
in the warmth of his heart, and in the genial sunshine of his presence, acquaintance soon ripened into friendship. I have never
before attended a meeting of this Institute, held for discussion or
for social enjoyment, where Mr. Holley was not present, and where
he was not,—and I am sure there is no man here who will think
himself disparaged when I say it,—where he was not *facile princeps*.
It was my sad but precious privilege to be present at the house of
one of our members when a few of the friends of Mr. Holley gave
him the little testimonial of affection and respect to which allusion
has already been made. As Mr. Shinn said, no one who witnessed
that scene can ever forget it. Standing upon what we all felt was
the brink of the grave,—for even then the coming event cast its
shadow before,—in accents that fell upon our ears and sank into
our hearts like a plaintive strain of sweet music, in words rendered even more touching by their modesty, we heard our friend
chant his own requiem. Then, and perhaps not till then, some of
us realized how dear he was to us. In the days of old, when the
Latin language was a living tongue, the words *de mortuis nil nisi
bonum* passed into a proverb. When applied to our friend, these
words have a new significance, for among the hundreds, or, perhaps,
thousands, who knew him in his own country or beyond the seas,
not one can say aught but good of him. Into the last twenty-five
years of his life he compressed half a century of the work of many
an able man. Many of the brightest of the dead whom the world
delights to honor, who reached the age of threescore-and-ten years,
left no deeper footprints on the sands of time than he. True, had
he been less unmindful of himself, had he possessed less of that
enthusiasm which alone makes great achievements possible, had he
been less prodigal of his strength and resources, had he, in a word,
not taken as his creed, "It is more blessed to give than to receive,"
he might have been with us to-day. But then he would not have
been the Alexander Lyman Holley whom we knew and loved, and
we would not be exclaiming from the depths of our hearts:

> "Oh, for the touch of a vanished hand,
> And the sound of a voice that is still!"

But, Mr. President, in the midst of our sorrow let us catch the key-note of the lesson of Holley's life. Let us profit by the example of our army friends when a comrade falls dead by their side. No matter how well he may have fought the good fight, no matter how bravely he may have died, or how much he may have been beloved, no matter how muffled the drum, or solemn the dirge, or measured the tread of his fellow soldiers as they bear him to the grave, the last rites once performed, the last tear shed, the last flower thrown upon the bier, they march briskly back, keeping pace to the music of an inspiriting quickstep, to the duties of life and the fight of to-morrow. Could our dear friend speak to us to-day, would it not be in this spirit? Would he not say, especially to you who must take up his fallen mantle, to you who were his co-workers for so many years, and with him organized this Institute, whose efforts in the field of applied science have been crowned with results which were a surprise almost to him as well as to you— would he not say, "Go on with the work so well begun, so successfully continued;" and might he not add in those familiar tones whose echoes will ever linger in our ears, "Thus will you best testify your remembrance of me."

O. CHANUTE, of New York city: My acquaintance with Mr. Holley dates back seventeen years, although that was eight years before I saw his face. It was in 1865. I was in the West, and in want of information which I failed to gain in the books. I knew that the information would surely be in the possession of Mr. Holley, and I took the liberty of writing to him and making the necessary inquiry. I took care to write the letter in such a way that he could answer it in a few words if he chose. Almost by return mail I got from Mr. Holley, who was a very busy man, a letter of five or six pages, by which he laid me under an obligation which remained so warm, that when, eight years later, I came East, I took the very earliest opportunity of hunting him up. At that time we were thrown occasionally into contact with each other, meeting in either this society or the Society of Civil Engineers, and I grew to know him better and love him more and more. And now that he is gone, I fail of words to express the regret I feel. I have listened to what has been said here, and each one upon rising has recognized the union of great talents, of the highest possible right living and integrity with the most lovable character, and I feel that all that has been said will be insufficient to make those, who knew him not, appreciate how this professional family feels for its lost brother.

CHARLES MACDONALD, of New York city: It is not for me to attempt to paint in words an enduring picture of Alexander Holley's life; but I may be permitted to dwell for a moment upon that wondrous wealth of loving light which illumined his intercourse with his friends—and who could ever have known him and not be his friend?

His character, as known to all of us, was the very personification of good-will to his fellow-man. Who could ever have looked upon that joyous face, and not feel his own petty cares fade away as a mist? or who could draw near to his inner life, and taste of the sweetness, the gentleness, the helpfulness, and withal the genuine nobility that was there, and not wish to be more like him?

Shall we ever forget—those of us who were fortunate enough to hear—that speech of his' at the Philadelphia banquet, when with exquisite humor he defined the "true basic lining," and then with equally exquisite pathos acknowledged the sympathy which, like bread cast upon the waters, had been returned to him again, as he lay upon a bed of sickness in a far-off land?

The foundation stone upon which Alexander Holley builded was love. Brilliant intellect was there; an indomitable will and perseverance to accomplish great things; but above and beneath all these was his ever-present willingness to spend and be spent for others.

The world will honor him for the great industries he has done so much to develop; for the stores of information he has left for the education of those who are to follow. But his friends will keep him in their hearts among the loved ones who have made life better worth the living. His memory will to them be ever fresh and green; and although we shall never see his smiling face again, or press his hand in friendly salutation, the recollection of all the good deeds he has done, and of all the kindly words spoken in the past, will ever prove an incentive to try to follow in his footsteps; to make those about us stronger to do the right for the sake of the right; and to spread abroad so far as in us lies the blessed doctrine of peace and good-will.

J. F. HOLLOWAY, of Cleveland, O.: In another and distant city, before an association of engineers, I spoke as best I could of the personal virtues of our dear friend; but while so doing I was em-

barrassed by the fact that of the large number present but few had
ever had the pleasure of his personal acquaintance.   As I rise here
to add my mite of tribute to his memory, to lay upon his new-made
grave a leaflet from the Buckeye State, I am still more embarrassed
by the thought that, owing to nearer residence and closer personal
relations of business and society, most of you knew him far better
than I possibly could; but there was about Alexander L. Holley a
cosmopolitan feature in all he said and in all he did, which so
broadened the scope of his influence, and widened the range of his
many manly virtues, so diffused that cheerful, genial, sunny atmosphere which was ever about him, that all who have ever met and
known him in any land or on any sea feel privileged to stand with
you as common mourners about his open grave.   I remember the
engineer of my youth, how uncommunicative he was, how closely
he kept the secrets of his craft, how even the setting of a simple
slide-valve was something to be done at night or reserved for a
Sunday, when no peering eyes were about to watch the proceedings
or seek to pry into the mysteries that lay locked up behind the cover
of the steam chest; how the terms "lap," "lead," and "compression" were as full of mystery as if they had been quotations from the
Arabian Nights; and I well remember that the first outgoing of
my heart toward him whose memory we have met here to honor
was when the first number of his paper, the *Railroad Advocate*, fell
into my hands, and for the first time in my life I learned that there
was a man who could not only lay out and set a valve, but could,
and better still would, tell plainly how others could do the same.
While this was in the very beginning of Mr. Holley's professional
life, it was ever afterward its characteristic.   He was ever noted for
the freedom with which he opened up the vast stores of knowledge
and experience he possessed,—knowledge and experience gained
only by hard study and much travel,—yet he gave of both freely
to his readers and his listeners; and how valuable both have been
to the industries of our country we all well know.   The generosity
of his nature, his frankness, and his open-hearted manner toward
all who came in contact with him disarmed all rivalship, and to-
day, without one tinge of jealousy or envy, all, with one accord,
unite to write above his honored grave, "Here lies America's
greatest engineer."   I cannot bring myself to speak of anything in
any way pertaining to our friend other than those events which so
well illustrate the loving traits of his character, and which have so
endeared him to us all; and no matter where my thoughts begin,.

or how widely they range, they never cease until they bring back that eventful night at Pittsburgh, where the darkness, the gloom, and the falling rain outside were only the forecast of what many of us then dimly foresaw and feared, and which, alas! has now fallen upon us all. What were the thoughts which so rapidly passed through his mind as he gazed upon that testimonial of love and esteem, and the names written thereon, can never be known. Beautiful as were the words he spoke, they doubtless failed to convey the depth and fulness of the thoughts which a busy memory conjured up before him. I ever think of him in connection with that event as if he were then standing beside a milestone in life's journey, upon the crest of a high eminence, to reach which he had travelled long and laboriously. As he leaned upon it, he cast behind him a wearied look down the long and rugged way over which he had passed, noting the while where friends had here and there joined him on the way; but he seemed alone now, and the way before him, as he looked into it, seemed dark, but through some opening rift in the clouded future he seemed to catch a glimpse of a resting-place not far beyond. You all remember with what touching words he summed up life's failures, and how appropriate was his beautiful simile of the converter,—the converter about which he had so much dreamed and planned,—how he spoke of it as taking the crude materials of the "earth, earthy," and through its alchemy transmuting them into a pure, a noble metal. So, too, of our lives; might not they, chastened, purified, and freed from all earthly dross and stains, come at last to be moulded anew into higher and nobler forms? But words fail to convey the beauties of his thoughts, while the pathos that was in his voice, the pallor that was on his cheek, the far-away look that was in his eyes, will never be forgotten by any one that stood among that group that night. When his biography shall be truly written, it will be found that while his accomplished work and deeds as an engineer will give him a place among the ablest in the profession he so well adorned, his highest and best monument will be found in the loving memory of him that will ever linger in the hearts of his friends.

ECKLEY B. COXE,* of Drifton, Pa., Ex-President of the Institute: The death of Alexander Lyman Holley means much more

---

* This and the following tributes to Mr. Holley's memory were contributed in writing, the authors being absent, or the lateness of the hour not permitting further speeches.

to the engineering profession than the loss of a great technical expert ordinarily would. There are not many, it is true, who possess his power of gathering and thoroughly digesting all the facts, theories, and other information bearing upon any great engineering problem they may have on hand, of opening the mind without prejudice to all sides of the question, and of reaching with almost unerring accuracy the true solution. He was one of a few men who have been distinguished not only as a civil, but also as a mechanical and mining, engineer. It is rare for any one to be eminent in a single branch of engineering, and almost unheard of that one should be, as Holley was, without a superior in all.

But it was in aiding in raising engineering as a profession to its present high position, in forming and strengthening that *esprit de corps* which of late years has grown up both here and abroad, that Holley exerted an influence which no other engineer has exerted, and which will be felt for years. He was a man whom to know was to love, with whom it was a privilege to have professional relations, to whom every true engineer delighted to communicate any new discovery that he might make; for no one who did so ever felt that he gave away anything for which he did not receive back full equivalent, not only in the treasures drawn from a well-stored memory of engineering facts and theories, but also in clear, sharp, unprejudiced criticism.

No one was quicker to acknowledge the merit of discoveries not made by himself, or slower to claim credit for himself for anything that in any way could be considered as the invention of another.

This characteristic showed itself not only in his intercourse with American engineers, but also with those whom he met in his many professional trips to Europe. When he went abroad, he was everywhere received with open arms, and information was gladly given to him which many others sought for in vain. All with whom he came in contact there found, as we all had done, that with him it was " more blessed to give than to receive;" that he came not as a beggar, asking alms, but as the generous fellow that he was, willing and anxious to give of the rich stores he possessed to those from whom he received. Thus he did more than any living man to break down the barriers and jealousies that separated the engineers of different countries. This he could do to great advantage, possessing as he did a mind which, after much reflection, I think was the broadest, best-developed, most complete that I have known. He loved not only science, but art; he could write well; he could speak well; whatever he was called upon to do, he did as a master; and it is hard to conceive of any sphere of life in which he would not have been distinguished. He was, in the highest sense of the word, a gentleman. To say that any person could have known Holley well, and not have loved him, seems to me impossible. Of him one can well say, "'Twere better to have loved and lost than never to have loved at all." The loss of Holley is something I could not at first appreciate; it grows upon me day by day, and I find myself constantly becoming more and more conscious of it; for when thinking over some problem or something of interest to the profession, I still say to myself, as I often did, "I must talk to Holley about this," and then suddenly remembering the sad truth, I realize how great, how irreparable our loss has been.

As I stood on that day at Greenwood, and saw him slowly lowered into his grave, I thought of all he had done for mining engineering, both in this country and abroad, and almost involuntarily I repeated to myself the old German *Bergmannsgruss*, which seemed peculiarly appropriate to him:

"DEN LETZTEN GRUSS BRINGT IHM DER BERGMANN DAR.

> "Leb' wohl, leb' wohl, Du Bergmannskind,
> Du hast vollbracht den Lauf;
> Treu warest Du und brav gesinnt,
> Drum rufen wir: Glück auf!

> "Zum letzten Male führst Du an,
> Und fährst nicht mehr herauf;
> Drum grüsst Dich auf der dunkeln Bahn
> Ein inniges Glück auf!

> "Doch schloss sich auch dein Auge hier,
> Dort thut sich's wieder auf;
> Wir Alle, Alle folgen Dir
> Und grüssen Dich! Glück auf!"

JAMES F. LEWIS, of Quinnemont, W. Va.: After all that has been written, and the many eloquent words spoken here to-day, it would seem impossible to find suitable words to express more. Yet I feel that the half has not been told, and that words cannot do full justice to the memory of our beloved friend and brother—certainly not words from me; but my feelings will not permit me to let this meeting pass without adding my testimony. The first time that I met Mr. Holley to know him personally was at the May meeting of the Institute, held in Dover, N. J., and it was through him that I became a member. My associations with him since then have been more of a social than of a business nature; yet so far as advice and information on business matters was concerned, I always found him ready and willing to impart it. I shall never forget the Sabbath I spent with him at his home in Brooklyn, directly after the Pittsburgh meeting and shortly before his departure for Europe to get the much-needed rest which he felt was essential at that time to prolong his life, and enable him to complete the great work he had marked out. In the long talk we had while riding that afternoon, he opened his heart, and spoke of the past and his hopes and fears of the future, with expressions of love and gratitude toward his friends for their many tokens of love and friendship to him. It was one of those seasons of delightful intercourse between men that come not frequently, and cannot be described, but are to be stored away in the heart as sweet memories—things to make us both happier and better. It also revealed to me the true manhood of A. L. Holley. But while we mourn the loss of our friend and brother, let us bear in mind that Holley still lives—not in the flesh, but in the spirit and in his professional writings, in the many interesting and most instructive papers read by him before this Institute, and in the monuments of industry at Troy, Harrisburgh, Johnstown, Bethlehem, Pittsburgh, Chicago, Joliet, etc. His spirit and example will lead others to take up the work where he has left it, and a monument will be built up to his memory that will be lasting as the ages.

JOHN FRITZ, of Bethlehem, Pa.: I much regret that I cannot go to Washington to attend the session in memory of our dear friend Holley; and I take this opportunity to express my heartfelt sympathy in the sorrow of his many friends. It was my good fortune to make his acquaintance some fifteen years ago, and for the greater part of the time I have been on the most intimate terms with him. While it makes me sad to think that I shall never see his bright and cheerful face again, yet I can with unalloyed pleasure look back to the time when we would sit for hours, and talk over the various problems of mechanical and metallurgical engineering with which he was so fully identified. It was in these quiet talks, which I so much enjoyed, that I learned to respect and love him. He was so brilliant, so frank, so communicative, and withal so modest, that it was impossible to withhold from him admiration

and affection. He is no more; his noble career on earth is ended;
and while in common with many others in his profession I shall
greatly miss him as a member of it, yet it is when I look back to
the enjoyable and instructive hours spent together with him, and
the thought comes that they will return no more, that I feel his loss
most keenly, and can most deeply sympathize with his many loving
friends.   But he did not live in vain.   His life was one of beneficence as well as of untiring industry and of herculean labor in the
development of the great mechanical and metallurgical progress of
the age.   Though his name is written in letters of steel all over
our broad, fair land, yet I think there should be some distinctive
memorial erected that will tell to coming generations of the work
and worth of our friend and brother, A. L. Holley.

W. R. JONES, of Pittsburgh, Pa.: In the death of A. L. Holley,
those who have been intimately connected with him in the development of the Bessemer process have lost not only their chief, but also
a valued and true friend.   To his genius and his mechanical ability
the wonderful development of the Bessemer process in this country
is largely due.   With far-seeing sagacity he urged development,
while others timidly suggested delay.   The perfecting of any new
process requires genius, enterprise, and force of character, all governed by sound wisdom.   All these elements he possessed in a
remarkable degree; and, combined with these, his frankness, his
generosity, his extreme modesty, his nobleness of purpose, rendered
him one of the grandest and greatest of men.   No wonder that we
entertained for him the highest respect, that we loved him with a
love strong and pure.

He has passed beyond, yet he has stamped the impress of his
great genius on our scientific and metallurgical enterprises.   No
longer will the drear monotony of our task be broken by a cheery
letter from our beloved Holley, or the roar of the converter, or the
clashing and clatter of machinery be made pleasant by his presence.
He did his whole duty while with us; let us, who still linger, see
that his memory is honored.

P. BARNES, of Springfield, Ill.: My acquaintance with our good
friend Holley began just before he went abroad to arrange for the
definite introduction of the Bessemer process into this country; and
after January, 1869, I was until the day of his death almost continuously employed, either as an attaché of his own private office,

or else in local charge of some one or other of the works with which he was associated as consulting engineer, and hence under his immediate professional supervision.

These works, in their varied extent, their large cost, and in their enormous product, are the best monuments to his skill; but no tribute to his worth can be framed in words clear enough to set forth his never-failing kindliness to his subordinates, his ever-ready considerateness toward their preferences, in the fulness which these qualities deserve.. He had a very rare faculty of impressing his own views upon others, and securing their adoption, even though at first there seemed to be wide differences to be overcome, in the innumerable details needing attention in construction-work; and probably a thousand instances could be found in which the correctness of conclusions formed by him almost by intuition, as it were, has been demonstrated by the rigorous proof of actual service of the details thus planned and executed.

One other thing may be most justly referred to at such a time as this, as showing the fully rounded character of our departed friend —the ever-ready zeal with which he would overlook and forget the unkindness of those who (in more instances than one) had, through heedlessness or through ill-will, forgotten the obligation they owed him of professional loyalty, to say nothing of kindlier personal regard. To every one, even to these, his heart was always open, his friendly advice and suggestion always ready.

To the offerings of those who may present more fitting memorials than this, I desire to add my own tribute of respectful and affectionate remembrance.

EDMUND C. PECHIN, of Cleveland, O.: What Holley has accomplished in the world at large does not so much interest me. I think of him only as the genial companion, the kindly, big-hearted man, the trusty friend. I can pay him no higher meed of praise than that in all the years of our acquaintance I never heard him speak an unkind word of any one. The Northmen make Odin say:

"We ourselves die, but the fair fame of him that hath earned it never dies."

Holly could afford to die; when he had enshrined himself in so many loving hearts, and had earned so fair a fame.

W. J. TAYLOR, of Chester, N. J.: I regret exceedingly my inability to be present, and unite with my fellow-members in expressing our great sorrow at the loss of our friend and brother, Alexander L. Holley, and in paying that tribute to his memory which his eminent abilities and noble character have so richly merited. Taken from us in the prime of manhood, when he was a vast store of knowledge, to which we all had the most kindly access, it is hard for us to be reconciled to the ways of Providence, and not rebel at the removal of one whom we not only loved, but loved to honor. Only those who knew him can realize the loss the whole metallurgical and mechanical world has sustained in his early death. But his earthly labors and trials are over, and we must not forget that our loss is his gain. God grant that there may be more Holleys.

W. F. MATTES, of Scranton, Pa.: I feel it a personal misfortune that my acquaintance with our late associate, Dr. Holley, was so limited, and that my opportunities for conversation with him so few. Therefore, in adding my trifle to this memorial, I will speak only of the impression made upon me by his writings, particularly in my repeated studies of his various reports to the Bessemer companies. These productions impress by their surpassing excellence for the objects in view, combining, as they do, in great masses of material the rare qualities of judicious selection and concise statement—an instinctive seizing of salient points with luminous expression. The strokes are bold, accurate, and graphic, revealing the extensive knowledge and working of a master-mind.

M. V. SMITH, of McKeesport, Pa.: As one of those whose own lives have received a benefit from the life of Mr. Holley, I am glad to avail myself of the privilege of paying a tribute to his memory. His more intimate friends will tell how he was endeared to each of them; they will also tell of those noble traits of his character by which he was best known to the world. A more favored few may speak of what he was at his own home and fireside. What I particularly wish to call attention to is the fact, that his nobility of character was exercised and found expression in noble words and actions, not only toward his kindred and his friends, but also toward those who had no claims upon him, either of friendship or of business, and from whom he could have no expectations of ever receiving any reward.

Some men may be generous from selfish reasons, because generosity, like honesty, is the best policy; but Mr. Holley's generosity sprang from no considerations of policy—it was only one manifestation of his natural disposition. I have a personal knowledge of one action of Mr. Holley's, in the Council of the American Institute of Mining Engineers, of which I cannot give the particulars, as they would involve the names of living persons; but suffice it to say that the action was a noble and generous one, for the benefit of one who could have had no claims even upon Mr. Holley's attention. I only mention this to show what I hope others may show in a better way, that Mr. Holley's heart was large enough to include not only his own kindred and friends,—and their number is legion, —but to reach out and do good in the outside world.

PROF. R. H. THURSTON, of Hoboken, N. J.: I had relied so greatly upon Holley in all the work and in all the plans in which we had a mutual interest, that his loss leaves me with a lonelier and more helpless feeling than I have ever experienced after the loss of the nearest of earlier friends. He was so just, so generous, and so absolutely trustworthy, so full of kindly impulses, so overflowing with noble enterprise; so kindly appreciative of the weaker attempts of his friends to inaugurate or to forward any useful work; so bright, cheery, happy, and sympathetic in his communion with us, that his departure seems like the passage of a summer's sun behind a winter's cloud. I only hope that we may, when we, too, "pass over," have something of this feeling of love and honor in the hearts of our friends, with somewhat less of the sadder sense of bereavement.

[Brief letters of condolence were also received from many other members of the Institute.]

The following telegrams were read by the Secretary:

LONDON.

The Council of the Civil Engineers, now sitting, desires to record its high sense of the eminent qualities of Mr. Holley, which won for him universal respect and esteem.

INSTITUTION CIVIL ENGINEERS.*

---

* The Secretary subsequently received the following letter:

THE INSTITUTION OF CIVIL ENGINEERS,
25 GREAT GEORGE STREET, WESTMINSTER, S.W.
22d February, 1882.

SIR: I beg to hand you herewith Extract from the Minutes of Council of this Institution, with copy of a telegram dispatched to you last night.

Having known Alexander Lyman Holley since his first visit to Europe in 1857,

LONDON.

As an English member I would testify to the unique regard in which Mr. Holley was held here as an engineer and man. I would add an humble personal tribute to his memory as metallurgist, brilliant engineer, and generous friend.

SIDNEY GILCHRIST THOMAS.

WORKINGTON, WEST CUMBERLAND, ENGLAND.

I express my deepest sympathy with Mr. Holley's friends and countrymen in the irreparable loss sustained by them, and by us, through his departure.

G. J. SNELUS.

MIDDLESBORO', ENGLAND.

I exceedingly regret that Mr. Holley has passed away from us. I join you all in spirit to-day in praise of his memory.

WINDSOR RICHARDS.

BLAENAVON, WALES.

We all mourn him, and shall miss him greatly.

E. P. MARTIN.

LONDON.

Having travelled with friend Holley all over Europe, few can better testify to his talent and amiable character, and how deeply

I may, perhaps, be permitted to add my own personal testimony to his worth and merits. His fascinating manner had a peculiar charm for all with whom he was brought into contact, while the uprightness of his character was beyond dispute.

I remain, sir,
Your obedient servant,
JAMES FORREST,
Secretary.

Extract from the Minutes of Council of the Institution of Civil Engineers, 21st day of February, 1882.

Moved, seconded, and

"*Resolved, unanimously,* This Council desire to record their high sense of the eminent qualities of the recently deceased member of the Institution, Alexander Lyman Holley, of New York city, which had won for him universal respect and esteem.

"*Resolved,* That in view of the Special Session of the American Institute of Mining Engineers, to be held in Washington on Wednesday afternoon, February 22d, in memory of the late Alexander Lyman Holley, the substance of the above Resolution be conveyed by telegram to Mr. Drown, the Secretary of the Institute."

his European friends show the sorrow felt at his loss. The friendship for Holley in Europe was strong as steel and good as Swedish iron. United in this mournful condolence are Schneider, of Creusot, France; Greiner, of Seraing, Belgium; Longsdon, of Krupp's, Germany; Akermann, of Sweden; and numerous friends in England from whom I have received letters expressing deep sorrow. Honor to the land that produced such a man. Our consolation is that Alexander Lyman Holley is now "formed in a better mould."

C. P. SANDBERG.*

DELORO, ONTARIO, CANADA.

You know the important work that detains me. Please express my regret at being unable to attend the meeting of the Institute. My whole heart is with you, and I desire especially to bear my testimony to the rare gifts which placed our Holley among the very first engineers of any age, and commanded the love, esteem, and admiration of all who knew him. Learned, skilful, discriminating, sound in judgment, and unprejudiced; unstinted in sympathy and appreciation for the work of his fellow-laborers; warm-hearted,

---

* The Secretary subsequently received the following letters:

PARIS, le 27 Fevrier, 1882.

Mr. C. P. Sandberg, ingénieur à Londres, m'informe qu'il a associé mon nom au témoignage de condoléance et de sympathie, dont il a près l'initiative au nom des ami de feu Alexander Lyman Holley en Europe.

J'ai l'honneur de vous faire savoir que j'approuve complètement les sentiments qui ont dicté la dépèche qu'il vous a adressée à cette occasion, et ji profite de la circonstance pour vous exprimer la part que ji prends personellement aux éloges et aux regrets des amis de Mr. Holley en Amérique.

Venillez agréer, Monsieur, l'assurance de ma considération la plus distinguée.

H. SCHNEIDER.

ESSEN, GERMANY, Feb. 27, 1882.

[To MR. SANDBERG.] Please accept my best thanks for kindly including my name in the cablegram of those who mourned the loss of our friend Holley. I had the profoundest admiration for the character of our late friend; for with all his excellent gifts that brought him prominently to the front, there was the true modesty of a gentleman. His judgment was always clear and distinct, while his knowledge was profound. America has lost much in losing him; and I am glad to see all that is being done to honor his memory. His friends will never forget him, and enemies I am sure he has none. Again thanking you, believe me,

Yours, very truly,
ALFRED LONGSDON.

brave, faithful, and incorruptible, our Holley has builded in his works and in our affection a monument such as few in any age have deserved or received.

R. P. ROTHWELL, of New York city.

READING, PA.

Regret I cannot be present to do honor to the memory of the lamented Holley. He always dispensed generously the knowledge he so easily and intelligently acquired, and was a benefactor of mankind.

W. E. C. COXE.

After the reading of letters and telegrams, Mr. Weeks spoke as follows:

J. D. WEEKS, of Pittsburgh, Pa.: It was not my privilege to know Mr. Holley as long as some of those who have spoken, but I remember that a few years ago, in this very city, at the time he was President of this Institute, I met Mr. Holley. As a newspaper man I asked him for those favors that newspaper men are accustomed to ask of men of influence and position. I found him kind, generous, friendly; and I have always found him so at every time that I have approached him. And I wish to bear testimony, in behalf of the technical and scientific press of this country, to their friend, to their fellow-laborer—for Alexander Holley was one of us in the early years of his life, and in his after-years as an author, also, he was one of us—I wish to bear testimony to the extreme courtesy, to the great kindness, and the great disinterestedness with which he has always met us, and with which he has always given us the best that he had to give. I thought, when reference was made to his connection with the Bessemer process, that he had merited and should have received as high honor as that man to whom he is only second.* And yet what matters it? He was Alexander the Conqueror in the arts; he is Alexander crowned king in our hearts, whose reign shall never end with the words, "The king is dead." When our chairman so beautifully referred to that sketch that our friend Holley made, there rushed to my mind that wonderful poem of Emerson, in which he describes the

---

* The Bessemer medal was subsequently sent by the British Iron and Steel Institute to the family of Mr. Holley.

feelings, thoughts, aspirations, and motives that animated the cathedral builders in those old times. You remember the words:

> "Himself from God he could not free.
> He builded better than he knew;
> The conscious stone to beauty grew."

and, as our chairman has so admirably said, has grown into the white glory of Milan or the stately splendor of York. I recalled the majestic cathedral of York as we saw its glories. We went down and down and down with the verger, and he showed us, beneath the foundation of the cathedral, another foundation that dated back in the Dark Ages, when they had builded a beautiful cathedral to testify to what their ideas of glory and grandeur were. In the coming days, in the grand social reform that has been spoken of, mankind will see a structure more grand and more glorious than that which exists at York. You and I may not live to help construct it, or to admire and explore it; but somebody else will have found the foundation that Alexander Lyman Holley laid, broad and deep and strong, and builded thereon a structure worthy of his thought. I wish, Mr. Chairman, in closing, to offer these

RESOLUTIONS.

Resolved, That in the death of Alexander Lyman Holley, formerly President of the Institute, we mourn the departure, not only of a great inventor and engineer, pioneer in the applications of science, and benefactor of mankind, but also and more keenly, of a true comrade and dear friend, the memory of whose strong and gentle spirit is indissolubly blended with the social history of this organization, as his genius, enthusiasm, and activity were potent factors in its professional success.

Resolved, That the chairman of this meeting be requested to deliver on some suitable future occasion an address in commemoration of the life and life-work of Mr. Holley.

Resolved, That the Council of the Institute be requested to take into consideration the publication of a memorial volume, to contain the above-mentioned address, the proceedings of this meeting, and such other matters as may be deemed expedient.

Resolved, That we extend to the American Society of Civil Engineers and to the American Society of Mechanical Engineers our sympathy in this great loss, sustained by them as well as ourselves.

Resolved, That a committee of five be appointed to take charge, after consultation with the Council, and in coöperation with such similar committees as may be constituted by our two sister societies, of the execution of the measures proposed in these resolutions, and to represent the American Institute of Mining Engineers in any further proceedings that may be taken for the same purpose.

Resolved, That a copy of these resolutions, together with the assurance of our profound sympathy, be transmitted by the Secretary to the family of Mr. Holley, and that copies be sent also to the Secretaries of the American Society of Mechanical Engineers and the American Society of Civil Engineers.

(Carried unanimously.)

The Chairman, in signifying his cordial acceptance of the task of preparing a memorial address, read a private letter written to him several years ago, in which Mr. HOLLEY placed at his disposal certain biographical memoranda, and proposed that, of the two, the survivor should render this service of friendship to the other.

The Chairman also read, at the conclusion of the meeting, the following letter:

89 JORALEMON ST., BROOKLYN, Feb., 1882.

MY DEAR FRIEND:

May I ask you to convey to my husband's friends in the Institute of Mining Engineers my deep sense of their kindness to me and affection for him? I have recalled so many times since his death their oft-repeated expressions of love for him. I never shall forget on one of the excursions at the Pittsburgh meeting the earnestness with which different members said to me, "Mrs. Holley, we do so love your husband." Those words pleased me then, but how much more precious they are to me now!

They all know the sad circumstances of his death and all the darkness and gloom that so suddenly enveloped *us*. At first there seemed no comfort; but I wish I could make them feel as I do, not only the *comfort* but the almost *joyousness* that has filled my heart as I have read all their words of love and sympathy. I never can express my gratitude.

Mr. Holley had the deepest interest in the Institute, and regarded its members as his *brothers*, and now their words make me feel that they had for him the same affection, and that at this meeting their tears are mingling with mine, because one whom we all loved so dearly has gone from us.

Will they think it presumptuous in me if I say that I shall always think of them as his brothers? I beg you and them to believe that any and all events connected with the American Institute of Mining Engineers will be of the greatest interest to

Yours most gratefully and affectionately,

MARY H. HOLLEY.

III.

MEMORIAL SESSION OF THE AMERICAN SOCIETY OF MECHANICAL ENGINEERS.

PHILADELPHIA, April 19th, 1882.

THE PRESIDENT, PROF. R. H. THURSTON, of Hoboken, N. J.: I feel that I have a peculiar right to speak in this place of the friend and colleague who has left us, to speak of him who was one of the most active among the founders of our Society, and of the man who was the ablest of his generation in our profession. As your presiding officer I stand in the place that he should have occupied, holding the position which he would probably have held had he not himself chosen otherwise, deferring an honor which he hoped, and of right may have anticipated, would be tendered him a little later, when, with improved health, he expected to pass an unbroken year among us.

The brotherly feeling that always unites men who have been taught within the same academic walls came to unite us a quarter of a century ago when we became alumni of "Old Brown." A mutual trust and confidence, such as rarely bind men seeing as little of each other as we did during the succeeding years, came to us, despite infrequent meetings, while the last few years had brought so many opportunities of intercourse that our friendship was cemented with a firmness and closeness of union that is still more rarely experienced among business men. Common tastes and closely related professional pursuits, similar interests, and pleasant memories of much that was common to our earlier manhood, led to a friendship of which the remembrance will never cease to yield sad pleasure to the survivor.

Mr. Holley was one of those who signed the call for the meeting for the formation of the American Society of Mechanical Engineers; he was the principal author of our by-laws and rules, and the leading spirit in the organization of the Society. He was a member of the Nominating Committee, and resigned in order to oblige his colleagues by accepting a nomination as Vice-President, while positively declining nomination as the first President. He was one of those among the officers of our Society who were always present at the business meetings of the Council, and at all regular meetings, and who never allowed even important private business to interfere with the business of the Society.

No member was more thoughtful in regard to its interests, more prolific of plans for the promotion of its welfare, or more active and earnest in enlisting others in its support, and in bringing the leaders of the profession into our ranks. Mr. Holley was among the foremost in the movement to resuscitate the United States Board to test metals, and to reorganize the great scheme of investigation planned so carefully·by that body, but hardly more than planned before the demise of the Board. He was the most active of our members in the organization of a plan for a gathering of European members of the several branches of the profession to meet our own representative men in convention in the United States, and to inspect, under the guidance of our committees, the public works and private enterprises of this country. This thought of a community of work, of pleasures, and of all interests, that should bring into contact all branches of the profession, and all members of our great guild, is illustrative of the breadth of his intellect no less than of his greatness of heart; and these qualities always became prominent in discussing those still weightier matters that had for us a common and more intense interest,—a rational system of education, and a general system of promotion of the useful arts and applied sciences by the united efforts of statesmen, men of science, and men of business,— matters that were always brought into view when, as was so often the case, "The Scientific Method of Advancement of Science" became the theme of our discussion.

Intellectually great, with a noble soul, and possessing the next essential, a powerful and vigorous yet graceful body, Mr. Holley was in all the days of his middle working life one of the finest illustrations of the type of man that Agassiz is said to have been. It was "the soul of a sage in the body of an athlete." But that soul has broken out from even such confinement, and that athletic frame yielded to the strain of the mightier soul temporarily confined within it; and to us is left only the hope of a future renewal of intercourse and the remembrance of the past.

Our friend Holley was an honest and an earnest man. But such a man is not always the most useful man either to the world, to his fellows, or to himself. The honest, earnest man, who, in the excess of his zeal, deceives himself, is often the most dangerous of characters. The greater his intelligence the more dangerous the man. The greatest crimes that the world has known have been committed by conscientious, zealous men. Such men must possess a better judgment and a greater power of self-control than their comrades if they are to live useful, happy, and successful lives.

Holley was an honest, earnest, intellectually great man, possessing that rare and sterling judgment, and having more than a common share of that woman's intuitive appreciation of the right, which is the best regulator of the earnest worker. The faith, the hope, the charity, the brightness, the earnestness, and the wholeness of heart that distinguished him, no less than his great mental powers and his professional standing, helped to place him in the high position which he held among men. Shakespeare's admonition in that well-named play, "All's Well that Ends Well," was unneeded by our friend. To "love all, trust a few, do wrong to none," was, with him, second nature. His charity and his love covered all humanity; his faith in those about him, once given, was never withdrawn, except when, by some such bitter experience as we have all occasionally tasted, it was extinguished by betrayal.

Do wrong to none! His whole life was a mission of noblest beneficence, not only to his friends and his acquaintances, to those who loved, and to those who came to him necessitous, but to all nations, to the whole race contemporary with and succeeding him. He was of those few great and fortunate benefactors of mankind to whom we owe the highest material benefits brought to us by civilization.

Our committees are considering how, where, and in what form a suitable monument shall be erected to the memory of this most honored of our colleagues; whether to mount a bust of marble or of bronze in Central Park; to erect a statue at the capital of the United States, or to place some more modest but not less fitting and expressive memorial at his tomb. We may adopt either scheme; if we were to measure his deserts, they would be beyond all these plans. It is of little consequence which is decided upon; his noblest monument is the memory which is implanted in the hearts of his friends, and in the memories of mankind. If these were not enough, we might erect in the midst of each of those great and wonderful industrial establishments built up so largely by his genius a tablet inscribed with his name, and the legend so familiar to the visitor to Sir Christopher Wren's tomb in St. Paul's, London:

"Si monumentum quæris, circumspice."

Let us hope that the time may come, and that soon, when a still nobler monument than any yet proposed may be built to perpetuate his fame.

The time must come, and that we will hope very soon, when a pressing want of this great country shall be supplied by the establishment of a complete system of thoroughly scientific practical education of the people for their work, a congeries of trade schools and of technical colleges, united into a thoroughly organized and well-administered whole. Such a system it seems now certain must be the work of private hands, and must be built up by the intelligent liberality of comparatively few wealthy and patriotic citizens. We have not yet statesmen in numbers, intelligence, and influence equal to the task of securing a governmental system of education such as has done so much for Germany and France. But the work is begun, and when it has so far progressed that the grand central, crowning, and directing member of the organization, a great UNIVERSITY OF THE ARTS AND SCIENCES, shall have been founded and endowed by some noble modern Vaucanson, or Worcester, or citizen more kingly than Ptolemy of Alexandria,—some one, perhaps, of the beneficiaries of the comrade whom we mourn,—let us hope that its most important department may be known as the HOLLEY MEMORIAL SCHOOL OF THE ARTS AND SCIENCES OF ENGINEERING.

If other inscription is needed upon any tablet that may be erected, or upon the pedestal of the monument that shall be raised to the memory of this great man, this worthy successor in fame to the greatest of the inventors of the steam-engine, we may write with fitness and justice a paraphrase of that splendid tribute which may be read on the base of Chantrey's statue of Watt in Westminster Abbey:

Not to perpetuate a Name
which must endure while the peaceful Arts flourish,
but to show
that Mankind have learnt to honor those who best deserve their
Gratitude,
those among the People of the United States and of Europe
who love, honor, and cherish his Memory have united
to raise this Monument to
ALEXANDER LYMAN HOLLEY,
who, directing the Force of an original Genius, early exercised
in Philosophic Research,
to the development of the modern Processes of Steel Manufacture,
enlarged the Resources of his Country, increased the Powers of Man, and
rose to an eminent Place
among the most illustrious Followers of Science, and the real
Benefactors of the World.

It is of this man that I am desired, that I myself desire, most
earnestly to speak in fitting terms. But I am unable to do so.
I have gone to my desk many times during these last sad weeks
with the intention of putting on paper words properly expressive
of the feelings that are awakened by the thought of our loss. But
the words would not fit the thought, and after repeated trials I gave
up the attempt. But one evening as I sat at my window, saddened
and disheartened, I saw Sirius, that most beautiful and bright of all
the stars, rising through the gray mists of the east, his sapphire rays
quivering with varying refraction, steadily sweeping upward into
the clearer space above, and finally shining out of the invisible dome
with the brilliancy of a thousand diamonds, only made the brighter
by contrast with the thousands of orbs of lesser magnificence which
besprinkled the whole celestial vault.

I watched the progress of that glorious star, from hour to hour,
as it so slowly, so steadily, so quietly rose toward the zenith, " Ohne
hast, ohne rast." After a time a thin cloud barely touched, without
concealing, its light, and presently it shone free and clear again, and
once more swung magnificently upward. Again, a broader and a
thicker veil passed before it, dimming its lustre, and bringing upon
me a startling fear lest the beautiful star should disappear forever
from view. And even when it reappeared the apprehension remained with me and dimmed the pleasure that its recovered beauty
should have given. How soon must a deep and impenetrable shade
conceal it forever! The star still rose, still bright, still beautiful,
still wonderful in contrast with the galaxy about it, shining down
upon the world with almost, if not quite, all its earlier splendor,
blessing the world with light gathered in space away beyond the
reach or ken of human minds, and impressing me with a feeling
of strength, majesty, invincibleness, such as can only be realized
in the presence of the most noble and incomprehensible of all
creations.

At last, when nearing the zenith, when in the very height of its
glory and beauty, those blue rays quivered again, struggling through
the cloudy veil for a little time, flashed through a rift in the black,
and disappeared. A shock came to my heart; a sense of deser-
tion, of loneliness, and of grief beyond remedy. Gone forever!
But a second thought brought relief. That great and glorious star
is still there! It is but a veil of mist, impenetrable to vision, but
hardly tangible, that has come between us. Another day will pass

and all its magnificence and all its beauty shall again be ours to enjoy.

Another thought brought greater relief: A friend passes from our sight when at the zenith of his fame, in the prime of his manhood, in the height of his usefulness. But why mourn, and why seek to express the selfish sentiments of grief? He still lives. His is still the glory and the splendor of a great soul. Let the tongue be silent! His is the story of the star.

And yet, after all, to many of us who have long known this eminent man, who have found in him a valuable acquaintance, the pleasantest of companions, and the truest and kindest of friends, who, ourselves no orators and feeble even in the every-day use of language, nevertheless feel " more than tongue can tell," or yet " heart can hold in silence;" to many of us it is an unspeakable pleasure to be able to intrust our duty to a representative of ourselves and of the Society, who can, and who will gladly, say what we would say had we the power. For this we gladly turn to one who can give suitable expression to the grief which weighs upon us while we contemplate our loss, and while, nevertheless, we are conscious that our utterances should rather take the form of a song of victory for this immortal, and of congratulation that our friend who has now " passed over," has won so gloriously the peace, and the love, and the happiness of the better life, to which we may hope he may, in due time, welcome all who are left bereaved.

I have the honor to introduce to the Society the eulogist chosen by our committee to express for us all a common grief, common recollections, and a common hope. I present MR. JAMES C. BAYLES, member of the Society.

Mr. Bayles then delivered the following

TRIBUTE TO ALEXANDER LYMAN HOLLEY.

Mr. President and Gentlemen of the American Society of Mechanical Engineers: I have been asked, on behalf and as a member of the Memorial Committee appointed by our Council, to formally express our deep sense of professional loss and personal bereavement in the death of our honored vice-president and dear friend, Alexander L. Holley. I have accepted this sad duty with satisfaction and with reluctance; with satisfaction, because he was my friend through

years of pleasant and, at times, intimate intercourse; with reluctance, because I know that nothing I can say will give fitting expressions to the sorrow we feel, each in his own way. Even the
language of exuberant eulogy, could I command it, would seem out
of place in this our lodge of sorrow, and inappropriate, because none
valued less than he mere phrases and declamation.

But how can we speak of Holley without eulogy? He was at
once so great a man and so dear a friend; we knew him so intimately and loved him so well, that we, at least, cannot speak of
him as of others who die crowned with honors gained in spheres of
usefulness different from our own. He was one of ourselves, but
now that he is gone we recognize as never before his immeasurable
worth. I do not mean that he was not appreciated and understood
by those of us who knew him best. We ever rated him far above
his own modest estimate of himself, and involuntarily paid him the
homage of an honor he never courted. But still he was *our* Holley,
and now that he has vanished we stand like Gideon beside the wine-
press, when, gazing at vacancy, he knew to whom he had offered
the meat and broth of his commonplace daily life. We realize now
as never before that in his high sphere of special usefulness, Holley
was one of the greatest engineers of his time, and that a generation
hence the student of science who scans the metallurgical and engineering literature of this century, will see better than we do now
the impress of his name on the cornerstones of more than one of
the great industries of the future.

I speak to many who in Holley's death have suffered personal
bereavement. To each of us the sad news came fraught with the
dread significance of irreparable loss. To each it meant the sever-
ance of ties far stronger than we had realized until a pang in the
heart revealed the truth. To each it meant a sorrow keen or dull
according to the intimacy with which we had known him. Each
of us has some legacy of personal reminiscence which, though better
worth remembering than telling, is none the less a precious possession—precious if only the echo of his gentle, kindly voice, or the
recollection of his earnest face beaming with a light which illumi-
nated all about him. I count it as one of the most striking evidences of Holley's greatness and goodness that we remember him
with an unconscious exaggeration of personal admiration. Who
has yet heard even calm and impartial comment on his work and
worth? When or where is he yet mentioned save with tremulous
voice? Who recalls aught but good of Holley, or names him with-

out such tribute of praise as few men merit while living, or receive when dead ?

In what is meant to be merely a tribute to Holley's memory, it will not be expected that I shall attempt to name or value the results of his varied, conscientious, and skilful professional work. With such knowledge of the subject as I possess, I can at most sketch freely and in outline the incidents of his phenomenal career. Had we time to look more closely, we should see that the genius we so greatly wonder at meant simply tireless industry ; that he moved upward step by step, in natural and regular development ; that the results he accomplished were worked out by close study and clear reasoning. Luck and chance were not factors in the equation of his success. What he did he first knew; what he knew he first learned. There was no happy accident to mark the turning-point in his professional career. His inventions and improvements were but the means by which he sought the attainment of ends kept steadily in view. Thoroughness characterized his habits of thought and of work, and those who knew him best, best knew how carefully he prepared himself for whatever he had to do. In this, probably more than in anything else, we find the secret of his uniform success in all the undertakings and duties of his brilliant career.

It detracts nothing from our estimate of his attainments to know that Alexander L. Holley began life under auspices peculiarly favorable. The child of exceptional parents, and born into a happy and virtuous New England home, the influences surrounding his early life were probably all which could be desired. He was a scion of the true American aristocracy—an aristocracy of intellectual and moral worth. Knowing neither poverty nor riches, he felt the inspiration of necessary self-dependence without the discouragements and limitations of want. Quick to learn, he completed his studies at school in 1853, choosing the scientific course at Brown University in preference to the classical course at Yale, for which he had been prepared. He was then twenty-one years of age. At once we find him seeking the knowledge which can only be gained in practical work, and without which technical training has so limited a value. He went direct from the school into the large locomotive works at Providence, and for about a year ran a locomotive on the Stonington road. Years after, as President of the American Institute of Mining Engineers, we catch a suggestion of his fruitful experience in this modest capacity, in the striking passage in his address on "The Inadequate Union of Engineering Science and Art," in which he thus describes the relation of the driver to his engine: "The thoughtful locomotive driver is clothed upon, not with the mere machinery of a larger organism, but with all the attributes except volition of a power superior to his own. Every faculty is stimulated, and every sense exalted. An unusual sound amid the roaring exhaust and the clattering wheels, tells him instantly the place and degree of danger as would a pain in his own flesh. The consciousness of a certain jarring on the foot-plate, a chattering of a steam-valve, a halt in the exhaust, a peculiar smell of burning, a sudden pounding of the piston,.an ominous wheeze of the blast, a hissing of a water-gauge, warning him respectively of a broken spring-hanger, a cutting valve, a slipped eccentric, a hot journal, the priming of the boiler, high water, low water, or failing steam; these sensations, as it were, of his outer body, become so intermingled with the sensations of his inner body, that this wheeled and fire-feeding man feels, rather than perceives, the varying stresses upon his mighty organism."

Thus, unconsciously perhaps, Holley tells us how he carried his responsibilities in all the details of his professional work. It was not perfunctory service for wages or for profit, but a living experience, subjecting mind and body to constant tension. He had put something of himself into every member of the Bessemer plant. The throb of its machinery kept time to his own heart-beats, and he felt, as well as perceived, all the stresses upon the mighty organism with which his life was so closely identified.

At the outset of his professional career, Holley began to write for publication. With an unselfish love of truth, he could not conceal or save for his own benefit the fruits of his study and experience. At twenty-three we find him a regular contributor to the technical press, especially to Colburn's *Railway Advocate*. About this time, I am told, there came a marked change in Holley's literary style. His earlier compositions, though enriched by occasional evidences of unconscious genius, were florid and sophomoric to a degree which cannot fail to excite a smile. At once he changed to the simple, earnest style which gave his literary talent the brilliancy of a cut and polished diamond. For this change, Holley was no doubt indebted in a great degree to his friend and co-worker, Zerah Colburn, and we can imagine what delight those wonderful young men must have felt in an association so fruitful of mutual benefit. Doubtless, Holley owed much to Colburn. Without the aid of such a collaborator he would have made his way to substantial greatness; with it the road was shorter and smoother. But journalism, under whatever guidance or in whatever companionship, is an excellent school, and one in which Holley learned much that better prepared him for his life work. At twenty-four we find him proprietor and editor of the *Railway Advocate*, which, founded too early and without 'an appreciative constituency, suspended during the crisis of 1857. This release from serious and unprofitable responsibilities gave Holley a chance to go abroad for study. At twenty-six we find him publishing with Colburn, as their joint production, a work on European Railways,* which had an immediate and important influence on American railroad construction and operation. At the age of twenty-nine we find him again started in what gave promise of a brilliant journalistic career. He went abroad as correspondent of the New York *Times*, and the scrap-books in which he preserved his writings is, I am told by Dr. Raymond, who now has them for examination, a mine of wealth from which might be compiled a brilliant and memorable volume. Of the value of his work as a contributor to the newspaper press we can have but little knowledge. That it was potent in stimulating invention and improvement we may be sure. Such work is often valued too lightly. It seems to possess but a transient interest, and to be pushed aside, almost before the ink is dry, by the fresh attractions of the next day's current literature; but every valuable article finds somewhere readers to whom it is worth more than a library of books. The writer for the newspaper press may often feel discouraged by the thought that what costs him so much is so soon forgotten, but every article which is worth remembering is remembered. Like the poet's arrows shot into the air and falling he knows not where, the work of the able and conscientious newspaper contributor exercises an influence he little knows. At twenty-eight, while still a journalist, we find Holley the author of a work on railway practice,† which at once

---

* The Permanent Way and Coal-burning Locomotives of European Railways, with a Comparison of the Working Economy of European and American Lines, and the Principles upon which Improvement must Proceed. By Zerah Colburn and Alexander L. Holley, with 51 engraved plates by J. Bien. New York, Holley & Colburn, 1858, 4to.

† American and European Railway Practice in the Economical Generation of Steam, Including the Materials and Construction of Coal-burning Boilers, Combustion, the Variable Blasts, Vaporization, Circulation, Superheating, Supplying and Heating Feed-water, etc., and the Adaptation of Wood and Coke-burning Engines to Coal-burning; and in Permanent Way, including Road-bed,

became standard. When we remember that the materials for this treatise were collected at a time when he seemed wholly engrossed in newspaper work, we can but wonder at his extraordinary industry. At thirty we find him going abroad for Edwin A. Stevens to study ordnance and armor; and at thirty-three he published a work on these subjects,* which was alone sufficient to give him a recognized position in the front ranks of engineers. Meanwhile he had secured for American capitalists the Bessemer patents, and built at Troy experimental works. He had thus reached professional eminence at an age when most men are but laying the foundations of a career. In this department of metallurgical engineering his extraordinary talent found full opportunity for its greatest achievements. How much he did to create the Bessemer steel industry in this country, and make our average practice superior to the best foreign practice, has been ably and frankly told by Mr. Robert W. Hunt, of Troy, in a paper before the American Institute of Mining Engineers.† When we remember in how short a time this industry has attained its present extent and prosperity, and with what giant strides it has moved forward to a point at which its statistics overshadow those of Great Britain, we cannot fail to find interesting the story of how this was brought about, chiefly by Holley's persistent industry and close study of details. Fully impressed with the possibilities of the Bessemer process as he had witnessed its workings in England, he inspired others with his own enthusiasm, and under his direction the original plant of the Albany and Rensselaer works at Troy was built. Previous experiments with the pneumatic process, as patented by William Kelly, had been made at Wyandotte, in which Mr. W. F. Durfee, of our membership, took a prominent part, and he and his associates are certainly entitled to share with Holley the credit of the

Sleepers, Rails, Joint Fastenings, Street Railways, etc., etc. By Alexander L. Holley, B.P., with 77 plates, engraved by J. Bien. New York, D. Van Nostrand, 1st edition, 1860; London, Sampson, Low, Son & Co., 4to., 1st edition, 1867; 2d edition, 1867.

* A Treatise on Ordnance and Armor, Embracing Descriptions, Discussions, and Professional Opinions Concerning the Material, Fabrication, Requirements, Capabilities, and Endurance of European and American Guns for Naval, Seacoast, and Iron-clad Warfare, and their Rifling, Projectiles, and Breech-loading. Also, Results of Experiments Against Armor, from Official Records; with an Appendix, Referring to Gun-cotton, Hooped Guns, etc., etc. By Alexander L. Holley, B.P., with 493 illustrations. New York, D. Van Nostrand, 1865; London, Trubner & Co., 1865, octavo.

† ransactions, A. I. M. E., vol. v., pp. 210-216.

first great improvement in the process, the substitution of the cupola for the reverberatory furnace for melting the iron to be charged into the converter. Mr. Durfee's failure to make this improvement successful was due to the small size of his cupola, the distance the iron had to be moved in the ladle, and the fact that, being low in silicon, it would not generate heat enough to produce the proper reactions when blown in the converter. Holley's success with the cupola was due to better and more convenient arrangements. Though not the first to make steel by the pneumatic process in this country, the Troy works were the first to approximate a commercial success. Early in the history of this industry, Holley seems to have concluded that the best foreign practice was merely a starting-point for an ingenious American engineer to work from. His talent was eminently practical, and in his judgment nothing was success-ful which did not give satisfactory commercial results. The task he had undertaken was a great one. Not only was the process to be adapted to the conditions here existing, but the popular prejudice against the product must be overcome by maintaining a standard of quality which should disarm criticism and command the confi-dence of consumers. Having made successful the melting in a cupola of the iron to be converted, he began to experiment with American irons, with enough success to encourage efforts on the part of furnace managers to provide a grade of pig suited to the process. The Troy plant was increased by the erection of a 5-ton converter, and Holley then assumed charge of the erection of the plant of the Pennsylvania Steel Company at Harrisburg, for which he had previously designed the machinery. In 1868 he returned to the management of the Troy works, which he partially remod-elled in the light of experience gained at Harrisburg, and the im-proved plant made its first blow in 1870. His next important improvement was the substitution of a 30-inch 3-high blooming train with lifting tables, for the cogging hammer, in the reduction of ingots. George Fritz, a great mechanic, between whom and Holley existed an almost fraternal love, subsequently devised an apparatus which displaced Holley's improvement, and carried economy a step further. Standing admittedly at the head of this branch of the profession, Holley was called upon to build or design one after another of the Bessemer works, or to assist with his advice and experience the engineers immediately in charge.

Mr. Hunt, in the paper before mentioned, thus summarizes the results of Holley's work up to the year 1877:

"The result of his thought gave us the present accepted type of American Bessemer plant. He did away with the English deep pit, and raised the vessels so as to get working-space under them on the ground floor; he substituted top-supported hydraulic cranes for the more expensive counter-weighted English ones, and put three ingot-cranes around the pit instead of two, and thereby obtained greater area of power; he changed the location of the vessel as related to the pit and melting-house; he modified the ladle-crane, and worked all the cranes and vessels from a single point; he substituted cupolas for reverberatory furnaces; and last, but by no means least, introduced the intermediate or accumulating ladle, which is placed on scales, and thus insures accuracy of operation by rendering possible the weighing of each charge of melted iron before pouring it into the converter. These points cover the radical features of his innovations. After building such a plant he began to meet the difficulties of details in manufacture, among the most serious of which was the short duration of the vessel-bottoms, and the time required to cool off the vessels to a point at which it was possible for workmen to enter and make new bottoms. After many experiments the result was the Holley vessel-bottom, which, either in its form as patented, or in a modification of it as now used in all American works, has rendered possible, as much as any other one thing, the present immense production."

Of what he has done since this was written we can learn only by a search among his papers. In the position of Consulting Engineer of the Bessemer Association, he worked with tireless industry, but with probably less advantage to his reputation and fortune than had he worked in another capacity. His responsibilities were great, and although his work cannot be said to have been profitable to him in proportion to its value to those for whom it was performed, he was too conscientious to consider his own interests to the sacrifice of theirs. It was not until a manifestation of their feeling of absolute ownership stung Holley's proud and sensitive nature, that he sought to sever this connection by resigning his position. But they were in no mood to part with one on whom they had learned to depend so absolutely. He remained to the last trammelled by a professional engagement he could not resign and was loath to sever, but which gave him a vast opportunity for usefulness in the line of his best abilities.

Considered as an inventor, Holley had fewer claims to recognition than many men whose lives have been of very much less benefit to the world. His talent was more fruitful of immediate results than that of the restless discoverer who is always pushing into the wilderness of possibilities as yet untraversed by the beaten paths of human endeavor. Holley cannot, I think, be called an inventor. He made no great discoveries, and, so far as I can learn, every invention claimed by him had for its object the provision of better means of reaching an end previously aimed at or attained.

His first patent was taken out in 1859, when he was twenty-seven years old. It was for an improved railway chair, and describes a device to preserve the continuity of the track by brackets so attached to spliced pieces and tension plates that the weight of the train wheels on the rail should keep the splices tightly in their places without the aid of plates, nuts, keys, or rivets.

In the same year he took a patent for cut-off gear for steam-engines, describing an apparatus in which a combination of the motion of an eccentric or its equivalent with the motion of a steam-piston for moving a valve, effected a variable cut-off of the induction-steam without interfering with a free exhaust.

Ten years passed before he again claimed protection as an inventor. In 1869 he patented a combination of crane, converter, and chimney, so placed relatively to each other that the crane could swing entirely around in its orbit over the converter without coming in contact with the chimney. One side of the converter was supported by a beam, in such a way as to permit a car to be run under it from one side; and it was claimed that by the arrangement of oven, crane, car, and lift for removing the bottom of the converter, special advantages were gained over those pertaining to the arrangement previously employed. A guide and hand screw were provided in connection with the improved arrangement of parts, so that the ladle stopper could be readily adjusted.

Again, in 1869, he patented a shield in connection with a Bessemer converter, for the protection of the workmen. A tuyere box is described in combination with the converter bottom, and the latter was so constructed as to admit of its introduction through the former.

In 1872, Holley patented the converter-bottom which bears his name. The patent described a construction of notched bricks shaped so as to be set below and around the tuyeres, the spaces between being rammed with ganister; and to more readily dry the mass screw plugs were provided, which passed through the ganister and boxes.

In the same year he took out two patents relating to the casting of ingots. The first of these describes a mould so arranged as to fill from the bottom to any height desired; the second described suitable moulds, in connection with a solid flask containing suitable runners leading from one mould to another, and lined with a refractory metal to prevent a too rapid abstraction of heat from the molten steel.

In 1873 he patented a stopper for ingot-moulds, supported at different points by elastic flanges or friction-springs, and on the same date an ingot-mould provided with an adjustable cast-iron stopper.

Towards the close of 1873 he obtained a patent on improved rolls, in which the middle roll was adjusted by two screws, one right- and the other left-handed, passing through the bolster at either end, and operated by worm-gearing connected with the pulley above. Fore- and catch-plates were fastened to lugs on the bolster of the middle roll, and carried by these when the roll was adjusted. A stop on the bolster limited the height to which the metal was raised by the table.

Three years later he invented and patented a furnace-construction, in the roof of which were spaces for air, water, or spray, conduits for cooling the same.

In 1879 he patented a feeding-device for rolling-mills, in which the feed-rollers were mounted on a special frame provided with suitable mechanism imparting a proper motion, and adapting the apparatus for feeding either long or short pieces. Another device consisted in a rocking frame attached to the housing. The feed-roller frame was carried by the rocking frame, and suitable mechanism is described to guide the pieces and impart a rotary motion to the feed-rollers.

Two years later, in 1881—scarcely more than thirteen months ago—he patented a steam-boiler furnace, in which the essential device consists of alternate ports, with a diaphragm so placed over them as to thoroughly mix the gases entering through the ports. The space below the diaphragm constitutes the combustion-chamber in which the gases are burned.

One year and seven days ago* his last patent is dated, which

* April 26th, 1881.

describes the removable converter shell, of which I shall speak somewhat more fully later on.

This, I believe, is a brief record of Holley's work as an inventor of new and patentable devices. The list is not a long one, and the casual reader will not find therein much to sustain a claim to great originality or a talent for discovery. But when we remember what some of these improvements have done for one of the great industries of the country, and how they have helped to place us in the front rank as steel-producers, we see that the world owes Holley more than it does many who anticipate industrial progress, and stake out claims which succeeding generations may perhaps work with profit, but which, when located, lie outside the busy circle of the world's activities and industries. I regard Holley's mechanical talent as eminently practical and characteristically American. He ever sought "convenient means." To facilitate, to simplify, to save labor, to economize where economy was profitable,—these were the ends he strove for and attained. Bessemer probably has more claim to recognition as a great inventor than Holley; but if we compare the two men we see strikingly exemplified the difference between the inventor and the industrious engineer. Where Bessemer left the process which bears his name, Holley's work began. It was full of possibilities which Mr. Bessemer, distracted by a restless ambition to do something new in marine architecture and other lines of experiment, not always judiciously chosen, seems to have aided but little in realizing. Holley was content to be useful; the typical inventor leaves the question of utility for others to answer, and pushes on. It is as an engineer, rather than as an inventor, that Holley must be considered great; and not alone as an engineer, but as a teacher of the accomplished facts of scientific progress. He had a faculty for imparting to others the fruits of study, observation, and experience, which is given to but few men. Not only was he lucid and clear in his description, but even around the dry details of mechanical proportioning and construction he cast a glow of color; and truth, when he presented it, became poetic. How much his writings have enriched the engineering literature of the two continents, I do not need to tell you. Holley's life and work merit all the honor we can pay his memory, and his title to substantial greatness is beyond the reach of question or criticism.

There is something very pathetic to me in all of Holley's death-bed utterances, but especially in those which touched upon his work. "I should like," he said, in effect, "to live ten or fifteen years longer to aid in realizing the possibilities of the open-hearth process. This would have rounded and completed my professional career; but I am satisfied." To long for an opportunity of further usefulness was natural to one whose life had been so full of great achievements, but to speak of rounding and completing such a professional career seems like wishing to gild fine gold. Not so to Holley! Death to him meant simply leaving undone that for which he had made earnest preparation, and which he desired to do because he could do it best. Others will do good work, great work, but not his work.

> "The unfinished window of Aladdin's tower
> Unfinished must remain."

Holley's connection with the Society of Mechanical Engineers is a memory of which we may well be proud. Perhaps to him, more than to any other member, its success is due. His active interest in the project was in itself an assurance that it would realize the objects of its organization, and his name created confidence in all departments of the profession. Some of us, but probably not many, know what effort he made to secure a good attendance at the Hartford meeting, and how anxious he was that the dinner should be a complete and memorable success. He knew better than most of us the value of recreation as a preparation for the serious work of life, and long experience had taught him that to make the social features of our society-meetings delightful was the surest way to make such meetings successful. In our dinners we have a perpetual memorial of Holley. On such occasions he enjoyed life at its best, and how much his presence added to our pleasure I do not need to say. Unfortunately, failing health deprived him of the opportunity of contributing liberally to our transactions, but, had he been spared, he would have aided materially in giving us a high place among the great technical societies of the world. I have lately re-read with pleasure and profit his address as chairman of the preliminary meeting in February, 1880, on "The Field of Mechanical Engineering," which is charming in its simple earnestness and brimming with valuable suggestions to officers and members.

We have also on our records the fullest, and, I believe, the first description of his last great improvement,* which is in a striking

---

* " An adaptation of Bessemer Plant to the Basic Process." Read at the Annual Meeting Soc. Mech. Eng., February, 1880.

degree characteristic. Convinced from examination that the basic process was a chemical success, he also saw that it presented difficulties which threatened to make it useless in this country. Having brought the Bessemer practice up to the high perfection which it had attained in the working of the so-called acid process, he recognized the impracticability of restricting a steel plant in the United States to the comparatively small productions which satisfied English engineers and capitalists. When Thomas was in this country, he and Holley were at Troy together. Thomas was greatly interested in all he saw, and while in the converter-house he remarked that he "should like nothing better than to sit down on an ingot-mould and watch the work all day." "If you want to find an ingot-mould cool enough to sit on," replied Holley, "you will have to send to England for it." Holley's improvements had rendered impossible the delays which would have resulted from the frequent relining of converters, and to perfect the basic process he had hit upon the clever expedient of making the linings detachable, so that with very little delay a new lining could be substituted for one burned out, and the work go on, enabling our steel-makers to adopt the basic process, when it is to their interest to do so, without sacrifice of product. This was the crowning work of Holley's life, and to us he gave the paper which would have been welcomed by the greatest technical societies of the world.

It is much to be regretted that petty jealousies led to the decision to withhold from Holley the Bessemer medal, which he, more than any engineer, had earned ; but he was too great a man to be made unhappy by the fact that he had excited in weaker minds feelings which found no place in his own great, loving heart. The consciousness that he merited the honor was worth more to him than to have had it grudgingly bestowed by those who knew, but dare not confess, that he towered high above those who sat in judgment on his claims to recognition. The love of his friends was always worth more to Holley than barren compliment, and he died without uttering a word to indicate that he had known a disappointment in life. Even in the detention of his stricken family, who were hurrying to his bedside, he saw a blessing for them which outweighed the satisfaction it would have given him to look once more upon those nearest and dearest to him ; and among his last words was a message that he died without disappointment, knowing that it would be less a shock to them to find their worst fears realized than it would be to find him unconscious, and see him die without even a look of recognition or a word expressing the infinite tenderness of his love. One capable of such forgetfulness of self in the presence of the awful reality of death could look with equanimity on the petty annoyances which make weaker natures unhappy.

Of Holley's personal character, I can speak only as a friend and best describe him as he seemed to me. Perhaps I owe him more than I would care to tell. He won my confidence and regard years ago, when with nothing but youth and inexperience to commend me to his consideration, I sought his counsel and was freely admitted to his confidence. You can estimate better than I can describe the value of such a friend to one weighted with grave and anxious responsibilities, and impressed with a sense of the inadequacy of his preparation for the work devolving upon him. It is the experience of the journalist that truth is sometimes difficult of access. The statements made to him are often colored by a regard for real or supposed self-interest, and misrepresentation masquerades in the garb of frankness and confidence. But when I met Holley and sat with him for half an hour in conference, I would have pinned my faith to his deliberate statement, otherwise unsupported, against the oaths of all the world. Holley was to me a revelation. Not only was he a man of whose sincerity no one could entertain a doubt, but he was one who dared to put confidence in the sincerity and honesty of others. It was as refreshing to talk with him as to pass from the gray shadows of a closed chamber into the full glow of sunshine, from the chill of reserve and suspicion into the genial warmth of outspoken frankness. Others I have found honest and true, others have won my love by unselfish service, others have given me wise counsel and judicious advice. Their sincerity I have proved; Holley's sincerity needed no proof.

During the twelve years of an acquaintance which I shall always remember with pleasure, it was my privilege to learn by observation and experience the generous side of Holley's nature. Never have I known him too busy to see one who needed his assistance; never did he promise aid without rendering it. In our great metallurgical establishments are scores of young men who have reason to bless the memory of this unselfish friend, whose timely assistance opened the way to honorable professional success. With Holley there was nothing perfunctory in this service for others. It was his pleasure in a peculiar degree to confer benefit, and he was never so happy as when it was in his power to bring happiness to others.

Of the irresistible charm of Holley's conversation, of his sunny temperament, his brilliant wit, and his genial good-fellowship, I need not speak; but remembering all these I am moved to write on the tablets of memory as his epitaph, a paraphrase of the remark of the old farmer of Marshfield as he stood beside the bier of Webster: "This is a lonesome world, and Holley dead."

THE PRESIDENT: I see among us a gentleman, who, although not a member of our Society, is a member of two of the great societies of Great Britain. I would like, if he is willing, to have him say a few words on this occasion—Mr. Fernie.

JOHN FERNIE, of London, England: Although not an intimate friend of Mr. Holley, yet I had the pleasure of meeting him in this city in 1876; and I know a good deal of his work, and I can bear high testimony, as an English engineer, to the very high appreciation we have in our country for his mechanical skill and genius. He commended himself to us in a great many ways, principally as a writer, as an inventor, and as a connecting link between English and American engineers. So, whenever Mr. Holley came to any of our meetings, we looked upon him as your representative, and treated him accordingly. I assure you that there is a great blank in our societies in England caused by the death of Mr. Holley, and that we mourn his loss as much as you do, for we considered that he belonged to us as he belonged to you. There are a great many small minds in our country, as I dare say there are in yours, who do not look at men with the broad feelings and respect with which they ought, and who regard them in an envious sort of way; but the general feeling of the engineers of our country as regards Mr. Holley was a feeling of genuine respect.

After the eloquent words which have fallen from the last speaker, the most eloquent memorial tribute which I have ever heard, it will be improper for me to express more than my deep regret for the death of Mr. Holley, and to say that we mourn his loss as deeply as you do.

One word in regard to a subject that came before your Society this morning. In respect to a meeting of Mechanical Engineers of England and America, I may say that two years ago I tried to get up a party to come to the United States. At our annual meeting, Mr. Barlow, our President, mentioned in his address the pleasure which a visit to the United States had given him. He was present here at your great Exposition. And after he made that statement, I thought it my duty, as having several times visited on this side, to try and get up a party to come across here and see your great works, and try to meet our professional brethren in America and have more fellow-feeling with them. But I found that a long time would be required for such a visit, and that considerable expense would attend it; and although I got Cook, the great excursionist, to arrange about a steamer for us, yet when we learned the length of time it would take, it was found impracticable to get up a party. I believe that is the great trouble with engineers coming to America. I wish we could shorten the road. I hope in a few years we will get it down to six or seven days, and at that time we hope to get a considerable number of English engineers over in America. We have a great many American engineers coming to England, but very few going from England to America. I wish there were more.

THE PRESIDENT: The road between England and America is being shortened very rapidly. The Alaska made her last passage in six days and twenty-three hours.

We have among us one of our old officers, who was also President of the Institute of Mining Engineers. Can we hear from Mr. Coxe?

ECKLEY B. COXE, of Drifton, Pa.: I have been at many meetings of the Civil, Mining, and Mechanical Engineers at which our dear old friend Holley was present. This, gentlemen, is the first one I have attended since he has gone. As I look around and see so many who have been with us when Holley was here, I feel as if I could say nothing. Holley was a man who made us better. He made us stronger. He made us act like men and feel like men; and I do not believe that there is a man worthy of the name, who has had the honor and the privilege of being well acquainted with Alexander Lyman Holley, who has not found himself a better man. Of him we may well say: " It is better to have loved and lost than never to have loved at all." I am not speaking of his great genius as an engineer; that is not necessary; he wrote his name as an engineer where none can efface it; but as a friend, as a man, as one who made engineering a profession: And I think to Alexander Lyman Holley the profession of engineering owes more to-day than to any other man who has lived on this side of the Atlantic. Those who were with him in the American Society of Civil Engineers know what he did for its advancement, and I, who labored with him for so many years in the American Institute of Mining Engineers, know what he did for that Society; and we all feel and must say, if we speak the truth, that but for him it is very doubtful if this Society would have come into existence, at least for some time. I feel that I should be but repeating what is in all your hearts were I to say anything in his praise; and I can only repeat that this is the saddest meeting that I have ever attended. I feel that I would like to go away, as I see his loved face before me there, and think that we are never again to meet upon this earth. I wish almost that I were not here. Gentlemen, let us all try to leave behind us a name like his,—*sans peur et sans reproche*,—the Chevalier Bayard of our profession. He did everything to advance and glorify engineering, and never anything to sully its fair fame.

THE PRESIDENT: We have among us another gentleman, who has watched Mr. Holley's work with more intelligence, more power of comprehension, than most of us could have done, and one better qualified to speak of his works than any man among us. We would like to hear from Mr. Hunt.

ROBERT W. HUNT, of Troy, N. Y.: I can hardly trust myself to speak of Holley. Yesterday I happened to be in the shops of the Corliss Steam-Engine Company, and mentioned to one of the workmen there that I expected to-day to attend the memorial meeting of the Mechanical Engineers on the death of Alexander L. Holley. The man exclaimed: "What! our Holley?" And so it is, whether it is among the workingmen or among the cultivated engineers, it is to "our Holley" that we to-day seek to pay our tribute.

Sadness is rendered less painful when the privilege is given us of making expression of our grief: "Out of the fulness of the heart the mouth speaketh." Oh, how full our hearts have been, and are, from the loss of our friend and fellow-member! In my reflections upon dear Holley's death, I have so many times thought of the death of his close friend, and one of our most cherished members, one who felt so much interest and filled such an active part in the organization and success of this Society,—Henry R. Worthington.

Many of you will remember that at our second meeting, the one held for the purpose of final organization, Holley was too ill to be present, and Mr. Worthington in his stead read the report of the Committee on Constitution and By-Laws. In a few weeks Holley, having partially recovered, sailed for Europe, where, later, he experienced the terrible sickness which so nearly ended his life. During this time, while his family and friends were anxiously awaiting each cablegram, several professional associates and myself had occasion to visit Mr. Worthington's office. We found him holding a message in his hands, and overwhelmed by grief. His feelings were so overpowering that speech was almost impossible. At last, in eloquent, heartfelt words, he pointed out to us his sorrow. Holley was dying!

What a beautiful tribute he paid to his character. Worthington himself, most genial of men, most pure, most talented, laid his garlands at the feet of one whom he loved for these same qualities. Would that I could to-day pay my tribute to Holley's memory by repeating Worthington's words!

How past all comprehension is fate! Worthington died; Holley came back to us apparently restored to health, and was himself the mourner at the tomb of his friend. And now both are gone. The world has lost much, and of the world this Society is among the heaviest sufferers.

Holley's character is best illustrated by the peculiar marks of affection and respect which have been paid to it since his death. Who would not live such a life? But few can. Such an intellect, such a simple, loving, all-embracing heart is seldom given. But while mourning his loss, we can all endeavor to prove ourselves worthy to have received his love, to have been of his friends.

Whether or no tablets of stone or monuments of brass are erected to his memory, the Memorial Session, at Washington, of the American Institute of Mining Engineers, this of our own Society held to-day, and the action of the American Society of Civil Engineers yet to come, are greater, better, sweeter tributes, tributes such as none but Holley could have called forth.

Nevertheless, let us do more, let the three Societies meet in rearing an enduring physical tribute—one alike appropriate to his genius, his love of art, and the good done by him for his fellow-men. Let it stand as an example of the value of practical science, of practical work, and as a beacon to the young men of our country, of whose welfare, of whose guidance, of whose fortune his great heart was so full.

THE PRESIDENT: I see there is another gentleman with us, who is also a member of this and of the sister Societies, who has worked with Holley on the Boards of direction of those Societies, and has himself been President of the Mining Engineers, and is one of our most active and most valued members. Will Mr. Metcalf address the Society?

WILLIAM METCALF, of Pittsburgh, Pa.: In 1874 I had the pleasure of first meeting the man we have to-day met here to honor. In 1874 it was my fortune one day, as I incidentally dropped into one of the machine shops of our city, to be directed to the pattern shop, and further into a little, dingy corner to find one of the employers. And there, in this little, dark corner of the place, I met a man who was introduced to me as Alexander L. Holley, and the bright face, and the sweet smile, and the clear, intelligent, flashing blue eyes that were set on me that day are just as clear in my mind at present as they were at that time, and that was my first meeting with Holley. Afterwards it was through his influence that I was induced to join the American Institute of Mining Engineers. It was partly through his influence that I became a member of the American Society of Civil Engineers, and it was altogether through his influence that I became a member of this Society. To him I owe the great honor of having the nomination to the office of President of the American Institute of Mining Engineers, and when called upon to-day, Mr. President, to speak of Mr. Holley, I hardly know what to say. Of his career, of his professional work, many gentlemen here to-day know far more than I do; and I have simply jotted down a few remarks to add as a tribute to the character of Mr. Holley, which I hope will be deemed at least worthy to go upon the records of this meeting, which is intended, as I understand, simply to be a tribute to the memory of a man whom we all love, honor, and respect.

We all know why we loved Mr. Holley,—simply because we could not help it. Not merely because he was sweet-tempered; many a man has a sweet temper, and is insipid. Not only because of his knowledge, for many a one is learned, and no one else is ever allowed to know it. Not because of his many-sided attainments, for many people acquire many things only to air their own vanity. Holley had sweet temper, profound knowledge, and a great variety of attainments, and he poured them out so lavishly, so persistently, and best of all so modestly, that he drew us all to him whether we would or not. But in what was Holley great? He was great in his far-seeing apprehension of the utility of things. He had the enthusiasm of a zealot, the courage of one convinced, and the energy of inspiration. He seized upon the great Bessemer process when capitalists were afraid, when old practices and ignorant prejudice derided it, and when a slumbering world had no idea of its own needs. He gave courage to capital, bent down ignorance and prejudice, and showed an astonished world what a poor world it was before. He was successful in probably the greatest of engineering feats, for his task was no wide chasm to be spanned, no great mountain to be pierced, no large river to be guided and controlled, nor a huge swamp to be filled up and made useful.

These are all great works, but their accomplishment depends mainly upon common-sense, and the knowledge and application of well-known and changeless laws of nature. Once completed they stand fulfilling their objects and requiring but little care for their preservation.

Holley went to the capitalists, and said, "Give me your money, and I will span the great chasm between now and to-morrow; I will blow to atoms the mountains of ignorance and prejudice; you shall float upon rivers of wealth; and old ways and old methods shall be completely swamped. I will take your dollars and convert them into buildings, and furnaces, and mills, and hammers; I will put all of these fair structures into the hands of the most ordinary men, and they shall do all they can to smash and tear them in pieces. They shall fail; I shall succeed, and you shall be rich." He did succeed, and why? How could this man, poet, artist, architect, lover of all that was beautiful, succeed in such a task? He did it because he was modest, and kept himself in the background. He pushed every one but himself to the front, and the front rank bore him aloft on its shoulders, and he fulfilled his promises. The little streams of thousands, invested in his many contrivances, united into a great river of millions, and his patrons still gather up the profits. And here is the great secret of his success. He never allowed his love of the beautiful to get the better of his sense of the useful; and he never allowed his ambition to overcome his faith to the trust reposed in him.

He was happy when he saw each new work completed and running successfully, but he was most happy when he could say, "They are working economically and making lots of money." All I have said seems as nothing, Mr. President, and I can think of no more fitting words to close than those of a friend whom I met the other day, who said : "I cannot tell you how I miss him."

THE PRESIDENT: We have with us a gentleman who has been in a certain way a co-worker with Mr. Holley, and who has helped him through a good many of his difficulties, and whom in turn he has helped very much. There was a sympathy between those two gentlemen, such as I am sure would justify me in calling for Mr. Charles T. Porter.

CHARLES T. PORTER, of New York city : In coming here, I confess to you, sir, it is not the great engineer, it is not the man of strong purpose and heroic endeavor, it is not the foremost figure in the band of giants who have created the great steel-industry of this country, neither is it the brilliant writer, nor the man of high and varied attainments, whom my memory most loves to dwell upon ; oh, no! Alexander Lyman Holley was all this ; but, sir, he was a great deal more than this. That beaming countenance with speaking eyes, upon which it was such a joy to look, and which, to every one who ever gazed upon it, it will ever be such a joy to remember, was the outward manifestation of a great soul, instinct with every feeling that, in the appropriate words of another, can ennoble or can adorn our nature.

The opportunity for studying Mr. Holley's character, which I enjoyed for the past few years, enabled me to form an estimate of it which is higher than I can very well express. It seemed to me, it always has seemed to me, as if Mr. Holley combined in a wonderful degree, strength and elevation of character, with warm, loving sympathies and sensibilities. It seems to me, sir, as if it could be fairly said of our dear friend, that whatsoever things were honest, whatsoever things were just, whatsoever things were pure, whatsoever things were true, whatsoever things were lovely, that to all such things he was ever loyal. These were the things which called forth all the enthusiasm of his nature, and with which his every heart-beat throbbed in harmony. Such a character, Mr. President, as that of Mr. Holley, must leave an unusually marked impress upon the great number of his co-workers, by whom he was admired and

loved: and it is a joyful thing to think that, as it ought, so it must,
tend thus to perpetuate itself in ever-widening circles, however
they may grow more faint, throwing its spell upon every one who
comes, however remotely, within the sphere of its influence. And
so we can write his name among the names of those who not only
have added to the material good of their fellow-men, who not only
have contributed largely to the advancement of our civilization,
but through whom men have been made better, have been made
more just, have been made more generous, have been made more
pure, have been made more loving.

THE PRESIDENT: I will next call upon Mr. Hoadley, of Law-
rence.

J. C. HOADLEY, of Boston, Mass.: I received information from
the committee having the commemoration in charge, that a few
minutes would be accorded to me to speak of my regard for Mr.
Holley, and I received this invitation with profound satisfaction,
and have spent hours in pleasing melancholy, thinking over the
associations that have taken place between us. When I consider
how few and how far between were the occasions when we met, and
upon how slender a foundation of actual personal intercourse was
based the strong and warm personal regard I have always entertained for Mr. Holley, I feel that it must be futile for me to attempt
to account to you for the feeling I express, which might seem, therefore, extravagant; and that it would be entirely idle for me to dwell
at any length upon his career, which is quite as well known to you
all as to me.

Almost twenty-five years ago, when Mr. Holley was a very young
man, I intrusted to him a delicate negotiation in England, when he
was about to go to England with Mr. Colburn to prepare their joint
work upon European railways and machinery. He performed this
negotiation with great tact and delicacy, but with characteristic generosity he declined to receive any compensation, and could only be
induced by considerable urging to accept a trifling remuneration for
personal expenses. A few years later, in 1863, I met him in London. I was almost ready to go home, and Holley had arrived but
a few days. He was seeking at that time to make arrangements
with Mr. Bessemer for the manufacture of Bessemer steel in this
country. With a perspicacity entirely characteristic of the man he
had perceived the transcendent importance of this invention, which

was almost unnoticed by the world, and before Mr. Bessemer had ever received a shilling of legitimate compensation for his invention. True, it was the year he had received a present from Sir John Brown of two thousand dollars. Mr. Brown told me that so far they had made no money, but he was confident there was money in the future. In that stage of the invention, Mr. Holley, perceiving its great importance, with his own true-hearted loyalty, went directly to the man who had invented the process to get at the very limit—the utmost outpost of the invention, and we all know how much further he has carried it.

Afterwards I occasionally met him, so rarely that of course we only entered upon the most ordinary themes of professional interest. Life, and destiny, and the loftier speculations of human thought were never even approached. His character was so lovely, so transparent, it spoke so plainly in his clear, calm eyes and in all his ways, that no one could doubt, at least I entertained no doubt, that he was a sound and true man in every respect, in heart and in character; as we all know him to have been in his chosen profession. As to his profession, as to the physical sciences generally, it is sometimes made a reproach to them that they fix the attention too exclusively upon phenomena, and therefore ignore essential verities; that appearances are much too opaque, and that behind the veil of appearances there is something undiscerned by the scientific eye. On the other hand, men of science say they see too clearly to be deluded by dreams and superstitions. And, therefore, these concurrent views of the same aspect of human life point in the same direction. They are like two sides of a tapestry. About all this, in connection with Mr. Holley, I know nothing, nor do I care. What is doubt but an ambiguous term? And denial itself is only negative faith, and the sign you know changes by transposition to the other side.

And though to us who "know in whom we have believed," doubt may seem dismal, and denial dreary and dark, yet when we see the hollow, shadowy forms that pass in the name of faith, doubt—denial itself—seems seraphic devotion, beatific vision, compared to that heartless assent and shallow acquiescence which give a too ready *credo* to the incredible. I do not know why I should have said all this of Mr. Holley, because I have not the slightest doubt that upon all that relates to the higher problems of life his mind was clear and poised, fixed upon firm conviction as upon all matters of physical science. I need not say that I loved him; all loved him. "None knew him but to love him, none named him but to praise." And if I should reiterate much that has been better said, as I should have to do to express my feelings, I should say that I have but little to give as a rational basis for those feelings; and therefore I will claim your attention no longer.

THE PRESIDENT: We have with us a gentleman who has come from the West, for the purpose of presenting a tribute to the memory of our friend. Mr. Holloway, I think, is in the room.

J. F. HOLLOWAY, of Cleveland, O.: It is now nearly twenty years since first I met Alexander L. Holley. At that time, at the request of some gentlemen who were about to establish works in Cleveland for the manufacture of steel by the Bessemer process, I made a visit to Troy for the purpose of witnessing its manufacture there, and to take note of the appliances by which it was accomplished.

Upon my arrival in that city I sought the location of the steel works, which, as I remember, was in a somewhat rural district below the city, on the banks of the Hudson. Arriving at the spot, I entered a small wooden building, which seemed to be office, drawing-room, and store-room combined; it contained among other things, as I well remember, a large table, and on one side a row of shelves upon the walls. Upon the table and upon the shelves were short bars of steel, sections of rails, lumps of iron-ore, specimen-pigs of iron, and pieces of boiler-plate. The bars of steel were bent and twisted into various shapes, and the boiler-plate was flanged backward, forward, and doubled upon itself, and the corners drawn down into small rods, which were tied into all kinds of fantastic loops and knots, all tending to illustrate the wonderful tenacity of the material from which they were made. I knew not where the specimens were made, or where the material came from, but supposed them to be from the newly discovered Bessemer steel as made in England. While looking over the contents of the table, Mr. Holley, who had been sent for out in the works, came in. I had read with great interest his paper, the "Railway Advocate," and his work on "European Railways," and had been charmed with his contributions to the New York *Times*, over the signature of "Tubal Cain," and I confess I was a little disappointed as I looked upon the slender, young-looking fellow who stood beside the table and before me; but the frank, open-heartedness of his manner, his bright, hopeful face, and his modest bearing, left an impression upon me years have only deepened, and time will never efface. I was taken through the works by Mr. Holley, and shown all that had been accomplished up to that time, and it was little enough. The works were then idle; they had built one plant and had tried to operate it by water-power, and had failed; they had then built another, and a larger one, expecting to work it by steam, but owing to insufficiency of boiler-power and for various other reasons, that had not been a success. I remember how fully and frankly he spoke of all these failures, and how hopeful he was of the future; he said that, when they had procured new boilers, and changed the blowing engines somewhat, and found a material that would stand for lining the vessels, and come across the right kind of pig-iron, he thought it would be all right. Knowing little or nothing of this new process for making steel, and seeing so little evidence of success in the surroundings, it seemed to me to be an almost hopeless undertaking. There were only two things about the whole place that looked at all encouraging; one was the table, with its twisted and bent bars of steel, the doubled and knotted specimens of boiler-plate that lay upon it; and the other was the young man who modestly stood beside them. A few days ago, after an interval of all these years, I again stood within the steel works of Troy. To you who are familiar with the Bessemer steel-plant of to-day no description of the place is required, but the contrast between it and its surroundings and the little experimental works I had visited there twenty years before was marvellous. The quiet, rural surroundings were all wanting; the peaceful air which had previously pervaded the spot had given place to a hum of industry, which encircled the whole country about. The very air quivered with the pulsations of immense fans and blowers, which swallowed up the atmosphere by tons and poured it into vast furnaces and converters; ponderous hammers shook the ground you stood upon; or as you picked your way about the works, amid the din of clashing wheels and the escaping steam from out a hundred panting engines, fiery little locomotives chased you over tortuous paths, dragging behind them cars laden with glowing ingots, whose passing left a fierce sirocco in the air; but amid the roar of leaping flames, the brilliant coruscations that filled the air with grandeur and beauty, I saw only the table of long ago with its curious specimens, and the young engineer standing beside it. The history of these intervening years is known to most of you to some extent, but to none have its trials, its disappointments, its struggles, and its failures ever been fully divulged. He who suffered them bore them bravely, uncomplainingly; and the study, the hard thinking, the patience, and courage which were so necessary, not only for himself, but for those with whom he was associated, can never be fully known by any one. How the metal that was in the man, as well as the metal he sought for and which lay within the reach of the process he introduced, both have triumphed in these later years, you all know. One has made all roadways safe and pleasant, and the other has opened up pathways in all our lives, which, lighted up by his genial wit and humor, no coming cloud can now obscure, and which only the twilight of our own lives will mellow ere its light goes out forever.

To the Society of Mechanical Engineers, in this the early stage of its existence, the death of Alexander L. Holley is a great loss. How earnestly he interested himself in its formation is known to you all; how valuable would have been his advice and counsel, his spoken and written contributions, had his life and health been spared, all can well imagine. It was ever his constant effort to raise the standard of engineering science, and to elevate to the high position he felt that the engineer was entitled to, all who made it a practice or a profession. You who still possess the engineering paper which, in connection with the late Zerah Colburn, he published in his youth, will find within its yellow faded leaves many an editorial in which he strove earnestly to incite the engineers of that day to make themselves worthy the position their high calling entitled them to. His helping hand was ever stretched out to lift upwards, his cheering words went through the ranks urging all to come up higher; and the rich legacy he has left us of an honored and world-respected name, is one which the Mechanical Engineers of America should ever prize. He was the Moses who led us out from the old bondage of cant and custom, which made the engineer a worker only, and not a thinker as well. College-bred as he was, donning the costume of the locomotive engineer, he mounted the footboard, and cajoled and manœuvred the rickety engine of that early day over the still more rickety roadbed over which they then ran. It was the saying of a celebrated and somewhat eccentric inventor and engineer, as illustrative of the various conditions of a life which fortune and misfortune had brought to him, that he had at times dined in the palaces of the great, where the plate upon the table was worth a duke's ransom, and so downward through every varying stage of descent to the twopenny bench under a bridge, where the battered iron spoons were chained to the table to keep the guests from stealing them. Inversely, our friend and associate from the footboard of the little Jersey locomotive made honest, manly strides upwards, until he became the honored, welcome guest in the highest circles in foreign lands as well as in our own. It was not because Alexander L. Holley was a graduate of a college or university that I loved him, it was not because he was a practical workman and engineer, it was not because he was a brilliant and graphic writer, nor was it because he was as well a learned and argumentative one; not because he could stand up before any society, no matter how technical or scientific, and deliver an essay which for its depth of research, originality, and comprehensiveness would rank with the best; it was not for the reason that at the social gathering, where wit, humor, and good fellowship held the hour, he was the plumed knight about whom all loved to gather, who from his well-filled quiver launched repartee and response, and who parried and thrust with his lance-like wit, hitting everywhere, wounding nowhere; neither was it because he was ever the kind, courteous, considerate gentleman; in short, it was not for any one of these things he won the high regard he so richly deserved; but it was because that he of all the men of his time and age, so far as I know, combined all these commendable qualities in one. The truest test of his goodness now is that in this steady upward march his noble manhood disarmed all criticism, allayed all jealousy, making no enemies, winning all hearts.

Let us remember his fame is our own, winning it as he did by hard study and toil; as he rose to the high eminence he occupied, he lifted the profession with him, and the standing of all mechanical engineers the wide world over is higher to-day for the labors of his life, and for the works he accomplished; and if there is any one thing more than another left us to do, it is to emulate his example and to keep his memory green.

THE PRESIDENT: I will call upon Mr. Coleman Sellers.

COLEMAN SELLERS, of Philadelphia, Pa.: I regret exceedingly that I was not able to come earlier to this meeting, so as to hear the addresses delivered by Mr. Bayles and those who spoke later. Probably they covered the ground better than what I can say now.

For want of particular knowledge as to what they have told you, it would probably be better for me to confine my remarks to some little instances that occurred in the life of Mr. Holley that may be interesting. My acquaintance with our dear friend began many years ago, when he was connected with Mr. Colburn, as the last speaker remarked, in that little paper which has now become yellow with age. I hardly know how to consider the different events of his life. Looking over a memorandum-book a few days ago for an entirely different purpose, I stumbled upon a period when Mr. Holley's name seemed to be written on almost every page, and that was the year 1861, at which time he was imbued with the idea that a locomotive traction-engine for common roads would be a very desirable thing; and in connection with Mr. Holley I worked for many months on this traction-engine. At that time our forts had been fired upon, and everything was confusion and fear, and it seemed that the whole attention of mechanics would have to be given to furnishing the Government with materials for war. It was then that Mr. Holley turned his attention to the more important work of making Bessemer steel. But there is a little incident that I should like to present to you. A gentleman some little while ago, writing from New York, asked me for a definition of "set-screw." Unfortunately, he said, he could not find a definition which he could use in a suit at law. I told him he was mistaken, and that the definition could be found in Webster's Dictionary; and the reason I knew it was because Mr. Holley had put it there. Mr. Holley called on me once to have one of those little chats that we used to enjoy so much. He said that he came for the purpose of getting my help in preparing the technical terms on mechanical science for Webster's Dictionary. So we went through the shop to get those words, and thus it came that the definition of a "set-screw" was one of the terms which Mr. Holley and I worked out together.

Now, all those little things are pleasant recollections to me. It seems as if there was no period in my life as an engineer into which Mr. Holley did not enter. He would come and have a long talk about this Society, what was absolutely necessary for its vital existence, and urging the preparation of various papers that would be required; and it was only a very short time before his death that we had one of those delightful conversations. But there was a little talk that I had with him on the Hudson River Road that was so characteristic of the man that I think, if I relate that alone, it will be sufficient for my contribution to this commemoration of Mr. Holley. We had been up to Troy, and we had gone over the Bessemer works there. We had dined together, and there was a party of ladies and gentlemen in an apartment of one of the cars. They did not know very well all the places along the road, and made inquiries about them, and finally the conversation turned upon the style of architecture that obtains in some of those beautiful buildings that stud the Hudson. Holley said: "Do you know I would like some day or another to deliver a course of lectures on architecture applied to mechanics." I said, "I hope you will. How will you handle it?" "Don't you know," he said, "that you and I have had a good many talks about the abominable practice of putting different styles of architecture, Gothic and what not, into steam-engines and other machines? We know perfectly well that what is the most fit is the most beautiful." And so he went on talking, in the way in which Holley only could talk, about the possibilities of the lecture, which would be of eminent use to mechanics in showing the law which obtains in regard to everything, that utility and fitness constitute beauty. Just what nature has done in adapting each tree and each part of it to its proper use is applicable to machinery, and each deviation from that is only an abnormal condition. This was soon after the fire in Chicago, and he said: "Have you seen Chicago since the fire? Have you seen the wonderful buildings that have been erected there? Chicago has risen like the Phœnix from her ashes, and yet you will find there the most striking instances of the barbarity of the American people, and their low condition in regard to fitness and propriety. In Chicago they have erected numbers of handsome buildings, and some of the noblest specimens of architecture have been put into their stores and warehouses, but what else have they done? All these beautiful pieces of architectural ingenuity are plastered from top to bottom with signs,—cigars, snuffs, tobacco, dry goods,— covering the whole city of Chicago with black and gold, after putting millions of dollars into those buildings in which the highest skill in construction has been displayed. Now," he said, "we must educate the American people up to such a condition that those things will be impossible. It certainly shows the very low condition of the æsthetic element in the country that they are capable of defacing these beauties with this mere advertisement of their goods in such a glaring way." That was so characteristic of Mr. Holley that I would like very much to see it put upon the record. Had

7

he lived, I think, because he frequently referred to it afterwards, he would ultimately have worked up this particular subject. He would have found many more willing ears to listen to him now than at the time he talked to me. The very thing he advocated so earnestly is having its effect.

It is useless for me to say anything to you about his genial quali-ties. You all know more about them probably than I do. It is very unfortunate that the city of New York is a great way off from the city of Philadelphia, and we did not see each other as often as we would like to,—Philadelphia being a suburb of New York, of course. But there were times when he would come over here. When he was in London ill, and every steamer was watched to bring the news of his condition, there was one very pleasing thing con-nected with it all, and that was that gentlemen connected with the paper which his former partner had originally founded,—I speak of the *London Engineering*,—had taken Mr. Holley to their own home; and when I heard of all the care and comforts that were thrown around him by these brethren of ours on the other side of the water, I must say that I felt heartily grateful to them for all that they had done; and if any word I am saying now ever reaches there, I hope it will convey at least my thanks for what the people of England did for Mr. Holley while he was in such deep distress. I think, Mr. President, that I can add nothing more, but I have given this as a little tribute to his memory.

THE PRESIDENT: In the formation of this Society there was a good deal of work done in preliminary organization, and, as I re-marked at the opening, Mr. Holley had a great deal to do in that preliminary work; but back of what is known and seen, there is a history under the surface of things unknown and unseen. You re-member that the call for the organization of the Society was issued with Professor Sweet, I think, as the moving spirit in the organiza-tion. He was assisted by two or three friends; and among those who have done so much in the preliminary work preparatory to organization is one whose name I find on the list presented by the committee as one of the gentlemen ready to speak, an ex-officer of the Society, the gentleman who took charge of our funds, and who in his connection with the Society became, even more than formerly, a very intimate friend of our deceased member,—Mr. Moore.

L. B. MOORE, of New York city: In accepting, with diffidence, and, I am not ashamed to say it, in accepting with tears, the oppor-

tunity to add a few words to the tributes already paid, if anything
can be·added that has not been better said, it has seemed to me that
there is no truer way to honor the dead than to point a moral for
the living.   In the illustrious life, the close of which we meet this
day to commemorate, there are two or three characteristics which
have especially impressed my mind.   One is the genial light-heart-
edness that not only made Holley so agreeable as a man, but that
also helped so largely to make him what he was as an engineer.
Nor was he one of those who, by nature doleful and sombre, strive
to cultivate a cheerfulness which they do not feel.   To me it has
always seemed that Holley was one of those men who could never
by any stress of circumstances be borne down, or become permanently soured, because he carried within him the ingredients that go
to make up mental health and moral sunshine.   His mind was not
burdened by the habitual croakings and uncertainties and dejections
that are so often mistakenly deemed the ripe kernels of thought,
when they are only the husks that hide or smother them.   Then,
too, closely connected with this trait of his character, and reacting
upon it, was entire freedom from the petty spites, and personal and
professional jealousies, which too often disfigure abilities of even
the highest order.   Holley's career is additional proof that it is
mainly the light-hearted and buoyant-minded men who rule the
world.   Another reminder that runs logically with this serves to
show us from Holley's example how largely the world's great enterprises are to-day in the hands of young men.   Before the age of
thirty-three, Holley had practically grasped the steel-making secrets
which have since changed the methods of trade and transportation,
and have influenced all the arts and sciences that are built upon
these two great foundations.   Let us learn anew from the life of
Holley, that though gray hairs are honorable, a great truth, or great
discovery, or great work, is not the less worthy because youth is
behind it, or at the bottom of it.

   The only other thought regarding which I shall presume to add a
word of comment is this: Holley's career well illustrates the broadened plane upon which men can in our day meet and study nature.
In our modern life creeds and customs are chiefly valued in proportion as we are content to accept at second hand.   A mind like
Holley's has little need of creeds, because it is one of the makers of
customs for mankind.   Living, as he did, close to the universal
heart of nature, and reading her secrets as in a half-opened· book,
it was one of the privileges of Holley's genius to show us that

there is in nature a beauty which even art cannot portray, because in this beauty are embodied the forces which make art possible.

With your permission I should like to conclude this thought by reading a few lines, the idea or suggestion of which, singularly enough, dates from a commemorative gathering, at which Alexander Lyman Holley was the moving spirit. Let me entitle it

THE NEW NATURE.

In the old days
Men walked with Nature in the quiet wood,
And found her features beautiful or good,
As were their ways.

Still do they look,
Painter and poet, seer and holy man,
For Nature's self, to find her where they can,—
In field or brook.

But these new days
Ofttimes entice from breezy dale and down
Her wandering feet into the dingy town
Where chimneys blaze.

Are forge and flue,
Steeple and street, becoming in her sight
More dear than all the joys of day or night
That once she knew?

That—none may know;
Her gifts are hers, to spend them as she will—
Changed, or the same, Nature is Nature still,
And chooseth so.

Of all who seem
To seek her face, one asks, whom do her eyes
Rest kindliest on? Nature herself replies
(So we may deem),

To him that asks:
"The wine is given to him that hath the cup;
Use is but beauty, girded strongly up
For kindred tasks."

ALBERT H. EMERY, of New York city: So much has been said that it would seem needless to add anything further; yet I should do great violence to my feelings if, when the opportunity is offered,

I should neglect to add at least a word towards giving them expression.

In the construction of the testing-machine, with which my name is identified, Mr. Holley was always ready to listen to my suggestions, and always ready to carry them out, and when the machine was finished he was the first to undertake to put its merits before the public. Unasked by me, he wrote and published at his own expense a little pamphlet, which he read before the Institute of Mining Engineers, at their meeting at Baltimore. He was one of the first to recommend Congress to pay me for the machine, and he has done much more than I can tell you to put its merits before the public.

Last summer, just before he started for Europe, I walked into his office one morning. He said, " Emery, I am glad to see you. I am going to Europe, and I want to know if you will allow me to go to some of the European Governments this summer and put that testing-machine before them, and get some contracts for you?" I said, "Some other time, Mr. Holley; but not now." I was so situated, pecuniarily, at the time, owing to the Government not having paid me as recommended, that I did not care to have him do what he proposed then. But he seemed very anxious to put that machine before those Governments. It was a work near his heart, and although he served on that Board a good many days of toil, he gave his valuable time to the public without a dollar of compensation, and when the Board was disbanded it went to his heart more than any other thing I ever heard him speak of. He spoke of it repeatedly, and with a great deal of feeling. He seemed deeply to regret that the Board could not be continued, and he go on with the others in the work which he had seen inaugurated. He has done more for me than I can tell you, and I would like to say a word in regard to this memorial which is proposed for him. It seems to me that the best monument of him is his own work. Mr. Holley has left a great monument, which must endure for all time. But as a member of this Society, and sister societies with which he was connected, as an American engineer, as one of those engineers with whom he was associated in a profession which he has done more to lift up abroad than any other man, as a citizen of this country, the wealth of which he has done so much to increase, I say much is due to Holley. I say it advisedly. None of us, I believe, realize to what extent—millions of dollars—hundreds of millions of dollars,—nay, I think, if a careful estimate was made, thousands of millions of dollars would be found to have been added to the wealth of this country—to its industries, because of the progress of Bessemer steel, which has given us that permanent way which enables us to take our wheat from the Far West and lay it down in the centre of Europe. Without that steel we could not have done this. Without it those millions which have flowed into this country for the last three or four years would not have so flowed. Without it we would not have had this flood of commercial prosperity. To Holley's individual efforts much of this prosperity is due; and I, for one, shall be dissatisfied if this Society, if the other two engineering societies, if those great Bessemer steel interests, which he has helped to build up, if this great prosperous country, which he has helped to make wealthy, do not unite in raising a monument worthy of one who has done so much for the world. I hope a monument may be put up which will be worthy of this country, worthy of these societies, and worthy of Holley.

WILLIAM C. PARTRIDGE, of New York city: Listening to all that has been said this afternoon, one who knew Mr. Holley only a little and at a distance, as it were, finds the single note recurring over and over again,—disinterested helpfulness. It seemed as though he had lifted everybody's load; and I think I can do little better than to give an instance of the way he would exercise his wonderful inventive ability to do even a little thing. When he wanted to make the Bessemer process known to the students— known to the world—I received through a friend a little card, saying that in Hoboken, at such a time, there would be a lecture, by A. L. Holley, on the Bessemer process. I went there and found a lecture-room arranged somewhat like this, with a goodly audience, and a quiet, pleasant man came on the stage at one side. The whole front was filled with a great screen for the lantern, and that pleasant man commenced reading a delightful story of steel and its uses, and began with the details of the Bessemer process, and referred to Figure 1, and the lights went down, and while his voice went on continuously, the lantern flashed out with a 15-foot diagram of Figure 1; and as he referred to letter after letter, or part after part, the black line of the pointer touched each one in succession. We had to look and to listen. It went on, and Figure 2 was necessary, and, without a pause, 2, 3, 4, and it went on to 7, 8, 9, and 10, and they made their appearance in their regular order, and every part that the lecturer mentioned was touched by that needle-like shadow.

It was teaching in its highest form. Only once in the whole lecture did Holley stop, and that was when, after referring backward to Figure 2, and forward to Figure 7, he turned round to see whether the man at the lantern was still keeping up the diagrams in order. There was not a hitch from the beginning to the end of the lecture. It was like magic. It was a system of illustrative lecturing so superior to anything that I had ever seen before, or ever heard of, that I thought it was enough to have made an ordinary lecturer's fortune, and all to enable the student to understand easily the Bessemer process.

Mr. SELLERS: I would like to ask if the Hon. Mr. Wayne MacVeagh is here.

THE PRESIDENT: Is Mr. MacVeagh here?

Mr. SELLERS: A few days ago I met him and told him of this memorial meeting, and he bowed his head with sorrow for his friend. He said that he would try to be here; that nothing would give him so much pleasure as to say a few words about one whom he valued so highly, not only as a personal friend, but as a man who had done so much for the industrial welfare of the country. If Mr. MacVeagh is not here, I should like at least that there may be a record of what he wished to say.

The following resolutions were unanimously adopted:

WHEREAS, We are called upon as a society to give expression to profound and sincere sorrow in the death of our Vice-president and friend, Alexander L. Holley,—

Resolved, That we mourn the death of our friend as an irreparable loss to the profession, and as a sad personal bereavement.

Resolved, That in the death of Alexander L. Holley, the country has lost an engineer whose genius and industry have greatly aided our industrial development, and to whom all branches of the engineering profession are profoundly indebted.

Resolved, That we shall ever hold Alexander L. Holley in cherished remembrance, as one whose life and example are an inspiration to high views and worthy motives, and who gave a new dignity to all branches of our profession, and that we remember our association with him as something which made our lives happier, and our work lighter.

Resolved, That the secretary be directed to forward a copy of these resolutions with a report of our memorial services to the family of Mr. Holley, with assurances of the deep and tender sympathy we feel for them in their bereavement, and that the committee of five appointed by our council be directed to coöperate with the committees appointed by other societies, in furthering the work of securing a worthy and permanent Holley memorial, in whatever form may be deemed most appropriate, and best calculated to keep his work and example before the rising generation of engineers.

IV.

MEMORIAL RESOLUTIONS OF THE AMERICAN SO-
CIETY OF CIVIL ENGINEERS.

AT a regular meeting of the American Society of Civil Engineers, held at the rooms of the Society, in the city of New York, March 1st, 1882, the following resolutions were unanimously adopted :

Resolved, That in the death of Alexander Lyman Holley, formerly Vice-President of the American Society of Civil Engineers, the engineering profession at large, no less than our own Society, has suffered a grievous loss. In him were combined not only the inventive genius to discover and successfully apply new methods of subduing the forces of nature for the benefit of mankind (as evinced in the great industries which have been developed under his direction), but a rare literary facility for arranging and distributing stores of information obtained through patient study of the works of others. By the example of his life, in his gentleness, his industry, his modesty, his deferential consideration of opposing counsels, combined with integrity, indomitable energy and power of work, the standard of our profession has been materially advanced, and a spirit of good fellowship engendered, which has had the effect to weld in harmonious continuity of interest the several branches of a profession destined to play an increasingly important part in the advancement of civilization.

Resolved, That a committee of five be appointed to act in conjunction with similar committees which have been or may be appointed by the American Institute of Mining Engineers, and the American Society of Mechanical Engineers, in any further measures that may be deemed advisable in honor of the memory of our departed brother.

Resolved, That we offer to the family of the deceased the assurance of our earnest and respectful sympathy in their affliction.

Resolved, That the Secretary be instructed to transmit copies of the above resolutions to the family, to the Secretary of the American Institute of Mining Engineers, and to the Secretary of the American Society of Mechanical Engineers.

V.

JOINT ACTION OF THE THREE SOCIETIES.

In accordance with the resolutions of the three societies, given in the preceding pages, the following committees were appointed.

For the American Institute of Mining Engineers—Messrs. R. W. Raymond, Chester Griswold, John Fritz, Thomas Egleston, and G. W. Maynard.

For the American Society of Mechanical Engineers—Messrs. W. P. Trowbridge, J. C. Bayles, James A. Burden, Eckley B. Coxe, and R. W. Hunt.

For the American Society of Civil Engineers—Messrs. Charles Macdonald, O. Chaunte, W. G. Hamilton, I. Newton, and T. C. Clarke.

These committees subsequently organized as a joint-committee, electing R. W. Raymond as President, and Charles Macdonald as Secretary.

A sub-committee, consisting of Messrs. Macdonald, Bayles and Raymond, was appointed to collect subscriptions for a memorial of A. L. Holley, to be placed in Central Park, New York City.

About ten thousand dollars has been collected for this purpose.

By the action of the three societies, it was determined that the Memorial Address should be delivered before the Societies in joint session, in New York City, November 1st, 1883.

VI.

MEMORIAL ADDRESS.

(DELIVERED IN THE TURF CLUB THEATRE, NEW YORK CITY, NOVEMBER
1ST, 1883, BY R. W. RAYMOND.)

MR. PRESIDENT; GENTLEMEN OF THE AMERICAN SOCIETY OF
CIVIL ENGINEERS, THE AMERICAN SOCIETY OF MECHAN-
ICAL ENGINEERS, AND THE AMERICAN INSTITUTE OF MINING
ENGINEERS; LADIES AND GENTLEMEN:

The memorial session in Washington, at which I was first desig-
nated for the duty of this evening, was chiefly devoted to the multi-
form expression of sorrow. From a score of speakers, who had
known Mr. Holley in various stages of his career, came tributes of
affection, honorable alike to him and to them. Among them all,
none uttered words more heartfelt and impressive than did the
venerable Ashbel Welch, who, by reason of official position, as well
as years and character, would doubtless have been called to preside
over this meeting, had not a potent message summoned him meanwhile to a higher seat. Nestor mourned over Achilles, slain in the
midst of the battle; and now Nestor too, from the peaceful life of
an honored old age, has passed away.

But neither this more recent, nor that earlier grief is the theme of
the present hour. However inadequate to the task the orator of to-
night may prove, it was fitting that some one, waiting until the first
outburst of emotion had died away, should attempt a calm review
of the life and works of Alexander Lyman Holley; that Friendship,
bewailing her loss, should give way to History, counting her gain;
that the achievements of the departed should be recognized and
valued, and his example studied. Was he greatly successful? How
did he win success? How much of it was born with him; how
much thrust upon him; how much earned by him? And if his
own hands wrought out his fame, is there anything in the method
of his preparation and practice that others might imitate with profit?

Mr. Holley was born at Lakeville, in Salisbury, Conn., on the
twentieth of July, 1832. His father, Alexander H. Holley, subsequently Governor of that State, was a native of the same village.

His mother, whose maiden name was Jane M. Lyman, was one of the Lymans of Goshen. The experts in New England genealogies will not need to be told that on both sides, he came of a good stock —such as, by a combination of enterprise, intelligence, and high principle, has made New England great. The mother could, indeed, bestow upon her son nothing more than the legacy of inherited character, for she died a few weeks after his birth. But her place was supplied by the second marriage of his father, three years later, to Miss Marcia Coffing, whose affection bestowed freely upon her stepson through twenty years, was as freely returned by him. Their correspondence, some of which has been preserved, shows that their personal intercourse was intimate, and that this excellent lady, though burdened with the cares of a large and hospitable household, never forgot to be a true mother to this son of her adoption, as well as to the children born of her. No doubt he was much indebted for noble impulses and principles to the influence of this devoted woman.

For two or three years of his early boyhood, he attended the district school near his father's house, and was then advanced to the Academy, to which he walked, a little more than a mile and a half every day, winter and summer. In later life, he was accustomed to allude to this regular exercise as having laid the foundation of the fine constitution which enabled him for so many years to work so hard and yet so easily.

From the Academy in Salisbury, he went to another under the care of Mr. Simeon Hart, at Farmington, Conn., and after a year or more, to Williams Academy, then directed by Mr. E. W. B. Canning, at Stockbridge, Mass. From Stockbridge he went to Bridgeport, Conn., to prepare for Yale College, under Rev. Henry Jones. According to the dates and internal evidence of his boyish letters, the above order is not strictly correct. I find him at Stockbridge in 1846 and 1847, at Farmington in 1848, at Bridgeport in 1849, and back at Stockbridge in 1850. For our present purpose, the question is not important, except as it shows an early trait in his character—a restlessness, born of versatility and genius, which under less judicious training might have wasted his life.

Ample and interesting materials tempt me to more detailed description of his boyhood. But I must be content to mention, and briefly illustrate, its leading characteristics. First among these must be named the normal, healthy physical activity and the overflow of mirth and high spirits which made him a leader in boyish sports

and adventures. Where the others climbed with ostentatious courage up to the belfrey of the academy, he, at the first trial, mounted
above it and stood on the gilded ball, which no foot had pressed
before. He hangs over precipices, takes long foot-journeys, and
revels in the mere consciousness of life and strength. Strikingly
handsome as well as athletic, he is naturally a leader among his
comrades. In all sorts of home amusements, too, his merry ingenuity makes him invaluable. Many of these, such as charades and
rhyming games, were intellectual; others were mere pranks—such
as the match between him and a friend, "who could eat the most
pancakes," of which the kitchen was the scene, the cook being
coaxed into complicity, while the dog, wagging his tail behind the
combatants, received from each as many segments as could be sur-
reptitiously bestowed without the knowledge of the other; or the
occasion when, having constructed a rustic bridge over the brook,
Holley forced the entire family to march over it in solemn proces-
sion, while he sat by, fantastically dressed as a troubadour, and
played the guitar.

Let no one despise this light-hearted gayety. It was the early
form of that courage which carried him afterwards through many
struggles and even defeats, with an air of victory that was in itself
the promise of victory to come.

To this quality must be added a keen observation and an inborn
talent for drawing. These were specially, but not wholly, directed
toward machinery, in which he took the liveliest interest. His
father having established the well-known knife-manufactory at
Lakeville, the boy made himself familiar with all the machinery,
and during his youth made innumerable proposals of improvement
—some of which, being really good, were adopted, while others—
no doubt the greater number—were crude and impracticable. When
but nine years old, he accompanied his father as far as Niagara, where
he was left for a few days with an uncle who was connected with
works employing machinery. During the father's absence, Alexander was repeatedly missed by his uncle, who always found him
on such occasions in some place where there was a steam-engine,
and who long preserved, as a memento of the visit, a little bundle
of papers on which the boy of nine had made drawings of the different machines he had thus studied. In a letter written at about
the age of fourteen, he describes an excursion with his school-mates
to the old Bristol copper mine, six miles from Farmington, and
says:

"The steam-engine attracted considerable of my attention, of course. It was splendidly made and fitted, and went so still that one would hardly know that it was in the room. Power, twenty-horse. Mr. S. Hart [his teacher] told the gentleman that showed us around that he would have me draw a plan of the engine from memory, which I have done, and which Mr. H. is much pleased with. He says he is going to send it to the aforesaid gentleman at Bristol."

His letters overflow with revelations of his passionate interest in machinery, and particularly in locomotives. In one of them, written after returning to school from vacation, he indulges in some of the truly good sentiments with which boys are wont to please parents, but which are in this case redeemed from platitude by this picturesque touch :

" It seems as if I should dive and dig and plow, and if that did not succeed, back out and plow again, in my studies, as faithfully as the locomotive, old ' Connecticut' did, this morning in the drifts, with seven long cars, all alone."

In another letter, he speaks of a locomotive which has been wrecked on the Housatonic road ; calls it by name, as an acquaintance ; says he has walked twice (a number of miles) to the place where it lies at the bottom of a steep embankment; introduces a pen-and-ink sketch of the scene, locomotive and all, to show how difficult will be the return of the engine to the track ; and concludes, " I guess the H. R. R. Co. will not make money by this operation."

He frequently declares his determination to master the science of machinery, and I find one sentence, in a letter written at fifteen, which seems to be an unconscious prophecy. He writes :

"I have seen, in a newspaper, an account of a man in England who makes steel that will cut iron or any other hard substance without dulling it. I should like to hire out to that man for a year or so. . . . . I wish I could learn the art of making steel."

Twelve years later, there was a man in England by the name of Bessemer, of whom he took, in this art, lessons that were not wasted !

In another letter, written from Stockbridge, he says :

"I have been devoting all my leisure time, for nearly two weeks, in making sectional and perspective views of the internal works, machinery, steam-works, etc., of the most improved locomotive engines, showing how the steam is made, applied, and cut off at half-stroke or not (a recent improvement); how the engine is worked every way, in some seventeen different pictures, with explanations filling some eight or ten pages. Mr. Canning is to have them framed and hung up in the Academy. I have explained them in such a manner that any one can understand them, and I really hope that people will look at them, for there is more ignorance among scientific and educated men on this point than on any other. People who pretend to 'know the ropes' can not explain the simplest form of a steam-engine, even with a model. Of mechanics and chemistry, I intend to get the most thorough knowledge, if I have the opportunity (and, in fact, I intend to get it any way), both practical and theoretical. These are. the studies I have always liked, and I am bound to investigate and become master of them."

One other characteristic deserves special mention—his talent for debate and literary composition, and his consequent love for them. Let it be said here that his was not an instance of dropsical precocity. His early efforts were not mature, or even surprisingly early. At fourteen he joined, I believe, his first debating society. I have found, in his handwriting, a constitution and by-laws of the Societas Literarum (symbolized by a Greek Sigma), which bear date about this time, and in their simplicity and brevity are worthy of imitation. The constitution runs thus:

" 1. It shall be the duty of each member to try to sustain the society.

" 2. Each member shall pledge his word of honor to keep all the proceedings a secret.

" 3. The business of this society shall be debating and composition reading.

" 4. This society shall support a semi-monthly paper, called the ——." [Name omitted.]

And the following are the by-laws:

" 1. The officers of the society shall be a Secretary and President.

" 2. There shall be as many as eight members in the society.

" 3. It shall be unlawful to use vulgar or profane language."

It was not long, however, before, in this congenial sphere, he developed extraordinary activity. I cannot forbear to introduce, at this point, the letter which appeared in the *American Machinist* of March 18th, 1882, from Mr. Canning:

" The universal sorrow in the inventive and mechanical world over the recent decease of A. L. Holley prompts me to jot down a

few particulars of his earlier school experiences, which go to prove
the truth of the proverb, 'the boy is father of the man.'

"Mr. Holley entered Williams Academy at Stockbridge, Mass.,
in the fall of 1848,* then under my charge.   He is still remembered
as a fair, fresh-cheeked, blue-eyed, wide-awake boy of sixteen, who
pursued studies preparatory to a college course.   His geniality, generosity, and overflowing good humor made him popular with his
school-mates, and soon gave him the lead, both in and out of school.
He excelled in every branch of study ; but his chief interest centred
in Natural Philosophy and Mechanics.   He was a prominent member
of a literary society of the institution called the 'Philologian,' in
which he manifested talent unusual for his years for debate and free
discussion ; while his fun-loving propensities found vent in conduct-
ing mock trials and in humorous essays and declamations.   He established and mainly conducted a periodical entitled *The Gun Cotton*,
issued fortnightly on a large sheet in manuscript, which was read by
myself from the desk, and afforded great interest and amusement by
the variety and spice of its contents.   This he edited during his stay
at the Academy.

"Though excelling in all the branches of study required of him,
his *penchant* for mechanics and invention developed itself markedly
when he attacked Natural Philosophy and Physics.   Dissatisfied
with the meagre description in the text-books of the steam-engine,
with which he seemed to be better acquainted than the author of the
treatise, he at my request made drawings in detail of a stationary
engine and of a locomotive, with an accuracy and skill that would
have done credit to a professional engineer or draftsman.   These I
used in demonstration, in preference to the imperfect model among
the school apparatus.   During one of his vacations, he came up from
his Salisbury home expressly to show me a miniature engine of his
own building.   It was complete in all respects, and of skilful workmanship ; and, on being fired up, ran with admirable success.   Thus
he foreshadowed the devotion to the mechanic arts which so eminently characterized his manhood.   One number of his *Gun Cotton*,
I remember, was devoted to the description of an aërial voyage made
by a machine of his own devising, whose practical workings were
related with as much interest as the details of the wonders of sight-
seeing it enabled its inventor to describe.   This, he prophesied,
would be substantially the vehicle of locomotion in A. D. 1950.

---

* Mr. Canning forgets his first sojourn at the school.   He was certainly there in
1846 also.

"His temperament prompted him to constant activity. There was not a lazy bone or muscle in his body. In fact, his mind was too powerful for his physique; and, beyond doubt, the continued high-pressure at which he drove his mental energy, during all his busy life, materially shortened his days.

"In his reading he was fond—though by no means exclusively so —of works of imagination. Every new invention that fell under his eyes received due notice in his *Gun Cotton*. Imaginative works seemed to be the whetstone on which he sharpened his own inventive genius. It is rare that good sense and sound judgment succeed in subduing the *imagination* to become the servant of the *practical*, to the extent realized in the case of Mr. Holley.

"Your brief but comprehensive article in the *American Machinist* of 18th of February follows the career of Mr. Holley subsequently to his college life. Doffing the student's toga for the workman's blouse, he put to the test the best theories of his book-learning, and showed the world, to its immense benefit, the unusual example of a man possessing the combination of enlarged education, inventive talent, and practical common-sense.

E. W. B. CANNING.

"STOCKBRIDGE, MASS."

To this life-like picture no improving touch could be added, unless by the hand of the subject himself. One or two quotations from Holley's letters of this period will be their own sufficient apology.

Writing from Bridgeport, at seventeen, and giving, as was his custom, an account of his doings, he says:

"I have written the following compositions:

"1st. A Dream, personifying Wisdom (a judge), History, Chemistry, Mathematics, and Philosophy, who speak of their respective merits. Philosophy wins the prize. 6 pages of foolscap.

"2d. A Fragment (revised from a former) containing a few thoughts like those in Gray's Elegy. 2 pages.

"3d. History of Audax Promptusque. A novel. 26 pages.

"4th. War (revised from a former). 4½ pages.

"5th. Pride (rather disconnected). 2 pages.

"6th. A Picture. 6¼ pages. On this I have spent in all at least twelve hours' hard study, and it is the best composition I ever wrote. I would like to have you read it.

" 7th. A Dream and Consequent Wish. The best I ever wrote, except No. 6.

" 8th. A composition in blank verse. Unfinished."

In January, 1850, he writes from Stockbridge:

" I write you in great haste, to say, that at the close of the term we're to have an exhibition. I was first chosen to write and speak a valedictory oration. Then I have to write the *Gun Cotton*, and a continuation of a treatise on the manufacture of pocket cutlery (which I have been at several weeks), for the *Experimentor*, another paper— all this for the day of exhibition. Then the forenoon of the day is to be occupied by a Lawsuit. The Philologian Society have, for that occasion, resolved themselves into a ' high court of inquiry,' and I am chosen for ' State's Attorney,' to prosecute a man for ' assault and battery.' This will be public. Besides this, I have to write a con- tinuation of my treatise on cutlery for the *Experimentor* next week, and to write two numbers of another paper I publish, called the *Locomotive*. Then I have to prepare also for a public trial next week in the Philologian, also to learn (probably) a part in a dialogue for Exhibition, and all this in addition to Latin and Greek. My request is this, that I may omit my music-lessons till next term, as I have my hands full, and shall burn some of my irons, if I don't look out.

" I shall also want a new coat to expatiate in on the great day. Please send as soon as convenient."

The treatise on cutlery, above alluded to, was subsequently ac- cepted by Poor's *Railway Journal*, and published in successive num- bers of that paper during the summer of 1850. It is a curious com- pound of learned extracts from such books of general chemistry, etc., as were accessible to the young author, and admirably clear and vivid descriptions of the actual processes of the manufacture with which he was personally familiar. In his ambitious view, the subject of pen and pocket-cutlery includes the natural history and chemical and physical relations of iron, steel, brass, copper, zinc, German sil- ver, tortoise-shell, etc. No element is mentioned without a consci- entious statement of its chemical equivalent, and the manner in which it is produced or found in nature. But these adornments of the essay, probably its principal merits in the author's opinion, are worthless in comparison with the practical details, which no doubt chiefly commended it to the publishers.

This was, I think, the first literary work for which he received pay. In an exultant but apologetic letter written in July, 1850 (after the publication of the treatise had begun), he confesses that he had made a surreptitious journey from Stockbridge to New York:

" I walked before sunrise to West Stockbridge, went to Hudson and down the river on the Alida. Called on Mr. Poor, who was sorry he had paid no attention to my dozen letters, and as a compensation gave me the equivalent of about sixty dollars for my essay. That is, he gave me $25 in cash, and 27 copies of every chapter of the article, thus making probably 243 *Railroad Journals*. . . . . He says I had better enlarge the essay a little, and come down in vacation to New York, when he will introduce me to a house in New York who are perhaps the largest publishing house in New York. He thinks I can sell the copyright. I saw the steamship ' City of Glasgow ' sail. City in mourning for General Taylor. Left city at three o'clock. We had two locomotives, and eleven cars full out."

One further trait, and our picture will be as complete as circumstances will permit us to make it. I have already alluded to the restlessness of Holley's mind. He is drawn by many tastes and ambitions in many directions, though, through it all, his dominating tendency may be perceived. He is impatient of processes, and longs for results. Sometimes his distaste for the drudgery of books and the discipline of school rises to despair. Thus, he writes from Bridgeport in 1849, to his father a letter from which I take the following extracts:

" I have had everything done for me that could be done—everything that kind parents could possibly do for a son. I have made three trials, and each one has proved unsuccessful—three trials to get an education; and now, having spent so much of your money and trouble, I wish to make one trial at work; and I know I can succeed. . . . . It is a waste, sir, I think, to send me to school. It is not in my nature to deprive myself of an education if I was able to get it; but I see the folly of it. I have tried as hard as I could to learn out of books, but it is folly in the extreme. *If* I have any talent at all, it is for writing. When I lay myself out, and spend many hours on a composition, I can, by copying all the good parts, make out quite a piece; but this is *all* the talent I have got, *any way*. Now I have got hands, and can work. . . . . There is John [his brother], a natural scholar, who could not bear hard work, and who will make, by his mind alone, a great man; but I can work, and do nothing else to any advantage. . . . . I am very anxious, of course, to hear your decision, and will come if you say so, with a right good-will; but if not, it all looks *dark* ahead, and I do not know what I shall do. . . . . P. S.—Please write to-morrow, as I am very anxious to hear."

The key to this exaggerated confession of failure doubtless lay in the fact, that at this time he was preparing for the classical course at Yale, and was giving a good deal of trouble to the Rev. Mr. Jones. Moreover, going home to work meant escaping from the bondage of Latin and Greek to the whirring wheels, the engines, the forges, the tools of *that knife-factory!* On one hand, purgatory; on the other, Paradise: what marvel that to his vision the disciplinary pains of the former took on the hopeless hues of utter despair?

I violate, in this one instance, the rule I have elsewhere pursued in the treatment of private correspondence intrusted to me, by quoting from the reply to the foregoing letter:

"I am very sorry to see you yielding to so desponding a tone of spirit. You are not quite the dunce you would attempt to make me believe you are; nor have all your experiments to secure an education failed, as you would intimate. You certainly know more than you did, when you commenced your career abroad, about books, and about men and things. I have certainly had two or three reports to that effect. Why then do you despond? I have not complained of your scholarship in writing to you. . . . . This complaint has been on your part and not on mine. . . . . No, my son, you must not despond. If dark days now appear, brighter ones will follow. . . . . Have you not often heard me say how grateful I always felt to my father, that he did not indulge me in my propensity for change? I think I should have been a ruined man if I had been permitted to hop from this thing to that, and hither and yon, just as fancy for the time might dictate. I wished to leave the store and engage in farming. He said no, and I felt hard about it; but I have often since thanked him for that *no*. Besides, suppose you were to leave school and engage in business systematically (which you never have done yet) and were subject to the drill which you must be, when that time does come, would not that after a while be as irksome as anything else? . . . . You are in the right way now, my son, and your future happiness, usefulness, and respectability depend upon a continuance in this. Of this I assure you, as a father most earnestly desiring your happiness as well as usefulness.

"If you are not ready to enter college at the next commencement, then go on till you are ready. There are more years to follow. Only make good use of your time, and we shall all be satisfied. . . . . You say you think you have *one* talent at any rate. I think you have more; but cultivate *that* at all events, and do all you can toward cultivating others. The cultivation of this very talent may yet be essential to your success in life.

"But always remember one thing, my son. It is an injunction of the Most High. Man is to earn his bread by the sweat of his brow. From this there is no escape. Therefore we must keep on in our employments, whatever they may be; and the more cheerfully we do so, the happier we shall be. Brighter days are before you, and you will so see it ere long. Be contented then, and make us happy and yourself happy, and all your friends happy, by a cheerful perseverance in the duties before you, which are not *always* study, but in after years the *fruit* of study, and all will be well."

An excellent letter; and there are many more of the same sort. But wiser than wise words, was the step that followed; for the father, while holding a firm hand upon these wayward moods, was not blind to the needs and impulses of the genius beneath them; and in 1850, Brown University having just established a scientific course, Alexander was entered at Providence instead of New Haven. From this time on, nothing was heard of discontent in study. In October, 1850, he writes:

"I have succeeded, by working nights and in odd hours, in making a painting of the fastest locomotive in the city, which I showed to the Professor of Mathematics. He was pleased with it, and asked me to go with him and look at the locomotive, and to explain to him a new invention in locomotive engineering, called 'link-motion,' which I did satisfactorily. I considered this quite an honor, as he has explained the steam-engine to classes for a dozen years or more. He then took me into several factories where I could not have gone without him."

Besides the picture above referred to, he finished a working-model of a steam-engine, which the professors assured him was the best they had ever seen. And, what was more important, he invented a new cut-off, concerning which the following extracts are interesting:

"Brown University, November, 1851.—. . . . I have noticed Professor Page's engine, of which father speaks. As he says, it will eventually do away with steam, but *not yet*. I understand his magnetic engine perfectly. It is just as capable of improvement as the steam-engine—and more so. Machinists' work is also quite as necessary for it as for steam-engines. At any rate, I have invented an improvement in steam-engines, and it is bound to be patented, if I sell the coat on my back to pay for it, and go without any. I have showed my plans to a man who was four years with Messrs. Corliss & Nightingale, of this place. These men have invented and are making the most improved cut-off engine of the day, and this gentleman says that my engine (that is to be) embraces all their improvements and none of its disadvantages."

" January 14th, 1852.—After many attempts to get time, I have at last succeeded in putting my new cut-off on paper. Professor Caswell says that it will work as well as Corliss's celebrated cut-off. Professor Norton says it is very ingeniously contrived, and is better than Corliss's. To-day I took it to Mr. Greene (of the firm of Thurston & Greene, the most extensive engineers of the city), and he said it would work as well as any cut-off he ever saw. He said I could not get it patented, for this reason : A man some years ago got up a cut-off, and in his patent it was provided that he should own all improvements in the cutting off of steam by the regulator, wherein the valve-motion was obtained by any *connection* with the working part of the engine. My cut-off is *entirely* different in principle and form from his, and from all others ; yet Corliss himself, whose cut-off is different from his and mine, is to-day involved in a lawsuit with the original inventor. . . . . I feel satisfied at all events, that my plan is entirely original, and as good as any body's. . . . . I can have a picture and description of ' Holley's Improved Cut-Off' circulated in *Appleton's Engineers' Journal* [he means the *Mechanical Magazine*], free of expense, and shall immediately do so. [This cut-off was illustrated and described in the *Mechanical Magazine* in July, 1852. It is a detached escapement, operated both directly by a cam (at the end of the stroke), and indirectly from the governor, at any point during the stroke.] . . . . You advised me when I was home, to consult Mr. Adams, C. E., of New York, about my oscillating engine. I did consult him, and found that my fundamental improvement, on which the rest depended, was patented in England by a celebrated engineer, some years ago. I thought it all out myself, and never heard of it till I had put it on paper myself."

Although such matters as these occupied much of his attention, he was active in the literary society to which he belonged. A letter to his step-mother pours out his wrath at the injustice to which the college societies were subjected by the President and trustees, when, desiring permission to meet in the evening instead of the afternoon, they were flatly denied. A rebellion followed, but though some of the hot-heads went so far as to incur the peril of expulsion, Holley stopped short. After all, what he wanted was to get an education, and to him these minor issues were not important enough to justify the risk of losing that.   So he declined to abet further the revolutionary movement with which he heartily sympathized, and turned his tumultuous feelings into the safer channel of a long, eloquent, and indignant letter home.

It was either before or just after his graduation, that he wrote an elaborate essay on " Water Considered as a Carrier," which was published in 1854 in successive numbers of the *Litchfield Inquirer*.   It is an exhaustive account of the functions and properties of water as a conveyer of gases, mechanical sediments, dissolved salts, germs, etc., in the vegetable, animal, and mineral kingdoms; of its agency in geological formations, volcanic eruptions, etc.   Curiously enough, water is considered as a carrier of everything except heat.   This aspect is omitted altogether, though it is the one with which the writer was at that time most familiar, and was afterwards to be most largely concerned.   The essay came from his reading, not from his experience.   It is creditable to a young collegian; but still more creditable is the fact that he never wrote another like it.

In September, 1853, he was graduated with the degree of Bachelor of Philosophy.   His oration, on "The Natural Motors," is in point of style not notably different from the fervid and florid efforts common to such occasions.   Yet it betrays throughout the passion of the speaker for locomotive machinery, terrestrial and marine; and two passages, describing respectively a locomotive and a steamship, show with what assiduous affection he has watched what he describes. Less clear and forcible is his allusion to electricity, the employment of which in the telegraph he represents with "commencement" rhetoric, as " ambitious man, grasping the red right hand of Jupiter ! " But he pays a compliment to the caloric engine, as an enterprise which " may yet be consummated in a future neither chimerical nor distant." This was just after the trial of Ericsson's steamer, and before the general recognition of the fact that heated air is useful and economical for small motors, though it cannot compete on a large scale with steam.   I use the words of the distinguished inventor of the caloric engine—a man whose brilliant list of great successes renders him well able to afford the confession of a failure, and who, in the true spirit of science, has drawn from this disappointment grounds for gratitude. "The marine engineer," writes Mr. Ericsson, "has thus been encouraged to renew his efforts to perfect the steam-engine, without fear of rivalry from a motor depending on the dilatation of atmospheric air by heat." (*Contributions to the Centennial Exhibition*, 1876, p. 438.)

Holley's faith in the genius of Ericsson was confirmed in later years, in connection with the triumphs of the screw-propeller and of the turreted iron-clad. And Ericsson's generous appreciation of Holley appears in a letter written since the death of the latter, and speaking of him as " the brightest ornament of American engineering."

After leaving college, Holley entered the shops of Corliss & Nightingale, at Providence. They were at the time engaged in the attempt to apply to the locomotive engine the principles of the variable cutoff, so successful in the stationary engine. Holley entered their locomotive department, where he served both as draftsman and machinist, and subsequently took the "Advance" out on the Stonington Railroad, where he ran it as engineer long enough to show the practicability of so doing, and, I believe, to effect a sale of the engine. In economy of steam, as shown by indicator-diagrams, the "Advance" was superior to existing link-motion and lap-valve locomotives. But the detached variable cut-off was too delicate an arrangement to endure the jar of such rough service. Another arrangement was substituted; but this, too, rattled to pieces; and even in the form finally adopted, the "Advance" was not practically a machine to be enthusiastically welcomed, particularly upon such road-beds as were then characteristic of America.

In his speech on "The Pursuit of Science," at the Hartford dinner of the Society of Mechanical Engineers, Holley revived his reminiscences of the "Advance." Said he:

"The idea began to obtain that science should be pursued not in books, but in things; and I commenced the pursuit of science in and on and under one of the awfullest *things* this world ever saw. It was Corliss's original locomotive, euphoniously called 'The Old Jigger.' This locomotive was possessed of a certain inborn cussedness, which could hardly be the attribute of a mere machine—her spiritual nature was a sort of Mephistophelian cross with a Colorado mule; and as to her physical constitution and membership, a cotton-factory 'mule' was simple in comparison. The Old Jigger had, as nearly as I can remember, 365 valves, one to break down every day in the year. And as to valve *motion*, well, nobody ever counted the number of its pieces. They were as the sands of the sea-shore. Most of them used to jar off, the first few trips of the week, after which all the men in the shop could comparatively keep track of the rest of them. I will say for the Old Jigger that she made the best indicator-card I ever saw from a locomotive; clean cut-off, almost a theoretical expansion-curve, and an exhaust as if she had knocked out a cylinder-head. Well, once in a while, after she had been jackassing over the road about four hours behind time, and we had pinch-barred her into the roundhouse, we used to pull out these indicator-cards of hers, and talk them over right before her, and we would look at her and ask one another why in thunder an engine that could make a card like that would act as if the very old— chief-engineer was in her. And next morning she would rouse up and pull the biggest train that had ever been over the road—ahead of time.

"But she was an inconstant old girl—and lazy, too—used to prefer to work with one side, and always made some plausible excuse for breaking down the other. I remember, one March morning, when nobody was looking, she kicked off about two dozen pieces of her starboard valve-gear, and brought up all standing, over a culvert about ten feet wide and full of ice-water. As I was standing in this culvert up to my middle, disconnecting her eccentric-straps, a college professor came along, and rammed his umbrella into me, and asked me to explain to him the difference between this locomotive and any other locomotive! I then delivered my first scientific lecture; and I am now of opinion that its diction would have been modified by a divinity student.

"Continuing my pursuit of science, I left Corliss's works with a knowledge of valve-motion which was simply sublime; and I then proceeded to engraft this knowledge on a locomotive works in the Middle States."

So far, the dinner speech, delivered in May, 1881. How lightly does memory pass over the sad hours of the past! Probably the witty orator would have been as much startled as his hearers, if any voice had recalled to him the period of despondency through which he had passed after leaving the Corliss shop, and before finding employment elsewhere. Messrs. Corliss and Nightingale wrote, under date of March 27th, 1855:

"Mr. Holley has been employed for nearly eighteen months in the locomotive department of our business. He is an accomplished draftsman, and exhibits talent in the designing and application of machinery. During the time he has been with us, he has enjoyed every facility for becoming practically acquainted with the working of locomotives. We should be glad to avail ourselves of his services in our regular business of manufacturing stationary engines. But his mind is on locomotives; and therefore, into that branch of mechanism will he carry that spirit and aim that will insure success. As we do not propose to pursue the locomotive-business at present, Mr. Holley leaves us, and carries with him our best wishes for his success."

Armed with this and other introductions, he visited the principal locomotive shops of the West in search of employment, with the result stated in the following letter, written about a month later, in St. Louis.

"I am completely discouraged. I have applied at every place in the Western country where they build locomotives, except one (at Milwaukee), and I am informed that I shall find no opportunity at that place. At Detroit, my letters were of no avail. They wanted no draftsman, only made the locomotive-business a minor affair, and did not propose to try to establish a reputation of their own—as nearly as I could understand it. Mr. —, of Cleveland, had no place for me, and said that if there was anything in the world he hated, it was patented improvements. Niles & Co., of Cincinnati, had a first-rate draftsman, and could not change. . . . .— & Co., of Cincinnati, . only built a few machines, and hired a draftsman, as they used a turning-lathe, for mechanical labor only. They get some poor fellow who will work a month or two, and then starve a month or two when they do not want to use him. The Covington, Louisville, and Chicago works have suspended. The shop at St. Louis is a good one; but they could give me no encouragement, though they seemed to be anxious to drive business. They have no draftsman at all, and think that people here are too ignorant to desire any change in the old form, even though it might be an improvement. I even offered to work for almost nothing, at almost anything, if they would take me in, but was unsuccessful. . . . . It is strange that when I have taken such pains to represent myself modestly, and am willing to do anything and work and persevere to the utmost extent, that when I have got such strong letters, and that when I know that I can build a better locomotive than all the rest of them put together—even in the face of all this, I cannot in the whole Western country get a place to earn my daily bread. The idea is damning to a man's spirits; though sometimes it looks so ridiculous that I cannot but laugh at the world generally. One thing is certain—I *will* build locomotives; and if my life is spared, I will ultimately place myself in a position where I can look down on every man who has neglected me, and laugh

with a good-will at the bad luck which the *improvements* they scorn
have brought upon them.   It may be a long time before I shall get
my head out of water, and I sometimes fear that my spirit will fail
me before I see the daylight.   If I sink, poor and unknown, I honestly believe I shall drag down with me some ideas of which, however humble they may be, the world is not worthy. . . . . . I want to
visit the Philadelphia, Baltimore, and New Jersey works, and see if
I can convince myself and my friends that I am good for something.
If I fail in doing this, I am ready to sink ; for if there is anything
certain in this world, it is, that I·will NEVER *do anything* permanently for a living, but just this one thing, namely, build locomotives."

It was at the very end of his hopes—in the locomotive works at
Jersey City—that he found employment at last.   And it was while
he was working there that he, most improvidently and most fortunately, married.   It is not my purpose in these remarks, devoted as
they must be to his professional career and works, to intrude upon
the sacredness of his domestic life.   Yet the two are not altogether
separable.   There are those who have not forgotten how the young
wife trudged daily with her husband to his experiments with coal-
burning locomotives on the Harlem road, or assisted him in the office
of the *Railroad Advocate,* or haunted the new Bessemer works at
Troy, until he was accustomed to say, when fears were expressed for
his health, "Don't be afraid; if I die, *she* can run the concern."
More than this : from the date of his marriage we find in his letters
no more outbursts of despair, but the cheerful and sanguine courage
of a heart anchored in a happy home.   Into that home trouble and
death came, as whither do they not come?   But they could not ban-
ish peace and hope.   Many of you will remember Holley's humorous and pathetic address at the Pittsburgh banquet of the Institute
of Mining Engineers in 1879.   Replying to the toast of " The Fellows' Wives," he said, among other things :

"Young man of the school, full of lore and anxious for hire, what
is the vista of probabilities that fills your eye?   Will you map out
the metalliferous veins under the fair landscape, from the ragged
outcrops of the upturned rocks?   Will you span the cañon, eroded
throughout æons, with your gossamer steel bridge of yesterday?
Will you compel a river which denudes a continent to build out its
own ship-canal through its own delta with its own *débris?*   Will
you sever continents to make a highway for commerce?   Will you
coax out of ores with your deft alchemy the metals which the evo-

lution of ages put in? Will you drive a train from the Orient to the Occident, following the sun, and keeping company with the hours? Ah, my dear boy! these things you may do; but they are only means to an end. And that end you shall see down the long vista of the inevitable. There, with eloquent eyes, and folded arms, sits a dear little woman. And, my boy, when those tender arms shall enfold *you*, and those eloquent eyes shall flash into your soul the potential caloric of a whole life, then you will know what it is to be the lord of a fellow's wife. . . . . Two thousand years ago, the philosopher Callimachus, wandering in the cemetery of Corinth, was arrested by a vision of prophetic beauty. It was only an acanthus plant, confined in a basket and covered with a tile, the struggling leaves curling through the meshes and wreathing themselves in graceful volutes under the covering stone. This was the decoration of a child's grave; but it was the prototype of the Corinthian capital. As out of a little grave grew the glory of decorative art, so out of, ah! how many little graves, struggling through the meshes and repressed by the cold marble, perennially bloom the graces and the virtues of the higher life—that long-suffering, that patience, that elasticity, that sweetness, that association of the good and the beautiful, which is but another name for *the fellow's wives!*"

While yet at Corliss's works, Mr. Holley had written, both for the *Polytechnic Journal,* and in Colburn's *Railroad Advocate,* articles on the Corliss engines, which displayed marked ability. Probably it was this which brought him to the notice of Zerah Colburn, the inconstant, erratic, unfortunate, but brilliant and wonderful engineer and author, whose fitful career would in itself be subject enough for a volume. Mr. Colburn had been superintendent of the New Jersey Locomotive Works, and had started in 1854 the *Railroad Advocate,* which may be said to have inaugurated a new era in the technical journalism of this country. From being a contributor to this paper, Holley became a partner and editor. The two men had many things in common. They were in love with the locomotive, and all that pertained to it. Their scientific knowledge had a foundation of practical familiarity with the topics of which they wrote. Colburn was the superior in the range and maturity of his professional knowledge, and it is impossible not to recognize the great advantage, intellectually, which his younger associate derived from this companionship. But in other respects, Colburn was no comfortable yoke-fellow. He could not bear harness. After a year, he sold out to Holley, and from April 19th, 1856, the *Advocate* was published by Holley

& Co. In August of the same year, the name was changed to *Holley's Railroad Advocate*, though Colburn still wrote for it occasionally, and for about a year the burden, both of editorial and business management, was borne by Holley. His letters show that it was not light. In January, 1857, he writes that the paper is "filling up with advertisements at $24 an inch;" in February, he is still sanguine, but says that "like all other things, it is slow at first." He adds, "I must be travelling most of the time, and picking up all that is new, to keep up the interest in the paper, and must keep it full of advertisements. I cannot edit the paper in New York, or in any less space than several millions of miles." In March, he writes from Lynchburg, Va., that he has progressed slowly, but thinks the trip will be pretty successful. He will have some $300 worth of advertising from Richmond. The country is not so dilapitated as he expected to find it. Things are lax and dirty, but there is a good deal of enterprise in the larger towns. He expects to go on as far as New Orleans and Cuba.

The *Railroad Advocate*, caught in the storm of a great commercial crisis, was sadly battered, if not wrecked. It never fulfilled his hopes, as a business; but we cannot fail to see what an education for its proprietor and editor was furnished by this active and continuous association with men and things as well as books and literary labor.

Meanwhile, Colburn, after several unsuccessful ventures in other directions, returned to journalism. In July, 1857, *Holley's Railroad Advocate* became Holley and Colburn's *American Engineer*, and in the following September was suspended and never revived. The cause of the suspension appears to have been the "hard times" of 1857; but the ingenuity and energy of the owners made this the occasion of a new venture. Securing from a number of American railway presidents and from private friends the necessary means, they went to Europe, to study foreign railway-practice and to report upon those features of it which would be most important at home. This was the first of thirteen journeys across the Atlantic, made by Holley, every one of which was fruitful of benefit to his country. No American ever went abroad more thoroughly furnished for such a work by nature and by training. If Colburn, on this first trip, showed him how to do it, he needed no teaching afterward.

It was on the return voyage that the Ariel, in which Holley was a passenger, was nearly wrecked, and obliged to put back. The following vivid description is taken from an unpublished fragment found in Holley's handwriting among his papers:

"We merrily sailed out of the Solent, past the Needles, against a stiffening breeze, just as eight bells sounded the New Year. But the barometer fell and the sea rose for six days, and on the tempestuous morning of the seventh, we were awakened by the joint sensation of ominous silence and new motion. The noisy but assuring heart-beat of the engine-room had stopped, and we were rolling over and over. The paddle-shaft was broken just outside the hull; one wheel was banging against the planking, and likely to go to the bottom with its counter-balancing weight; the ship was in the trough of the sea, and the gale had grown to a hurricane. They tried to make sail enough to get steerage-way, but the fore-yard snapped in two. Then the gallant Ludlow threw out a floating anchor called a 'drag,' a big basin, made of a stout and weighted sail, stretched on four spars. This, with our spanker, held her just so far out of the trough that we only got 'pooped' once—then came in the stern-windows, and a foot of water over the cabin-floor, washing away babies, furniture and—hope. I knew the engineer professionally, and I crawled down to his den, and begged him to let me do something to occupy my mind, for I was afraid. But he said there was little to do, except to keep the bilge-pumps running, for she had sprung a leak. Then I crawled up into the cabin again, and saw some men crying and wringing their hands, and some dear women, brave and quiet, taking hold of each other's hands, and looking like angels. That took away my fear; and I made a sort of nest for some little children who were tumbling about with the Ariel's lurches; and I told them stories and worshipped their innocence and their ignorance of engineering which I had spent half a life to learn. So passed the dreadful day and night. We had no regular meals, of course; but the cook scalded some potatoes and himself; and a few of us went into his galley and cooked ourselves and some chops, and in that fun we almost forgot our condition. The next day was Sunday. The hurricane had not abated. The pumps had simply kept the ship afloat. The greater number of the passengers wanted to have a prayer-meeting, and ask the Deity to stop the storm. There was no authorized representative on board, except a Catholic priest, and he was one of the best and truest men I ever met. He kneeled down in the cabin among us all, and, without any ritual or any Latin, he described our peril and our wants in a few graphic and fervent words, which put us in harmony with the situation. Then the storm broke, and the next morning was bright and sunny. For ten days, we sailed and paddled with our well wheel back to Queenstown."

Colburn and Holley's report—a handsome folio, with 51 engraved plates—appeared in 1858, under the title, *The Permanent Way and Coal-burning Locomotive Boilers of European Railways, with a Comparison of the Working Economy of European and American Lines, and the principles upon which Improvement must Proceed.* This title is admirable, because it exactly expresses the three-fold nature of the work, which comprises a description of foreign plant and practice, a demonstration of American inferiority, and a recommendation of practicable improvements.

The book reflects much credit on its authors in many ways. With characteristic courage and ambition, they issued it in a style which they could ill afford, and which makes it even to this day one of the handsomest of engineering books. It was a bold venture, even outwardly, and its contents were bolder yet. When we remember that Colburn and Holley were abroad less than three months, collecting the materials for it, we are astonished at its completeness and accuracy. They were "tremendous workers." Holley's letters show that after a few days given to the new delights of travel, and the sights in London, he settled down to intense labor, visiting railway-shops and offices, and devoting days and nights to writing and drawing. The excellent descriptions thus prepared might, however, have fallen unnoticed in the presence of a public little able to appreciate mere engineering details. It was the "Comparison," made by Colburn, which appealed directly and irresistibly to American railway managers—"counting-room engineers," as Holley was wont contemptuously to call them—with its overwhelming demonstration of the financial economy of the best construction and the best machinery. In 1860, Holley wrote:

"The first half of the last decade was distinguished by the *opening*, as if by magic, of thousands of miles of railway; the last half has been distinguished in revealing the fact that the roads thus open are yet to be built."

This revelation was effectually made by Colburn's "Comparison." It was not enough to show that the annual operating expense of American railways was $120,000,000, against $80,000,000 for the same mileage in England—an excess of $40,000,000; that the annual maintenance of the road-bed cost $33,000,000 here, against $12,500,000 there—an excess of $20,500,000; that the cost of fuel was $18,000,000, against $7,500,000, thus giving as total expenses, $171,000,000 in America and $100,000,000 for the same mileage abroad. Any industrious compiler could present such figures; and the counting-room answer was ready. " Such comparisons could not be made. The conditions were utterly different in the two countries. English lines were very expensively built, and what was saved in current expenses was paid out in interest on first cost. The grades were lighter than ours ; the traffic was more favorable ; there was cheap fuel and pauper labor." This sort of vague *qualitative* talk is what all reforms encounter ; and it must be met with *quantitative* demonstration. In all such questions, there is " truth on both sides ; " but the scientific inquirer weighs the truth, and ascertains on which side is the ultimate overweight. In this case, Colburn proceeded to discuss in detail all the varying conditions, and to give a precise value to each. He showed that of the superior English economy of nearly sixty per cent. in the maintenance of permanent way, only about half was due to favoring circumstances ; that of the 44 per cent. superior economy in fuel, only 15 per cent. could be thus explained ; that the necessary difference in first cost was far less than had been supposed. By an exhaustive analysis, he tracked the saving to its sources, and proved these to be chiefly the locomotive and the permanent way. This was an argument which financiers could understand. The press took it up, and drove it home. The leading New York dailies came out with long leaders (mostly contributed by Holley) on the causes of the depreciation in railroad property, and drew from this book overwhelming proofs. The English press, of course, rejoiced in its acknowledgment of English superiority. Even the patriotic rage displayed by some of our journals, regarding this conceited attack on American institutions, helped to advertise the book. Taken together with its successor, Holley's *Railway Practice* (of which I will speak presently), it inaugurated, and did much to effect, a revolution. As to the completeness of the mechanical part of it (which was Holley's special portion), I may here quote a remark once made to me by a leading railway engineer of this country. Said he, " I keep the book in my office still ; and frequently, when inventors call on me with their new ideas about rails, and joints, and sleepers, and boilers, and so on, I open Colburn and Holley, and show them their inventions, already described and discussed."

From Holley's letters during 1858, it is evident that he travelled extensively, soliciting subscriptions from railway companies to defray the cost of publishing the report, and also selling other scientific books on commission to cover his expenses. Probably during this period he made the acquaintance of Mr. Henry J. Raymond, founder and editor of the New York *Times*. His first article in that paper was a vigorous editorial on railway management, published November 9th, 1858.

Mr. Raymond was characteristically quick to recognize, encourage, and attach to his corps of editors, reporters, and correspondents young men of talent and ambition. He realized that he had found a prize in Holley, who speedily became a frequent contributor to the *Times*. I have found 276 articles from his pen, published in that paper, of which about 200 appeared between 1858 and 1863, and the remainder at rarer intervals to 1875, the last being the leading editorial of April 27th, 1875, on the recently-appointed United States Testing Board. The range of these articles is indicated by the following classification: Setting aside 52 miscellaneous articles (descriptive, political, etc.), and 30 which may be called "scattering," though devoted to engineering topics, we have 194, divided as follows: Railways (including street railways), 49; steam navigation, 42; war ships and armor, 30; the Stevens battery, 22; arms and ordnance, 19; boiler explosions, 11; and steam engines, 7. The most important and remarkable of these articles were, perhaps, those on the Great Eastern, written under the signature of "Tubal Cain." In 1859, he accompanied Mr. Raymond to Europe as a *Times* correspondent, made the acquaintance of Brunel and Scott Russell, and thoroughly studied the structure and details of the great ship. His description (October, 1859) of the vessel and its machinery (accompanied with drawings), his account of the trial trip, the accidental explosion occurring on that occasion, the coroner's inquest, etc., and his discussion of various engineering and commercial questions thus suggested, present a wonderful combination of technical, critical, and literary skill. The articles attracted attention on both sides of the Atlantic, and the *Times* assumed a position of authority on engineering topics not before or since occupied by a New York daily newspaper.

In 1860, Holley again went to Europe for the *Times*, and returned on the first transatlantic trip of the Great Eastern. This time his equally remarkable letters were divided between the *Times* and the *American Railway Review*, of which in the mean time he had become editor of the mechanical department. The *Review* was a New York weekly. His connection with it began with its second volume in January, 1860, and lasted about eighteen months. Among the first things he contributed to it was a description and explanation of the Giffard injector, then a novelty. An examination of the col-

umns of this paper and of the *Times* throws an interesting light on
the manner in which he contrived to do so much literary and professional work. He made one hand wash the other. The topics
treated for the general public in the *Times* were served up in more
technical form in the *Review*. The anonymous editor in the *Times*
frequently quoted and commented upon the avowed editor of the
Review, and *vice versa*. But all this was merely the incidental,
though necessary, occupation of this period. He wrote to earn
money, and he wrote with the rapidity and versatility of a Bohemian ;
but all the time his eye was upon his profession, and his articles
were but the chips thrown off in the labor of preparing his American and European Railway Practice, which appeared at the close of
1860. This was, so far as the subject of permanent way is concerned, a digest of the report of Colburn and Holley ; but it was a
great deal more. The subjects of the combustion of coal, its use in
locomotives, the economical generation of steam, the proper construction of boilers, etc., were thoroughly discussed, and the whole
problem was treated with the precision of a judge combined with
the earnestness of an advocate. The defects of American railway
management in these particulars were exposed with satire and in-
dignation. The book was, in even a higher degree than its prede-
cessor, an epoch-making one. Our railway practice in the branches
of which it treats has done little more than follow its guidance, and
its recommendations and warnings are not yet out of date.

In the preface to this work, Holley acknowledges assistance received from Mr. J. K. Fisher, well known to New Yorkers as an
engineer of talent and an inventor who tried hard—and failed—to
introduce steam-carriages on common roads. In the latter experiment, Holley gave him some professional and financial assistance.
The money was lost ; but out of this, as out of all other experiences
of his life, he drew a dividend of added knowledge. I believe he
never ceased to consider the steam-carriage and traction-engine as
technically an accomplished success, and certain eventually to find a
wide use in this country. To discuss the causes which have fal-
sified, thus far, that expectation, and have left us apparently more
distant than ever from its fulfilment, would be beyond the limits of
this occasion. Suffice it to say, that in my judgment, the immense
extension of railroads is one of them.

Another matter to which Mr. Fisher had given great attention
was that of steam fire-engines. How quickly and thoroughly Holley appreciated this problem may be seen in several of his *Times*

articles—notably a long one, published December 10th, 1858. It
is a model of clear and epigrammatic statement, abounding in such
sentences as these :

" The size of a fire-engine is limited by the size of the men who
handle the hose. We can build an engine that will throw a river
over a mountain—*who will hold the butt ?* " . . . .

" Boilers which can raise steam from cold water in three minutes,
can do almost any thing else in the next three minutes, if they are
not closely watched."

There is ample evidence that the outward rewards of all his
labors so far had been mainly in growing reputation, not in money.
He was still struggling for a living. In April, 1859, he took out
two patents, one for a variable cut-off gear for steam-engines, and
the other for railway chairs.

Of the railway-chair patent he writes at the time, " My rail-joint
seems to be liked ; and I shall doubtless make something out of it."
It preserved the continuity of the rail-ends by brackets, so attached
to the spliced pieces and tension-plates that the weight of the wheels
of the train on the rail kept the splices tightly in their places,
without the aid of plates, nuts, keys, or rivets. It was illustrated
in his *Railway Practice*, and in the *Railway Review*. It was tried
by one or two roads (I believe with satisfactory results); but it did
not come into wide use, partly, as I judge, because reforms in rail-
sections and permanent way made the simple fish-plate adequate to
all demands. As Holley wrote in the *Review*, " The practical difficulty with the fish-joint is not the form of the fishing-piece, but the
form of the rail."

Meanwhile, the pressure of outward necessities continued, but
Holley's courage and hope rose to meet it. The denser the medium
through which he made his way, the greater his relative buoyancy.
In March, 1861, he writes :

" I have an engagement with the publishers of Webster's Una-
bridged Dictionary, to write a lot of engineering words and definitions, to make some illustrations, and to correct engineering definitions, for a new edition of that work, for which I get my name put
in the book, and $200. The former part of the pay will be pretty
valuable, and the latter part very timely in these awful days of panic
and poverty. I am at work at this as hard as possible, to get it
done in time, and to get the money."

A few days later he writes, referring to the slow sale of his book,
and other difficulties :

"These unexpected hard times have certainly and *fairly* interrupted my plans. Under normal circumstances, things would have come out as I expected they would. Therefore, I do not think it bad management, but bad luck, that I am still in an undesirable position. But I am making my expenses as light as possible, and getting what professional work I can to do. I yesterday completed an arrangement with the Camden & Amboy Railroad Company, to alter an engine of theirs to burn coal. I am to be paid eight dollars per day, and to be employed thirty or forty days. Mr. Stevens, the President, has been for some years engaged on a battery for the Government, about which you know, of course. He says he shall probably be called on to finish it by this administration, and that he may want to employ me, here and in Europe, for this and other matters. I am also getting some business as an expert, which pays first-rate—am writing for the dictionary, and gradually getting the business offered, after which I have so long been seeking. So, on the whole, I do not despair of getting back the money I have been investing for the last ten years in *education,* and of securing something to live on."

Up to this time I find no proof that Holley interested himself specially in politics. He seems rather to have regarded with disgust the manner in which the slavery question, in one form or another, engrossed the attention of Congress, leaving great matters of internal improvement, the regulation of commerce, the safety of travel, the construction and maintenance of public works, to be dealt with by crude and hasty legislation. Thus he writes in the *Times,* May 3d, 1860:

"As the law-makers tread the decks of steamers, they will need no expert to unfold the probable causes of danger. Let them but look and tremble: a single compartment with a wooden shell—Heaven only knows how weak and rotten—quivering with each stroke of the engine—between them and death: fires roaring and lamps swinging within the very embrace of seasoned combustibles—boilerplate of questionable tenacity, straining under undue pressure—firepumps and hose, bilge-pumps and life-boats, lashed and stowed away for the voyage like so much cargo or permanent ballast; sailing vessels, without light or signal, bearing down into our very path: should sudden danger overtake us, what are the probabilities of deliverance? The chances are, that there will be a collision—that a hole in any part of the hull will admit the sea to every cranny of the fabric; that the furnace-fires will be quenched before the steam-pumps can be set at work; that the ship will founder before all the boats can be cleared and launched; that all the boats will not hold half the people; that there is no material for rafts; that the vessel will take fire; that the fire will get the advantage before the pumps can be got at work and the hose adjusted; that the deficient means of overcoming danger, and especially the delay in applying the means provided, will give accident and carelessness the winning start of defence and caution.

"Urgent and reasonable as are the demands of the case, it is found practically impossible to meet them fully and fairly with legislative enactments. Sectionalism, State rights, spoils, corruption, selfishness, and the whole catalogue of personal and party motives and influences, menace alike the interests of the white man and the negro—the African traveller and the Red River slave."

Like the vast majority of our citizens, he did not realize the serious and instant peril of the country. As late as March, 1861, after the inauguration of Lincoln, when the government of the Southern Confederacy under Jefferson Davis had been fully organized, Holley became a candidate for the position of U. S. supervising inspector of passenger steamers. The letters forwarded in recommendation of his appointment to the President were subsequently returned, and after his death I found them among his papers. I do not wonder he preserved them. They constitute an astonishing testimonial to the professional standing of a man not yet thirty years old. A host of firms and individuals, including the presidents and engineers of the principal American railways, and the managers of great shops for the construction of steam machinery, bear witness to the extraordinary ability and fitness of Mr. Holley. If I repeat before this audience the names of J. Edgar Thomson, Erastus Corning, John Taylor Johnston, Sam Sloan, Charles Minot, Allan Campbell, S. W. Roberts, Amasa Stone, John C. Cresson, W. H. Clements, David Hoadley, George H. Corliss, J. S. Rogers, M. W. Baldwin, Richard Norris, W. W. Fairbanks, Horatio Allen, Benjamin F. Thurston, Peter Cooper, Abram S. Hewitt, Edward Cooper, J. G. Barnard, William G. Hamilton, Cyrus W. Field, Samuel J. Reeves, Montgomery C. Meigs, to say nothing of college and West Point professors, or editors like Henry J. Raymond, and personal friends of the President and cabinet, I need add nothing to prove the unusual force of these credentials. In a private letter, dated April 3d, 1861, Mr. Holley says:

"I was in Washington the other day, about the inspectorship; but

I do not expect to get it. I have as fine a list of engineering names as could be offered; but I have no hard-working New York City political backers, except Mr. Raymond. Another candidate is more of a politician than an engineer, and he will probably get the place. However, I may get it. I shall certainly *not* go and bore the President and departments. If they can't take my papers as evidence, they ought not to take my own statement."

Those who remember him in the brightness of his youthful prime cannot but feel that his personal application, adding magnetism to the weight of the professional indorsements he presented, would not have bored even the tired officials at Washington, but would have inspired them with the desire to win for the public service his skill and enthusiasm—would have enabled them to find delight in duty. But it was not thus to be—and so far as we can now discern, what was to be was better.

The letters of those gentlemen I have named, with many others, were subsequently recovered from Washington, and arranged and filed by Mr. Holley. On a blank page at the end, he wrote in his bold hand these significant words : " What came of it? Mr. Holley was not appointed." Yet through all his life he was proud of the indorsement he had thus received ; and to-night we may safely say that those who gave it need not be ashamed.

Besides the ordinary fatuity which presides over Governmental appointments, and the special pressure of party politics in the case of a new administration, receiving the powers and privileges of federal office for the first time from the hands of its party opponents, there were in this instance peculiar reasons for the apparent neglect of Holley's application. Events were then occurring which might well cause those in power to overlook the inspectorship of steamboats. The attention of all was concentrated, not upon the possible accidents that might happen to vessels navigating the Hudson or the Sound, but upon the beginnings of civil war in the South. The firing upon our flag in Sumter and Baltimore excited to their highest pitch the feelings of the North. Many of you must remember the scenes that transformed the metropolis : the vast meeting at Union Square, with its many platforms and orators, and its surging, shouting multitude of hearers and spectators. What enthusiasm attended the passionate appeal of Mitchel and Baker, as they pledged their lives to the service—pledges redeemed by both, after a few short months, in blood ! And what frenzy of applause followed the reply of one of the orators, when, being asked from the crowd, " How about the Seventh Regiment?" he answered, "They have just been heard from by telegraph at Philadelphia. It is proposed that they go by sea to Washington; but *they prefer to march through Baltimore!*"

The sudden change in the sentiments of many who up to that time had hoped for compromise, is well illustrated in the case of Holley. In January, 1861, he had written:

"I suppose we have got to have a war; but it is a pity to fight for what isn't worth fighting for. It seems our duty to have a general convention of the people and let the beggars go."

But the events of the next three month were for him, as for the majority of his Northern countrymen, a rapid political education; and on the 23d of April, 1861, he wrote to Secretary Chase the following letter, substantial duplicates of which were sent to the War and Navy departments also:

"I am an applicant, indorsed by a large number of prominent engineers, for the office of United States Supervising Inspector of Steamers.

"In the present state of affairs, I am anxious to bring such engineering facilities as I may command into the service of the Government.

" I have an intimate acquaintance with Mr. Scott Russell and many other English engineers and shipbuilders, having been sent to Europe several times on engineering business.

" If I can do the Government any good with reference to the construction or purchase of ships or arms, the construction of batteries, gun-boats, or iron vessels of light draught, the application of armor to ships, etc., I hereby offer my services, *without compensation,* desiring only that my necessary expenses be paid, as I have not the money to pay them.

"I know that I have peculiar facilities for gaining the latest information relative to the construction of iron ships and boats and their engines, without waste of time.

" I refer you to the names appended to my application aforesaid. I am ready at an hour's notice."

On the same sheet, Mr. Raymond added these words: "I know Mr. Holley *intimately,* and KNOW him to be in every respect one of the very best men whose services the Government can command."

From another source, I learn that at this time Mr. Holley was ready—as what patriotic young American was not?—to enlist in the Army or Navy, but that a little reflection convinced him of the greater usefulness which lay in his professional skill.

The letter I have quoted was filed at the Treasury department (as the clerical indorsement upon it shows) together with the other papers concerning Mr. Holley's previous application for office. Neither it, nor the similar letters addressed to the Navy and War departments, were ever acknowledged. Probably there was no time in those crowded days for mere politeness and thanks. Probably thousands of other men were tendering their services, even without pay. Moreover, experienced administrators know very well that the acceptance of such gratuitous service is in most cases no advantage to the public. Officers under salary, and no others, can be held to strict responsibility. The honorary employés of the state demoralize the rest. They despise red tape, which is, on the whole, essential, however harmfully it may now and then be tangled; and, to speak plainly, no tangle is so mischievous as that produced by a volunteer shuttle, flying lawlessly across the web of a regular system. Railroad engineers know how many trains must be delayed, when some swift "special" demands the track, in spite of the time-table.

Doubtless these calm considerations did not comfort the soul of the ardent young volunteer, conscious of the power he freely offered to his country. There is a touch of bitterness in the words he indorsed upon the papers I have quoted: "What came of it? The letters received no attention. The foregoing application to Secretary Chase was found filed with the application for the Inspectorship, at the Treasury. The End." To which, indeed, History adds, "Not the End, but the Beginning."

Both his patriotism and his professional ability found an immediate object in the Stevens battery, and in other plans which Mr. Edwin A. Stevens proposed to the Government. That remarkable man and his brother, Robert L. Stevens, were the originators of most of the modern improvements in naval warfare. Their father, Col. John Stevens, built in 1805 a steam-vessel with twin screws—a feature adopted in the Stevens battery, and in the Naugatuck (a vessel presented to the U. S. Treasury Department during the war by Edwin A. Stevens), and subsequently employed in the war-ships of England. The armored ironclad known as the Stevens battery was proposed by the brothers Stevens to the United States Government as early as 1841. It was not until 1854 that the work was commenced; and in 1861, twenty years after its suggestion, it was still unfinished, the Government having refused for more than eighteen years to do anything about it. Half a million of public money had been spent upon it; Mr. Stevens had spent $200,000 besides; and he now asked from Congress an appropriation of $500,000 to finish the whole work. The proposal met with unexpected opposition. Holley states the case in a *Times* editorial, August 13th, 1861, as follows:

" Here is an iron screw ship of 6000 tons, made of the best selected material, with as beautiful a model as ever floated, with engines and boilers of a pattern superior to that of most modern steamers, and capable of developing the whole horse-power of the Great Eastern, and a speed of twenty miles an hour—a ship that can turn on her own centre in perhaps a minute—outrun any known enemy—fire with her eight guns a heavier broadside than the Warrior—fire three of these guns at a time parallel to the keel—sink to the gun-deck during action, and so leave only her cover, as it were, to be protected by plates—carry $6\frac{3}{4}$-inch armor, inclined at 30°, and coal enough to cross the Atlantic at ordinary speed—a ship up to the best commercial practice in every important detail, and ahead of the best naval practice in nearly all—and this is the vessel that some of our contemporaries advise the Government to abandon as a *failure*, while Congress debates bills for the construction of *modern* ironclad ships ! "

It is impracticable on this occasion to trace the course of the discussions, examinations, reports, negotiations, and intrigues which constitute the subsequent history of the Stevens battery. Holley's work, in connection with it, turned out to be rather literary than technical. Mr. Stevens, whose age and health disinclined him to engage actively in a fight for the privilege of serving his country with his knowledge and experience, left this part largely to Holley, who wrote memorials, arguments, criticisms, editorials, with untiring zeal, bringing to bear science, wit, eloquence, and anger in a manner peculiarly his own. Whatever may be said of Stevens's battery, Holley's battery was unquestionably a powerful one; and so far as words could win the battle, he won it. But the victory cost too much time, and when won, it was fruitless.

The peculiar features of the Hoboken ship have been elsewhere adopted and in turn superseded. The principal effect of this episode upon Holley's career was the attention it caused him to give to the subject of ordnance and armor.

Sent abroad in 1862, by Mr. Stevens, to investigate this subject, he found the facts he needed scattered in official documents, monographs, unpublished records, etc., and speedily his own note-book became a more comprehensive and accurate collection of them than any printed book. He obtained his information with some difficulty. I find, for instance, the following letter from his friend,

J. Scott Russell, referring to certain ordnance works or experiments of the British Government:

September 24, 1862.

"MY DEAR HOLLEY:

"I have applied in the proper quarters, and find that special instructions have been given that *you* are to be refused admittance.

"As you have achieved this distinction, you will, I am sure, have no wish to put yourself in a false position. . . . .

Yours sincerely,

J. SCOTT RUSSELL."

On another occasion, Holley desired to study the lines of a new British ironclad, then in process of construction. One of the contractors, whom he had made (as usual) first an acquaintance and then straightway a friend, said to him, "If you can manage to get into the yard, I will show you all you want to see. But I am powerless to procure admission for you, and I am sure it will be refused if you ask it." It must be admitted that, in spite of the confidence of his friend, Mr. Scott Russell, Holley did, on this occasion, "place himself in a false position;" for he hired a stylish carriage, arranged himself in solitary state with folded arms on the back-seat, gave the necessary instructions to the coachman, and drove straight through the big gate into the yard, acknowledging with a bow the presented arms of the guard, as proudly as any other Lord of the Admiralty. Once inside, he found his friend, and satisfied his curiosity. This story, now published for the first time, is respectfully dedicated to Her Majesty's Government!

We can hardly wonder at the occasional exclusion of Holley from important works at that time. He was certain to send to his own Government whatever new facts he observed. On the whole, however, he was treated with liberality, and his note-book became, at the close of 1864, a treatise on Ordnance and Armor.

This work has, perhaps, been overrated. It is in reality a clever piece of book-making, remarkable as showing with what rapidity and accuracy a trained reporter, employing both pen and pencil, can collect and arrange a mass of data. Holley's independent criticisms and suggestions are not made prominent; though, when they occur, they are sensible and timely. The book is simply an attempt on his part to supply the need which he had felt on approaching the subject of ordnance and armor—the need of a summary of the existing state of the art. It was translated into French, and became everywhere a recognized authority—just as a dictionary or a directory is recognized authority, particularly if it is large and thorough, and intelligently arranged, and the only one to be had. It is out of date now. The arts of warfare have made great progress since it appeared; and though it is still indispensable as a record, it is, to me at least, chiefly interesting as a specimen of Holley's method of work; his ability to grasp the leading principles of any mechanical problem; the facility with which he seized the details of an apparatus or an experiment, putting them down for future reference in words or in sketches, as might be most convenient; and the system with which he indexed everything he had once noted, so that he could at any moment recur to it again without delay.

While he was thus studying ordnance and armor, the columns of the *Times* coruscated with brilliant articles from his pen on these topics, and the bureaus at Washington had frequent reason to regret that his genius was not directly enlisted in their assistance, instead of employing the free lance of destructive criticism.

An interesting and able summary of this subject appeared in the *National Almanac* of 1863, under the title, "Iron-Clad War Vessels;" and the *Atlantic Monthly* of January, 1863, contained an article from his pen on "Iron-Clad Ships and Heavy Ordnance." At the close of this article, he speaks of a more extended work, about to be published by Van Nostrand, of New York, thus showing that at that time Ordnance and Armor was almost completed, though it did not publicly appear for nearly two years.

Before it saw the light, his activity had turned into a new and still more important channel. In May, 1863, he writes:

"It is a matter of regret to me, on many accounts, that I have to go to England again this summer; but this is no pleasure-trip, but a trip preparatory, I hope, to something settled. Precisely what I am going for, I am not at liberty to say, except that I am going to get information for Corning, Winslow & Co. about a new manufacture. If I succeed, they are going to establish the business, which will be in nature allied to, but in a business way separate from, their present manufacture. They then wish me to become a partner in the new business, ... and expect, if I succeed, to spend about $30,000 in establishing the new manufacture."

Imagine starting in the Bessemer business with $30,000!

His mission was successful. The Bessemer patents were purchased, and subsequently combined with the conflicting American patents of Kelly. The works at Troy were built and started in 1865, and en-

larged in 1867. From this time on, the career of Holley was substantially the history of the Bessemer manufacture in the United
States. In 1867, he built the works at Harrisburg. About a year
later, he was recalled to Troy, to rebuild the works there, which had
been destroyed by fire. Still later, he planned the works at North
Chicago and Joliet, the Edgar Thomson works at Pittsburg, and the
Vulcan at St. Louis, besides acting as consulting engineer in the designing of the Cambria, Bethlehem, and Scranton works.

It is not my purpose to describe in detail the improvements he
introduced into the Bessemer plant. They have been admirably
summarized by Mr. Robert W. Hunt, in his paper ('Trans. Am. I.
of M. E., Vol. V., p. 201) on the History of the Bessemer Manufacture in America. It is fair to say that they put an entirely new face
on the commercial relations of that manufacture, by enormously increasing its productive capacity, and proportionately decreasing its
cost. Whoever would appreciate their nature and effect, need do
but two things : First, compare the pictures of the Bessemer plant
and its arrangement, as given in English text-books and journals of
that period, with the plans of American works ; secondly, compare
the records of foreign works with the records of our own. Mr. Hunt
says :

"The result of his thought gave us the present accepted type of
American Bessemer plant. He did away with the English deep pit,
and raised the vessels so as to get working space under them on the
ground-floor ; he substituted top-supported hydraulic cranes for the
more expensive counter-weighted English ones, and put three ingot
cranes around the pit instead of two, and thereby obtained greater
area of power ; he changed the location of the vessel as related to the
pit and melting-house ; he modified the ladle-crane, and worked all
the cranes and vessels from a single-point ; he substituted cupolas for
reverberatory furnaces ; and last, but by no means least, introduced
the intermediate or accumulating ladle, which is placed on scales,
and thus insures accuracy of operation by rendering possible the
weighing of each charge of melted iron, before pouring it into the
converter. These points cover the radical features of his innovations.
After building such a plant, he began to meet the difficulties of details in manufacture, among the most serious of which was the short
duration of the vessel-bottoms, and the time required to cool off the
vessels to a point at which it was possible for workmen to enter
and make new bottoms. After many experiments, the result was
the Holley vessel-bottom, which, either in its form as patented, or in

a modification of it as now used in all American works, has rendered possible, as much as any other one thing, the present immense production."

Concerning the increasing productiveness of the American Bessemer plant, it may be said in round numbers that it has been raised from the capacity (per two converters) of about 900 tons per month to more than 10,000 tons for the same period—an exceptional maximum of over 14,000 tons of ingots in a single month having been reached by the Edgar Thomson works.   Holley's arrangement of · buildings and machinery, to secure convenience in handling materials, and his movable converter-bottom and other devices, to reduce the time lost in repairs, were undoubtedly the basis of this great advance, though valuable contributions have been made by the able engineers who followed his lead.

But turning for a moment from technical details, I cannot forbear quoting from an article written by Holley, in 1865, for the Troy *Daily Times*, the description of a Bessemer "blow" at night.   It is not only admirable in itself, but interesting as a proof of his keen perception of the picturesque and artistic elements in his profession :

"The cavernous room is dark, the air sulphurous, the sounds of suppressed power are melancholy and deep.   Half-revealed monsters with piercing eyes crouch in the corners, spectral shapes ever flit about the wall, and lurid beams of light anon flash in your face as some remorseless beast opens its red-hot jaws for its iron ration. Then the melter thrusts a spear between the joints of its armor, and a glistening, yellow stream spurts out for a moment, and then all is dark once more.   Again and again he stabs it, till six tons of its hot and smoking blood have filled a great caldron to the brim.   Then the foreman shouts to a thirty-foot giant in the corner, who straightway stretches out his iron arm and gently lifts the caldron away up into the air and turns out the yellow blood in a hissing, sparkling stream, which dives into the white-hot jaws of another monster—a monster as big as an elephant, with a head like a frog, and scaly hide. The foreman shouts again, at which up rises the monster on his haunches, growling and snorting sparks and flame.

"What a conflict of the elements is going on in that vast laboratory !   A million balls of melted iron, tearing away from the liquid mass, surging from side to side, and plunging down again, only to be blown out more hot and angry than before—column upon column of air, squeezed solid like rods of glass by the power of five hundred horses, piercing and shattering the iron at every point, chasing it up and down, robbing it of its treasures only to be itself decomposed, and hurled out into the night in roaring blaze.

"As the combustion progresses, the surging mass within grows hotter, throwing out splashes of liquid slag; and the discharge from its mouth changes from sparks and streaks of red and yellow gas to thick, full, white, howling, dazzling flame. But such battles cannot last long. In a quarter of an hour, the iron is stripped of every combustible alloy, and hangs out the white flag. The converter is then turned upon its side, the blast shut off, and the recarburizer run in. Then for a moment the war of the elements rages again; the mass boils and flames with higher intensity, and with a rapidity of chemical reaction, sometimes throwing it violently out of the converter-mouth; then all is quiet, and the product is steel—liquid, milky steel, that pours out into the ladle from under its roof of slag, smooth, shining, and almost transparent."

It is scarcely possible to exaggerate the importance, to this country and to the world, of the Bessemer manufacture, and particularly of that manufacture on the vast scale which Holley's improvements helped it to assume. The end is not yet. The structural uses of steel are still in their infancy. But in one branch of engineering—the branch of Holley's early choice and love—a world-shaking revolution has been accomplished. The permanent way of which he wrote so much has received its final perfecting touch in the steel rail —and cheap transportation has been the result. The farmers and cattle-breeders of Great Britain find themselves brought into competition with regions of the very existence of which they had scarcely heard before. The invention of an English chemist, perfected and applied in America, reacts upon the whole social fabric. The gigantic spectre of the land question itself reveals through its dread garments a skeleton of Bessemer steel!

To Holley personally, the entrance upon these new labors was the greatest change of his life. His chance, for which he had so patiently waited and so thoroughly prepared himself, had come at last. His work changed from the critical to the creative; and a whole side of his genius, repressed hitherto, sprang into joyous power.

All his life he had been fond of designing. The fertility of his imagination and his artistic taste were shown in a thousand ways— in the drawings with which he adorned albums and scrap-books; in the design he made for the charter-oak chair of state, which still wins admiration in the capitol of Connecticut; in his love of old cathedrals and masterpieces of painting and sculpture. But he was not bewitched by the surface of beauty alone. Looking below the surface, he recognized the beauty of adaptation. He recognized the great scientific truth that the line of economy is the line of grace. The arch, the truss, were no unmeaning forms to him. And beneath a strong, light roof, or before a well-designed machine, or in the midst of a well-arranged plant, he found the satisfaction of an artist as well as an engineer. I think he took more pride in the Edgar Thomson works than in any other which he helped to build, because, as he once said to me, he began at the beginning with them, taking a clean sheet of paper, drawing on it first the railway-tracks, and then placing the buildings and the contents of each building with prime regard to the facile handling of material; so that the whole became a body, shaped by its bones and muscles, rather than a box; into which bones and muscles had to be packed.

Yet this new activity was not substituted for the older ones; it was rather superadded to them. In January, 1869, he took charge of Van Nostrand's *Eclectic Engineering Magazine,* which he edited for a year. In August of that year, he wrote from Troy:

"I have not got along far enough in life to look back on much work or much fruit from it; but I have lived long enough to conclude with certainty, that leisure is the hardest thing in life to get along with. I try to have as little of it as possible."

In the subject of technical education, as I need not tell the members of these societies, he was deeply interested. Elected in 1865 a member of the Board of Trustees of the Rensselaer Polytechnic Institute, he made his influence felt in favor of an improved curriculum, keeping pace with the demands of the times. While it is impossible to discuss at this time the views on technical education which he subsequently announced, it is worth mention, in passing, that the system he so eloquently advocated, of a practical training preceding the scientific instruction, was not the one under which his own genius had developed itself. He went from the school to the shop, not from the shop to the school.

If I pass swiftly over the latest and most fruitful years of his life, it is not because I fail to recognize their importance. They were in every way his best working years. His rapidly growing fame, his widening circle of friends, his own matured power, combined to give value to his labors and to win for them adequate reward. In fact, this is the answer to those impetuous ones who think it better, as they say, "to wear out than to rust out," and declare that if they do twice as much, and only live half as long, the world at least will be no loser. This is not true. A true man's last work is his best. Two bushels of green apples to-day are not the adequate substitute for one bushel of ripe ones, when Time shall have brought them to perfection. And this ripening effect of Time is in human character the one thing that cannot be hurried. Wisdom—the degree conferred upon faithful students in the University of Life, cannot be had in the sophomore year.

But the work of these wisest and intellectually strongest years of Holley's life is, for the most part, either familiarly known to all of you, or it is still under the lock and key of his professional relations, in confidential reports. His papers and addresses in the Institute of Mining Engineers, of which he became a member in 1872 and President in 1875, the Society of Civil Engineers, of which he was a Vice-President in 1876, the Society of Mechanical Engineers, of which together with the honored chairman of this meeting he was a founder, and the British Iron and Steel Institute, and Institution of Civil Engineers, of, which he was a member; the admirable paper on Iron and Steel, contributed by him to the Reports of the Judges of the Centennial Exposition in 1876; the series of illustrated articles on American iron and steel-works, prepared by him together with Mr. Lenox Smith for London *Engineering*, from 1877 to 1880; his masterly treatise on steel, published in 1880 in Appleton's Cyclopædia of Mechanics; and, in another sphere, his breezy description in *Scribner's Monthly* for May, 1878, under the title "Camps and Tramps about Katadin," of a health-giving summer excursion, in genial artist company, to the forests and mountains of Maine—these are both familiar and accessible to you all. But more voluminous, and in many respects still more valuable, were the reports which he printed and issued confidentially to his clients (for the last five years to the members of the Bessemer Association only) on the various branches of steel manufacture. No doubt, when the immediate business value of these reports shall have passed away, they will become accessible to engineers generally; and they will be found a mine of clear, precise, well-arranged, and well-discussed information. I know that he regarded them as his best work, and that he put his life into them.

Of all the later labors to which I have alluded, and of other works of his pen, I shall publish as an appendix to this address a catalogue, which I believe is complete, and which in itself constitutes a striking picture of his intense and various industry.

It was probably about 1875 that his elastic strength began to fail. In that year he wrote: "I have been so hard at work for so long that I am getting pretty tired and 'played out.' I am going in a week to one of the Elizabeth Islands, off New Bedford, where there is neither mail nor telegraph, to lie on the sea-shore for a week and try to get strong and *sleepy*." That last word tells the story.

In June, 1875, he was appointed a member of the United States Board for Testing Structural Materials. He had been unweariedly active in promoting the formation of this Board; he was not the least laborious of its members; and down to the end of his life, he ceased not to strive that its work, so promising, so fruitful, so unfortunately interrupted, should be revived and continued. In our endeavors to advance that great work against ignorance, indolence, and prejudice in quarters high and low, we shall sorely miss henceforward his voice and pen.

In 1879, he accepted an appointment to lecture at the School of Mines, Columbia College, on the manufacture of iron and steel. He wrote these lectures with great care, printed a complete synopsis of them for the use of the students, and took as much pains to assure himself of the proficiency of his class, by rigorous examinations, as if he had been a resident-professor, and this his chief business.

Besides the two early patents which I have already mentioned, Mr. Holley obtained fourteen others. Ten of these refer to his improvements in the Bessemer process and plant; two of them to roll-trains and their feed-tables; and the remaining two are those of July 18th, 1876, and March 1st, 1881, the first for a water-cooled furnace-roof, and the latter for a steam-boiler furnace, with gaseous fuel. These are both important; and the first of them, in which the pipes cooling the arch of a furnace constitute at the same time the skeleton supporting it, is highly ingenious in conception and detail. It is not unlikely to be the "furnace of the future" for many purposes. The last of his Bessemer patents (purchased since his death by the Bessemer Association), that of the detachable converter-shell (April 26th, 1881), is perhaps the most important of all, after the old converter-bottom patented August 9th, 1870. I will not describe it here. It is discussed by its inventor in a manner to leave nothing more to be said, in a paper read in November, 1880, before the American Society of Mechanical Engineers.

It is pleasant to remember that in these later years he began to receive the public and professional recognition which his genius and

perseverance deserved.   In 1878, on the twenty-fifth anniversary of
his graduation, his Alma Mater bestowed on him the honorary degree
of Doctor of Laws.   A still more appropriate honor, the Bessemer
medal, given in cordial though late appreciation of his services and
merits, can be placed, not, alas! in his hand, but only on his tomb.   But
these things are but trivial symbols of the warm, unanimous, universal love and respect with which he was regarded by the engineers
of two worlds.

This has been more adequately shown by the outburst of sorrow
and of eulogy on both sides of the Atlantic, which followed his death.
Yet scarcely less significant was the cordial welcome which, while he
yet lived and labored, awaited him everywhere on his journeys.   All
doors—even those which were inscribed with "No admittance"—
opened before him.   One of his friends who has been travelling this
year among foreign iron and steel-works, writes that Holley's name
has been everywhere a potent charm, securing for him an eager
courtesy of reception.

I have resolved to make this address, as far as may be, purely
professional and critical; and there has been no lack of testimony to
Holley's private virtues and personal magnetism, so that I need not
dwell at length upon these.   But even in a cold estimate of his professional achievements, these qualities cannot be passed over.   Generosity, honor, tact, unselfish interest in the welfare of others, high
devotion to great causes, unstinted service to the interest of employers, a full performance—nay, an overflowing performance—of
every duty: these qualities win love and trust; and to win love and
trust, in our profession, as in every other, is the very heart of success.

We may answer now the questions with which we began.   This
life *was* successful.   It was filled with the joy of labor; it was surrounded at the last with comfort and fame and troops of friends.
But the success was not of accident, or luck, or sudden growth.   It
was earned, inch by inch; won out of innumerable delays and
defeats; held at the cost of constant vigilance and toil.   Homer
sings of warriors who were invulnerable and irresistible; but Homer
gives them the assistance of the gods, fighting invisibly beside them;
and to my mind, his noblest heroes are those who stand up bravely
against such odds, and die where they stand.   Again, the tales of
chivalry are full of triumphant champions, whose lances in *melée* or
tourney nothing can resist.   But history tells us that, apart from
the exaggerations of the legend, these all-conquering heroes were
arrant humbugs—princes, whose prowess it was the part of courtiers

to help them to exhibit; that their invariable triumph was the farce of hired players. *Our* hero was no such gay cavalier. Neither miracle nor connivance made his lance omnipotent. His armor was bruised and dented in earnest; he knew the shock, the overthrow, the retreat, the struggle again and again renewed, the victory that called for new conflicts with new risk of defeat.

If Holley's genius was such as to forbid us from hoping by mere effort to attain equal heights, yet, on the other hand, there is ample encouragement and instruction in his career for all young engineers. Let me, in closing, barely mention its chief lessons.

The first is the great benefit of uniting theory and practice. It is less important how these are to be combined than that the student of either should not despise the other. Every word that Holley spoke, every line he wrote, betrayed his familiarity with the practical operations, tools, difficulties, and needs of his business. A great inventor once said to me (when I talked to him of some fancied discovery of my own): "My boy, half the art of invention consists in knowing what needs to be invented." Holley's career illustrates this principle, and bears witness also how deeply he felt what he called the inadequate union of engineering science and art, and how ardently he labored to make it closer and more complete. Not his eloquent words merely, but the eloquence of his whole life speaks one language—the language of the brotherhood of brain-workers and hand-workers. And what he was, even more than what he said or did to promote such union, wrought mightily to that great end. For the end is to be found in the multiplication of such men as he—men who do not merely preach harmony to the two classes, but actually belong to both.

It is important to observe that the foundation of his training was wholly American. Far be it from me to disparage the advantages of foreign study. I would not speak such treason to my own Alma Mater in a far land. But I say without hesitation, that he brings most from travel and study abroad who carries most to them. Many a precious graft they have furnished, and will yet furnish, to our native stock; but the stock is as important as the shoot, and there are too many young men returning with their hands full of scions and nothing to graft them on. How illustriously different was Holley's career!

Another important matter is the early cultivation of the observing powers, and, as incidental thereto, the art of drawing. Holley's facility in these respects was an inestimable advantage to him. He inclined to graphic methods of stating and solving engineering problems ; and his eye, thus trained, became an intuitive judge and calculator.

Then comes, in natural succession, the habit of instant, rapid, accurate, methodical recording of observations.   It was Holley's practice to do this constantly; to make every record so clear and complete that it could be comprehended and used after years had passed ; and to index his note-books and scrap-books so that they became thoroughly available at any moment. This is no trifling matter.   When the officers of our Corps of Engineers are examined as to their fitness for promotion, they are obliged not only to an-swer questions and prepare " projects," but also to exhibit the note-books they have kept during their terms of service.   No other rev-elation of character is more significant, no test more severe.   The work that a man does in a hurry, and unobserved, and for himself, not the public, tells the story of his method and temperament. Hol-ley's note-books are models of fullness and order.

But neither observing, nor recording, nor studying, nor the com-bination of all these with practical training, completely furnish the engineer for the highest place.   For he has to deal, not merely with matter and mathematics, but also with men.   They must be made to recognize his skill, to back his enterprise, to coöperate in his achievements.   Influence, *influence*—that is the secret of power. Genius may seize opportunities; influence brings them.   And the chief vehicle of influence is language.   The mastery of language, therefore, is no superfluous accomplishment to the engineer.   The young man who deliberately and of choice says, "I mean to be scientific, but not ' literary ; ' " or the parent who says, " My boy is not going to need a liberal culture; he is going to be an engineer," is ignorant of the most potent principle of modern life—the solid-arity of the race, the dependence of each upon all, the necessity of a wide foundation for a high fame, the universal law that every occu-pation deals ultimately with men even more than with things, and that the ability to shape things is almost barren without the power to move men.

But language, as the means of this power, is effective in propor-tion as it is filled with appeals to the responsive associations of human minds.   A host of things in fancy, poetry, history, and gen-eral literature, concerning which people are interested, may be trivial in themselves : it is nevertheless worth while to know them and to use them, as a means of commanding the interest and assent of men.

In other words, a wide culture, in sympathy with the age in which we live, is an element of power. It is true that all this, belonging to the art of expression, is wasted in the hands of him who has nothing to express. Men may be arrested to listen, but they will soon find out that behind the skillful utterance there is neither character nor knowledge. They may be fascinated by the instrument, until they find out there is nothing in the tune. But when real genius and noble ambition utter themselves through the channels of art in language, how gladly hears the world!

Holley's versatility and intellectual sympathy with many lines of thought prevented him from sinking to the level of drudgery, though he worked harder than many a drudge; they made him, not merely a bricklayer, but an architect for his generation. Controlled and reinforced by a mighty perseverance, softened and brightened by an unfailing gentleness of soul, they added to his genius that which made him great. For what we call greatness in any sphere is simply *recognized excellence*. The excellence may be spurious, the recognition may be factitious and ephemeral—then the greatness is false, and the great of to-day are forgotten to-morrow. But when a noble character has been nobly exhibited; when genuine power has won genuine praise; when fame soars not for a brief flight into the windy air, but stands firm-footed on the solid pyramid of achievement, to sound through her silver trump the name of her victorious son—conqueror of nature, leader of men—this greatness will endure.

Build him a monument that shall testify our love and his renown. Let the world understand that not alone the plots of politics or the luck of war may give title to such public memorials. This witness, addressing as it does the imagination, the ambition, the worthy pride of the greatest number of men, is conspicuously appropriate to a life so many-sided and complete, so simple and sincere, yet so popular and influential.

He did not, as once he feared he might, go down poor and unknown, carrying with him thoughts of which the world was not worthy. He was heard, believed, accepted, rewarded—with no greater delay or difficulty than sufficed to bring out to their full extent his own best powers. It was given to him to do grand things in the sight of all men. And beneath all our words and pictures and statues of him—lies forever, a sure foundation, the work that he did for his time.

Foresters tell us that a tree once marked will retain the mark, though a hundred years of growth may have overlaid it with later coverings. What may be the future spread and stature of the stately oak of American engineering we cannot presume to foretell. But there will come no time when the historian, stripping off the bark, and cutting through the rings of many generations, will not find at the heart that name which with keen blade and skillful hand was carved by Alexander Lyman Holley.

VII.

CATALOGUE OF THE BOOKS, PROFESSIONAL PAPERS, ETC., WRITTEN BY ALEXANDER L. HOLLEY.*

I. Books.

THE PERMANENT WAY AND COAL-BURNING LOCOMOTIVES OF EUROPEAN RAILWAYS ; *with a Comparison of the Working Economy of European and American Lines, and the Principles upon which Improvement must Proceed.* By Zerah Colburn and Alexander L. Holley. With fifty-one plates by J. Bien. New York : Holley and Colburn, 1858. Folio, 168 pp. of text.

AMERICAN AND EUROPEAN RAILWAY PRACTICE *in the Economical Generation of Steam, including the Materials and Construction of Coal-burning Boilers, Combustion, the Variable Blast, Vaporization, Circulation, Superheating, Supplying and Heating Feed-water, etc., and the Adaptation of Wood and Coke-burning Engines to Coal-burning ; and in Permanent Way, including Road-bed, Sleepers, Rails, Joint-fastenings, Street Railways, etc.* By Alexander L. Holley, B. P. With seventy-seven plates, engraved by J. Bien. New York : D. Van Nostrand; London : Sampson Low, Son & Co., 1860. (Second Edition 1867.) Folio, 192 pp. of text.

A TREATISE ON ORDNANCE AND ARMOR : *Embracing Descriptions, Discussions and Professional Opinions concerning the Material, Fabrication, Requirements, Capabilities and Endurance of European and American Guns for Naval, Sea-coast and Ironclad Warfare, and their Rifling, Projectiles and Breech-loading. Also, Results of Experiments against Armor, from Official Records. With an Appendix,*

---

* Mr. Holley's articles in the Railway Advocate, the American Engineer, and the American Railway Review, and his editorial paragraphs in Van Nostrand's Eclectic Engineering Magazine are not included in this list. Their number, and the difficulty of identifying them with certainty, forbids the attempt to catalogue them. But the files of the Railway Advocate for 1855, 1856 and 1857, the American Engineer for a brief period in 1857, and the mechanical department of the American Railway Review for 1860 and the first half of 1831, abound in his work. He was editor of Van Nostrand's from its foundation in January 1869, for one year.—[R. W. R.]

Referring to Gun-Cotton, Hooped Guns, etc. With 493 Illustrations. New York: D. Van Nostrand; London: Trübner & Company, 1865. Octavo, 900 pp.

II. ADDRESSES AND PROFESSIONAL PAPERS.

An Essay on Pen and Pocket Cutlery, Embracing a Detailed Description of the Mechanical, Chemical and Manual Operations Performed on Certain Raw Materials, to Convert them into the Means, Implements and Materials for Manufacturing Pen and Pocket Knives. By A. L. Holley. Published in Poor's *American Railroad Journal,* New York, during May, June and July, 1850.

The Natural Motors. Graduating Oration (unpublished), delivered September 7th, 1853, at Brown University, Providence, R. I.

Water Considered as a Carrier: the Properties upon which its Qualification for the Office Depends. By Dr. Hugag. Published in the *Litchfield Enquirer,* January 26th, 1854.

Corliss's Stationary Steam Engine. Published in the *Polytechnic Journal,* New York City, 1854. 10 pp., with diagrams.

The Dominion of Mind. An Oration, Delivered before the Theta Delta Chi Fraternity at their Annual Convention, by Alexander L. Holley, June 1st, 1855. Providence, B. T. Albro, Printer, 185:'. Octavo pamphlet, 18 pp.

Ironclad War Vessels. By A. L. Holley. Published in the *National Almanac* for 1863. About 6 pp., small octavo.

Ironclad Ships and Heavy Ordnance. Published in the *Atlantic Monthly* for January 1863. 10 pp., octavo.

Steel, and the Bessemer Process. A paper read before the Polytechnic Association of the American Institute, New York City, October 12th, 1865. Published in the *American Artisan.*

The Bessemer Process and Works in the United States. (Originally an Article in the *Troy Daily Times,* July 27th, 1868.) New York: D. Van Nostrand, 1868. Octavo pamphlet, 39 pp.

Rolling versus Hammering Ingots. A paper read before the American Institute of Mining Engineers, February 21st, 1872. Published in the *Transactions*, Vol I., p. 203. Octavo, 3 pp.

Three-high Rolls. A paper read before the American Institute of Mining Engineers, October 17th, 1872. Published in the *Transactions*, Vol. I., p. 287. Octavo, 6 pp., with plate.

Tests of Steel. A paper read before the American Institute of Mining Engineers, October 22d, 1872. Published in the *Transactions*, Vol. II., p. 116. Octavo, 6 pp.

Bessemer Machinery. A lecture delivered before the students of the Stevens Institute of Technology, Hoboken, N. J., in 1873. Published in the *Journal of the Franklin Institute,* Vol. LXIV. Octavo, 30 pp., with plates.

Recent Improvements in Bessemer Machinery. A paper read before the American Institute of Mining Engineers, February 24th, 1874. Published in the *Transactions*, Vol. II., p. 263. Octavo, 10 pp., with plates.

On American Rolling Mills. A paper read before the Iron and Steel Institute of Great Britain. Published in the *Journal* of the Institute, No. II. for 1874. Octavo, 19 pp., with plates.

Setting Bessemer Converter-Bottoms. A paper read before the Iron and Steel Institute of Great Britain. Published in the *Journal* of the Institute, No. II. for 1874. Octavo 6 pp., with plates.

The Porter-Allen Engine: Report on its Practical Performance, Economy, Durability, etc., with a View to Establishing its Manufacture. By A. L. Holley, C. E. New York: D. Van Nostrand, 1875. Octavo pamphlet, 11 pp.

On the Use of Natural Gas for Puddling and Heating, at Leechburg, Pennsylvania. A paper read before the American Institute of Mining Engineers, May 27th, 1875. Published in the *Transactions*, Vol. IV., p. 32. Octavo, 3 pp.

The Form, Weight, Manufacture and Life of Rails. Remarks before the American Society of Civil Engineers, June, 1875. Published in the *Transactions*, Vol. IV., p. 233. Octavo, 8 pp.

Tests and Testing-Machines. Remarks before the American Society of Civil Engineers, June, 1875. Published in the *Transactions*, Vol. IV., p. 265. Octavo, 44 pp.

Some Pressing Needs of our Iron and Steel Manufactures. Presidential Address before the American Institute of Mining Engineers, October 26th, 1875. Published in the *Transactions*, Vol. IV., p. 77. Octavo, 23 pp.

What is Steel? A paper read before the American Institute of Mining Engineers, October 29th, 1875. Published in the *Transactions*, Vol. IV., p. 138. Octavo, 12 pp.

The Inadequate Union of Engineering Science and Art. Presidential Address before the American Institute of Mining Engineers, February 22d, 1876. Published in the *Transactions*, Vol. IV., p. 191. Octavo, 17 pp.

Iron and Steel at Philadelphia. A series of articles by A. L. Holley and Lenox Smith, published in London *Engineering* as follows:

    I. Iron and Steel at Philadelphia, November 10th, 1876.

    II. Swedish Exhibits, December 6th, 1876.

    III. Belgian and French Exhibits, January 5th, 1877.

    IV. German Exhibits, January 19th, 1877.

    V. The Exhibits of Great Britain, February 9th, 1877.

    VI. American Exhibits, March 2d, 1877.

American Iron and Steel Works. A series of illustrated articles, by A. L. Holley and Lenox Smith, published in London *Engineering*, as follows:

    I. An Analysis of the American Bessemer Plant, Illustrated by the Vulcan Works, St. Louis, March 9th, 1877.

    II. An Analysis of the American Bessemer Plant, Illustrated by the Vulcan Works, St. Louis, March 16th, 1877.

    III. The Midvale Steel Works, Philadelphia, March 30th, 1877.

    IV. The Works of Park, Brothers & Co., May 4th, 1877.

    V. The Union Iron Works, Buffalo, N. Y., June 22d, 1877.

    VI. The Otis Iron and Steel Works, Cleveland, O., July 27th, 1877.

    VII. The Works of the Bethlehem Iron Co., Bethlehem, Pa., August 24th, 1877.

VIII. The Works of the Bethlehem Iron Co., Bethlehem, Pa., August 31st, 1877.

IX. The Works of the Bethlehem Iron Co., Bethlehem, Pa., September 14th, 1877.

X. The Works of the Bethlehem Iron Co., Bethlehem, Pa., October 19th, 1877.

XI. The Works of the Bethlehem Iron Co., Bethlehem, Pa., October 26th, 1877.

XII. The Crescent Steel Works, Pittsburg, Pa., November 23d, 1877.

XIII. The Cedar Point Iron Company's Works, December 21st, 1877.

XIV. The North Chicago Rolling Mill Company's Works, January, 18th, 1877.

XV. The North Chicago Rolling Mill Company's Works, February, 8th, 1878.

XVI. Rail Mill of the Philadelphia and Reading Railroad, Reading, Pa., February 22d, 1878.

XVII. Mines and Works of the Crown Point Iron Company, N. Y., March 15th, 1878.

XVIII. Mines and Works of the Crown Point Iron Company, N. Y., March 22d, 1878.

XIX. The Diamond Furnace—Ferro-manganese Manufacture in the United States, March 29th, 1878.

XX. Works of the Cleveland Rolling Mill Company, O., April 5th, 1878.

XXI. Works of the Edgar Thomson Steel Company, Limited, Pittsburg, Pa., April 9th, 1878.

XXII. Works of the Edgar Thomson Steel Company, Limited, Pittsburg, Pa., April 26th, 1878.

XXIII. Works of the Edgar Thomson Steel Company, Limited, Pittsburg, Pa., May 17th, 1878.

XXIV. Plate Mill of the Bay State Iron Company, Boston, Mass., May 24th, 1878.

XXV. The Cambria Iron and Steel Works, Johnstown, Pa., May 31st, 1878.

XXVI. The Cambria Iron and Steel Works, Johnstown, Pa., June 21st, 1878.

XXVII. The Cambria Iron and Steel Works, Johnstown, Pa., July 12th, 1878.

XXVIII. The Cambria Iron and Steel Works, Johnstown, Pa., July 19th, 1878.

XXIX. The Cambria Iron and Steel Works, Johnstown, Pa., August 23d, 1878.

XXX. The Cambria Iron and Steel Works, Johnstown, Pa., September 30th, 1878.

XXXI. The American Iron Works of Jones & Laughlin, Pittsburg, Pa., November 1st, 1878.

XXXII. The Lucy Furnaces, Pittsburg, Pa., November 22d, 1878.

XXXIII. The Union Iron Mills, Pittsburg, Pa., January 10th, 1879.

XXXIV. The Works of Cooper, Hewitt & Company, Trenton, N. J., and Riegelsville, Pa., January 31st, 1879.

XXXV. The Works of Cooper, Hewitt & Co., Trenton, N. J., and Riegelsville, Pa., February 21st, 1879.

XXXVI. The Works of the Meier Iron Company, April 18th, 1879.

XXXVII. Salisbury Iron; and the Works of the Barnum Richardson Company, May 30th, 1879.

XXXVIII. The Works of the Phœnix Iron Company, Phœnixville, Pa., February 6th, 1880.

XXXIX. The Springfield Iron Works, Springfield, Ill., May 14th, 1880.

XL. The Albany and Rensselaer Iron and Steel Works, Troy, N. Y., December 24th, 1880.

XLI. The Albany and Rensselaer Iron and Steel Works, Troy, N. Y., December 31st, 1880.

Notes on the Salisbury, Conn., Iron Mines and Works. A paper read before the American Institute of Mining Engineers, October 23d, 1877. Published in the *Transactions*, Vol. VI., p. 220. Octavo, 4 pp.

Notes on the Iron Ore and Anthracite Coal of Rhode Island and Massachusetts. A paper read before the American Institute of Mining Engineers, October 24th, 1877. Published in the *Transactions*, Vol. VI., p. 224. Octavo, 3 pp.

The Strength of Wrought Iron, as Affected by its Composition, and by its Reduction in Rolling. A paper read before the American

Institute of Mining Engineers, February 27th, 1878. Published in the *Transactions*, Vol. VI., p. 101. Octavo, 24 pp.

Solid Steel Castings for Ordnance, Structures and General Machinery by the Terrenoire Process. Published in the *Metallurgical Review*, New York, May, June and July, 1878. Octavo, 48 pp.

Chemical and Physical Analyses of Phosphoric Steel. A paper read before the Institution of Civil Engineers (England). Published in the *Proceedings*, Vol. VIII., Session 1877–78. Part III. London 1878. Octavo, 28 pp.

The United States Testing Machine at Watertown Arsenal. A paper read before the American Institute of Mining Engineers, February 18th, 1879. Published in the *Transactions*, Vol. VII., p. 256. Octavo, 9 pp.

The Pernot Furnace. A paper read before the American Institute of Mining Engineers, February 19th, 1879. Published in the *Transactions*, Vol. VII., p. 241. Octavo, 14 pp., with plates.

The Tessié Gas Producer. A paper read before the American Institute of Mining Engineers, May 13th, 1879. Published in the *Transactions*, Vol. VIII., p. 27. Octavo, 7 pp., with plates.

Washing Phosphoric Pig-Iron for the Open-hearth and Puddling Processes. A paper read before the American Institute of Mining Engineers, September 17th, 1879. Octavo, 9 pp., with plates.

The Field of Mechanical Engineering. An address delivered at the preliminary meeting of the American Society of Mechanical Engineers, February 16th, 1880. Published in the *Transactions*, Vol. I., p. 7 (in the earliest copies it is at p. 28). Octavo, 5 pp.

Notes on the Siemens Direct Process. A paper read before the American Institute of Mining Engineers, February 19th, 1880. Published in the *Transactions*, Vol. VIII., p. 321. Octavo, 4 pp., with plates.

Engineering, the Intermediate Power between Nature and Civilization. An address delivered at the banquet in honor of Count Ferdinand de Lesseps, New York, March 1st, 1880. Published, with other addresses on the same occasion, by D. Appleton & Company, New York, 1880.

An Adaptation of Bessemer Plant to the Basic Process. A paper read before the American Society of Mechanical Engineers, November, 1880. Published in the *Transactions*, Vol. I., p. 124. Octavo, 8 pp., with plates.

Steel. An article in *Appleton's Cyclopædia of Mechanics*, New York, 1880. Octavo, 15 pp.

On Rail Patterns. A paper read before the American Institute of Mining Engineers, February 17th, 1881. Published in the *Transactions*, Vol. IX., p. 360. Octavo, 16 pp., with plates and tables.

The Bethlehem Iron and Steel Works. An article in London *Engineering*, October 28th, 1881.

VIII.

ACTION OF THE CLEVELAND CIVIL ENGINEERS' CLUB.

At a meeting of the Club held at Cleveland, O., February 14th, 1882, the following resolutions were unanimously adopted:

Resolved, That the members of the Cleveland Civil Engineers' Club have heard of the death of Alexander L. Holley with profound sorrow and regret.

Resolved, That in the death of Mr. Holley, the engineering profession of the world has lost one who not only contributed largely to the success of all industries connected in any way with metallurgy, being the father, as it were, of the Bessemer steel process in this country, whilst he also added largely to the highest order of our literature.

Resolved, That while he held a position among the highest of our profession, he will ever be remembered and mourned on account of his great personal worth and purity of character.

In presenting these resolutions, Mr. J. F. Holloway spoke as follows:

Mr. President: In presenting the resolutions at the opening of this meeting, I felt certain that I was but giving voice to the feelings of all members of this club who have had the pleasure of Mr. Holley's personal acquaintance, as well as those who knew him only by his published books, and by his accomplished works in the various steel and iron-mills of our country. To those of you who have felt the warm, hearty grasp of his hand, who have seen upon his face the ever-present genial smile, and who have listened to the sympathetic tones of his voice, a voice no less pleasant when expounding the most intricate theories of science, as when it sparkled with wit and humor, the news of his death will come with peculiar sadness. It is not my purpose to occupy the time of this Society with a recital of Mr. Holley's professional career; the technical journals and magazines that lie upon your tables have with more or less accuracy informed you respecting that. Neither do I intend to speak of his standing as an engineer in other and foreign lands; the papers that will in a few days reach you, will tell of that also far better than I would be able to.

There is one aspect of his life and mission—I think I may call it a mission—about which I would gladly speak; and that is the rare combination there was in him, of the science of the savant, the practical knowledge of the workman, and the courtliness of the gentleman. Not content with possessing these rare qualifications in himself, he occupied the later years of his life in bringing about a new and better era of fellowship between science and practice in others. Standing as he did, the peer of anyone in the ranks of either, he made himself the connecting link between men whose lives had been passed among books only, and the man of practice, who picked his uncertain way over hard and flinty roads, with patient toil and trial. It was his mission to bring the scientific man out from the libraries, colleges, and the laboratories, into the smoke and grime of the world's workshop. On the other hand, standing beside his fellow-workmen in the mine, the furnace, and the workshop, he told them that by study, by investigation, and by interviews with men of science, they could find many a clew to the difficulties that beset them from day to day. He told them, if they would go with him to the laboratory with their troublesome ores and metals, that the man of science would, by ways of his own, hunt and drive out the demons that so troubled and baffled them in the furnace, the forge, and the foundry, and in the various processes through which they so blindly chased them. And the man of practice, though ever distrustful of science, taking the advice of a fellow-workman, took his ores and his metals to the laboratory, where the man of science calcined them, triturated them, and sublimated them; he bathed them in acids, dried them in alkalis, and, melting them in crucibles, brought out a tiny button of metal, and a folio of profoundly written formulas, replete with figures which divided a unit into ten thousand parts. Out of all this, by comparing the results without understanding them, the workman saw that the more he had of some things, and the less he had of others, the better would be his iron and his steel, and in the end he had a higher regard for science, and a greater respect for the man of books; while on the other hand, the college professor, wandering among the mills, furnaces, and workshops, was struck with the ingenuity and good sense displayed by the engineer, and thought the more highly of him.

But the mission of Alexander L. Holley meant more than this.

He was not satisfied to simply bring each class to a better understanding and admiration of each other, he interested himself in the
formation of societies where men of different professions but kindred
pursuits, might meet together to tell of the work they had in hand.
Sometimes to speak of their success, often of their troubles and their
failures. By the discussions which have taken place in these societies,
all have been made wiser. Indeed it is safe to say that out of the
greatest failures often has come the greatest good. In these societies
are often found members who, in long years of practice, have gathered valuable stores of knowledge, but being unaccustomed to put
their thoughts into words, were simply silent though interested
listeners. These were induced to write papers which also came before the societies for discussion, and record, and thus their printed
transactions have come to be volumes of rare and valuable information, which not only does credit to their authors, but as well to the
engineering literature of our country.

But there was still a further step taken. Mr. Holley in his numerous trips abroad, oftentimes the guest of similar societies, early
saw the advantage that would accrue to the industries of our country,
as well as to the men to whose labors these industries owe their ori-
gin and success, if they could only be induced to leave their daily
round of duties, and joining with others, make excursions among the
mills and workshops of their fellow-workmen. Just how much good
has grown out of this new departure can never be fully known. But
it was not enough that the members of the societies should go, they
must bring their wives with them, and those only who have availed
themselves of these excursions, which have so happily combined
business, instruction, and social intercourse, can in the least manner
understand how enjoyable they have been, or how pleasant the acquaintances thus formed. I have spoken thus somewhat at length,
but by no means exhaustively, of the modern scientist, engineer, and
workman, that I might the more fully exemplify the part Mr. Holley has taken in bringing about so pleasant a state of affairs between
them; and I do not hesitate to say that no man, no matter how high
his position or his attainments, has done as much as did Alexander
L. Holley to bind in one bond of kindly feeling and fellowship those
who, as members and associates, have thus mingled together.

Among the many things he had doubtless planned for the future,
and which, alas, are now unaccomplished, there was at least one, of
which I knew, that it must have pained him to have left undone.
It was this: he had hoped at some time in the near future to have

11

brought before the various scientific and engineering societies of America, of which he was a member, a scheme by which they, joining together, should invite similar societies in England and on the Continent, to send large delegations of their membership to unite in a grand tour through the United States, to be passed from State to State, and from city to city, seeing in each their different and distinct industries, to be taken down into our mines, carried on our broad rivers, borne upon our vast inland seas, and across wide prairies, far westward through States and Territories teeming with untold wealth, to the very portals of the Golden Gate. It was to be the excursion of all excursions, it was to excel by its extended field of observation, its immensity of proportions, and the standing and character of its members, the grandeur and brilliancy of all past time. It was to be a millennium of good feeling, and of good cheer. All of you who have come in contact with, and enjoyed the companionship of that wonderfully genial and kind-hearted man, can easily imagine what a success it would have been, and how largely his personal endeavors would have contributed to make it so. But the times were not yet ripe for its accomplishment. Perhaps the severe illness that overtook him abroad a year or more ago and the enfeebled state of his health since had warned him it was not to be; but let us at least give him credit for that largeness of heart which conceived the idea.

I have not said, neither did I intend to say, anything about what Mr. Holley has accomplished as an engineer. His works are his monuments. In many a valley from the Hudson to the Mississippi, from the mouths of numerous converters the lurid flames light up the hillsides, and write upon the midnight sky the wonders of his achievements. It was of Mr. Holley the man that I wished to speak; and as I remember his cheerful humor, his ready wit, the keen retort that left no wound behind, I feel how powerless I am to convey to ears unaccustomed to his voice, the magic of its tones. There was ever about him a coterie of choice spirits, and to have been a listener to the flow of good things that fell so unpremeditated from his lips was indeed a treat. There are times and occasions when words fitly chosen, harmonizing with the circumstances which surround speaker and listeners touched with a cadence of feeling and earnestness, bring to the heart of the hearer something deeper and wider in their significance than the same words would do spoken by other tongues and with different surroundings. And yet, knowing this as I do, I am tempted to relate an incident in Mr. Holley's life which I, in common with many others, witnessed and which none will ever forget. It was on an occasion during the Pittsburgh meeting of the Institute of Mining Engineers, when a few personal friends of Mr. Holley who had been engaged with him one way and another in the study, erection, and working of the modern Bessemer steel plant, desired to present him with a beautiful and costly piece of plate. The presentation was to take place at the elegant country seat of William P. Shinn, at that time the president of the society. It came at the close of several days of most enjoyable meetings and excursions; but, as the evening upon which it was to take place came on, there came with it a drizzling rain-storm. Mr. Holley, who had not been well during the meetings, seemed quite used up, and making up his mind to forego the pleasure of the evening reception, went to bed at his hotel. So quietly and carefully had the projected presentation been planned, that neither Mr. Holley nor his wife, and but a very few members of the Institute had any suspicion or knowledge of what was about to be done. With the rain falling outside, and Holley sick in bed, the promoters of the scheme were at their wits' end. At last, as they saw no possible way out of it, they took Mrs. Holley into their confidence, and told her all that they had hoped to do, and how disappointed they all were. Realizing as she did the generous feeling and love for her husband, which prompted the act, and seeing, too, how sadly disappointed they all felt over the situation, she promised to see what could be done. Going to the bedside of her husband she told him how disappointed Mr. and Mrs. Shinn were that he could not attend their reception; and that many of the members, hearing that he would not be there, were half inclined to stay away also. Holley heard her in silence. At last, with an effort he roused himself, and, thinking only of his disappointed friends, said, "Help me to dress, and send down word that we are coming." A close carriage was procured, and, carefully wrapped up, he made the journey and appeared in the parlors of his friends amid a wild huzza of delight from all present. I need not recount the strategy by which he was at last brought up to the table, whereon, inclosed in a beautiful case, the still more elegant present lay enshrined. I could not, much as I might desire to do so, repeat the beautiful and touching address made him by Mr. Shinn in behalf of the donors. As he closed, and, uplifting the cover, revealed the testimonial beneath, enriched as it was with the memories that clustered about the names written thereon, Holley was for a moment silent; the ever-ready tongue failed to interpret his thoughts: at length, amid a silence that was profound, he began his reply. He spoke of the love

he had for his profession, and of his earlier efforts as an engineer;
then, coming to a later period of his life, he accorded high and generous praise to those friends who had so much aided, and encouraged
him in his various undertakings.   As he proceeded, it seemed as if
a gleam of the future opened up before him; and he spoke of his
work as about accomplished ; then casting, as it were, a retrospective
glance over the past, thinking doubtless, as indeed we all must at
times think, how it might have been purer, better, there flashed across
his mind the beautiful simile of the converter, the converter about
which he had so much dreamed, and planned, and he remembered
how it, taking the impuré and crude materials of the earth, earthy,
through its alchemy, transmutes them, purified and purged from all
defects, into a pûre and noble metal.   So, too, of our lives; might
not they, chastened, purified, and freed from all earthly dross and
stains, come at last to be remolded anew into higher and nobler
forms?   But words fail to convey the beauty of his thoughts.   The
pathos of his voice, the pallor that was on his cheek, the far-away
look that was in his eyes, will never be forgotten by those who with
tear-dimmed eyes stood grouped about him.   But he is dead ; and
as a warm friend and an eminent writer has well said : "Tears shed
for such a man are no evidence of weakness.   The world will go
on, and another will take up the work he has left unfinished ; but
Holley's place in the hearts of his friends will never be filled."

IX.

ACTION OF THE BOARD OF TRUSTEES OF THE RENSSELAER POLYTECHNIC INSTITUTE, TROY, N. Y.

AT a meeting of the Board of Trustees, held Friday, February 10, 1882, the following resolution was adopted.

Resolved, That the accompanying memoranda respecting Alexander L. Holley be adopted, and that they be entered on the records of this Board, and that a copy of them be sent to his family.

Alexander L. Holley was born at Lakeville, Conn., in 1832, and died at Brooklyn, N. Y., January 29, 1882. Having become temporarily a resident of this city, he in 1865 was elected a member of this Board, which position he held until his resignation, two years later. He was again elected a trustee in 1870, and served in that capacity until his death. His connection with the Bessemer manufacture, commencing in the autumn of 1862—when, being in England, he became convinced of its great importance—and extending through his whole subsequent career, has given him a place, among iron scientists, of high honor, and distinguishes him as the most efficient among those who have developed the Bessemer process in this country.

In Mr. Holley's character were combined thought and use, in well-balanced proportion. Every theory which followed as the evolution of thought, was tried in the alembic of resultant use, and was either abandoned, modified or adopted, in accordance with the event. Thus it happened that men came to place confidence in his opinion, whenever he gave to it expression, and to value his judgment above that of every contemporary in this broad land, in all matters pertaining to the process already named. Beneath his manipulation, the deification of iron among metals has been rendered complete.

While connected with this Board, he undertook a great part of the labor of preparing the "Report of the Committee of the Trustees," concerning the Rensselaer Polytechnic Institute, which report was published in 1870. This very thorough treatise exhibits at once the logical character of Mr. Holley's mind, and manifests his power of presenting a given subject in varied aspects and with aggregation of valuable suggestion.   Starting with the statement that "the objects for which the Institute exists are, not merely to provide young men with a knowledge of mathematics, and to familiarize them with learned text-books, but to qualify them for the practical application of science to the useful arts"—starting with this comprehensive definition of the work of the Institute, the report, with admirable clearness, developed step by step the most efficient modes of realizing and effecting this "practical application."

Endowed by nature with a pleasing person, which enshrined a mind to which came easily and gracefully the development that follows a lofty training; respected and beloved among men for his manly, noble and definite avowal, under all circumstances, of devotion to right principles and right action; renowned among scientists for the thoroughness of his investigation in fields of novel research, and for the certainty with which he builded upon theories which he had adopted; cheerful, modest, brave and determined;—thus realizing his gifts and his acquirements, and knowing his great worth, we ask the young men of this generation, and especially the young men of the Rensselaer Polytechnic Institute, to study his career and reflect upon the valuable work he has accomplished during a well-spent life.

X.

ACTION OF THE CENTURY ASSOCIATION, NEW YORK CITY.

At a meeting of the Century, held February 4, 1882, the following resolutions, offered by Mr. R. W. Raymond and seconded by Mr. O. Chanute, were, after appropriate remarks by Messrs. S. H. Wales and Charles Macdonald, unanimously adopted:

Resolved, That in the death of Alexander Lyman Holley the Century Association deplores the loss of one of its most honored and beloved members, whose varied accomplishments and great achievements commanded the admiration, as his tireless activity and stainless honor won the respect, of all; while to innumerable friends, privileged to know in cordial intercourse his brave, joyous, generous character, the sense of public and professional bereavement is hidden in the deeper shadows of personal grief.

Resolved, That the Secretary be instructed to enter these resolutions in the minutes of the Association, and to communicate them to the family of Mr. Holley, together with the assurance of our heart-felt sympathy.

XI.

ACTION OF THE IRON AND STEEL INSTITUTE OF GREAT BRITAIN.

At the annual meeting of the Iron and Steel Institute, held at London, May 10, 1882, the General Secretary read the thirteenth annual report of the Council, in which the following passage occurs:

"In Mr. Holley's recent decease we have to deplore the loss of a member who occupied a most conspicuous place in connection with the iron and steel industry of the United States, and whose active interest in the affairs of this Institute was shown on many occasions during his membership, which extended from 1873 to the time of his death.

"In recognition of Mr. Holley's great services, the Council have decided to forward to his family the Bessemer medal for 1882."

Upon the presentation of the report of the Council, the President, Josiah T. Smith, Esq., spoke in part as follows:

"The report unfortunately indicates the death of a very large number of members; but it would not be wise or desirable on these periodical occasions to harrow the feelings of friends by alluding at length to the losses they have sustained. At the same time, there are names amongst those who have gone to which it would be highly improper not to allude before adopting the report. Amongst these, I refer more especially to the death of the distinguished American, Mr. Holley. That gentleman gave himself an infinite amount of trouble to attend our meetings; and the clear and straightforward manner in which he always explained to us the development of the trade of his own country, at the same time modestly keeping in the background his own efforts, elicited our admiration and thanks. Those efforts were so highly appreciated that the Council felt that the Bessemer medal was due to Mr. Holley, and hoped to have the pleasure of presenting it to him at this meeting. They have now, however, to hand it to his representatives."

On the same day, the Bessemer medal was delivered by a deputation of the Council to Hon. J. Russell Lowell, the American Ambassador, and was subsequently transmitted, through the Department of State at Washington, to the family of Mr. Holley.

The Journal of the Iron and Steel Institute (No. II., 1882) contains an extended obituary notice of Mr. Holley, which concludes (after biographical and professional details which need not be repeated here, since they are contained in greater fulness elsewhere in this volume) with the following words:

"Of Mr. Holley's many-sided character, apart from his career as an engineer and metallurgist, the scope of this too brief sketch does not allow of much being said. The universal esteem in which he was held has been sufficiently evidenced by the manifold tributes of sorrow and regard which have been paid to his memory, since his decease, by the leading men of the iron trade on the two continents, between which his genius and his amiability tended so greatly to establish an *entente cordiale.*"

XII.

THE PITTSBURGH TESTIMONIAL.

REPEATED reference having been made in the foregoing pages to this testimonial, it is deemed proper to insert here a brief account of it, and a report of the remarks made on the occasion, taken from a volume printed at the time for private distribution.

The "testimonial" itself consisted in a handsome silver pitcher and salver, presented in token of appreciation and regard to Alexander Lyman Holley from his friends,

William R. Jones,	Daniel J. Morrell,	James Park, Jr.,
Erastus Corning,	William P. Shinn,	Charles C. Teeter,
Chester Griswold,	William Metcalf,	D. S. Hines,
Robert W. Hunt,	S. T. Wellman,	John E. Fry,
Charles Kennedy,	Daniel N. Jones,	Selden E. Marvin,
John W. Hartman,	Alexander Hamilton,	John H. Ricketson,
Thomas H. Lapsley,	James Hemphill,	Robert Forsyth,
Henry R. Worthington,	O. W. Potter,	E. V. McCandless,
William A. Perry,	John Fritz,	John Rinard.

The occasion selected for the presentation was a social reception given to the American Institute of Mining Engineers, during its Pittsburgh meeting, at Home Lawn, the residence of Mr. William P. Shinn, East End, Pittsburgh, on the evening of Thursday, May 15th, 1879. The affair was kept secret from Mr. Holley until the last moment; and indeed, there was a narrow escape from disappointment through his absence; since, exhausted by the labors of the meeting, he had decided not to attend the reception, unconscious that so much depended upon his presence. Being persuaded at last to change his determination, he left his bed to join his assembled friends.

Mr. Shinn, in making the presentation, spoke in behalf of the donors as follows:

Ladies and Gentlemen: Allow me to claim your attention for a few moments. A once prominent railroad official was known to define an engineer as a " man who knew what he wanted to do and how to do it," and he added, by way of illustration, that he was an engineer in that sense. The definition is not so wide of the mark as the application. This gentleman was well known as never knowing either what he wanted to do or how to do it. It must, therefore, be evident that a " mining engineer " is one who wants to mine, and knows how. In this sense, I fear that many of us are in the same category with the railroad official referred to. Some of us sport the title of "civil engineer." It is presumably a reasonable requirement of all engineers to be civil, yet some of us find even that task difficult. There are yet others who masquerade under the designation of "mechanical engineers," and there is one of our number who has imposed upon a too credulous and confiding public with this title and sundry others, to which I will refer, until " forbearance has ceased to be a virtue," and it has fallen upon me to expose him before this intelligent audience.

This gentleman appeared in this vicinity some years ago and his theme was " blowing Bessemer steel." His ambition appeared to be to blow about something, and his greatest desire was to " blow a heat." This gentleman was always descanting upon converting things—and people. He made some converts and some converters, but such a failure was he in this direction, that those who came in contact with his converters found themselves consigned to a hotter place than they had ever reached before. The most remarkable characteristic of the converts of this gentleman's converters, is that they are always inclined to steel. This gentleman also indulges in the title of " consulting engineer," and frequently favors his victims —whom he is pleased to call his " clients "—with a visit for consultation. This visit results in his finding out all we know, and in return he confidentially tells all that he don't know ; and there is so much of the latter, that he seems to doubt whether what he gets from us is a full equivalent !

He occasionally goes abroad, to England and the Continent, and favors our foreign friends by " consulting" them in like manner. Anon, he talks of " basic linings," as if his ordinary schemes were not base enough ; and you have heard him, at this very meeting, hold forth upon " economical gas-producers," as if such articles were valuable anywhere outside of Congress and our State Legislatures. But his propositions are so plausible, his manner so winning, his countenance so frank and " open-hearth " like, and his gas so overpowering, that he has admirers who still insist upon doing him honor ; and it is because of this that I have sought to place before you the facts in regard to this gentleman's true characteristics, lest you might be misled into that confidence, the burden of which these misguided persons have laid upon me this evening.

This gentleman's name you perhaps have heard, for it has a habit of getting into print—it is Alexander Lyman Holley. After all, Mr. Holley's blowing has been for Bessemer, for Siemens, for Tessie du Motay, for anybody and everybody except Holley, and that victimized few, as whose representative I appear here to-night, have resolved that one blow at least shall be struck for Alexander Lyman Holley.

Mr. Holley! In behalf of a few of those whose lives you have made a burden by teaching them the pathway to success in making Bessemer steel, and then leaving them to the mercy of the mathematician and the chemists—with their "analyses" and their "formulæ," their "moments" of this and their "units" of that—I present you this testimonial, which I find characterized in the official catalogue as a "pitcher upon a plateau." Which is the "pitcher," you can doubtless perceive; which is the "plateau," I leave for your patient and careful investigation, believing that, as in other cases which you have undertaken, science will finally triumph and the "plateau" will be discovered. The catalogue further states that the figures on the pitcher are a symbolical representation of "art chasing nature." It is an undoubted fact that nature needs chasing, as witness the too plentiful phosphorus in the convenient pig-iron; and as the art of Thomas and Gilchrist has now succeeded in chasing it out, so has your art chased nature out of many of her strongholds and forced her to deliver up her secrets to science.

In behalf of those whose names are recorded herein, I beg that you will accept this testimonial as but a slight evidence of their appreciation of your great professional ability, your high moral worth, and as an indication of their steadfast friendship.

The gift was uncovered, and after a moment of embarrassed silence, Mr. Holley, with tremulous voice, responded as follows:

I thank you for the kind and elegant manner in which you have presented this lovely gift; it is not only a surprise but an astonishment, so much so that I am utterly unprepared to properly respond.

My kind friends have intended this delightful presentation as a recognition of my contribution to the development of our Bessemer manufacture. I am disposed to be a modest man; but there is one thing which I certainly do claim to know more intimately than most people, and that is, Who contributed to that somewhat remarkable development, and what each one contributed. I am proud to be recognized as one of the dozen men—here (pointing to Captain W. R. Jones) is a conspicuous member of that dozen—who, in the way of good mechanical engineering on the part of some of us, and good management on the part of others, have put the Bessemer process in the high and successful position which it occupies to-day.

But, sir, one of the first principles of our profession is to make constructions only upon mature working-drawings. This surprise is so complete that I have had no chance to work up drawings and specifications of a suitable response; but that I will endeavor to do when I can more completely express my overwhelming feelings.

Among us all who are working hard in our noble profession, and are keeping the fires of metallurgy aglow, such occasions as this should also kindle a flame of good fellowship and affection which will burn to the end.

Burn to the end!—perhaps some of us should think of that, who are "burning the candle at both ends." Ah! well, may it so happen to us that when at last this vital spark is oxidized, when this combustible has put on incombustion, when this living fire flutters thin and pale at the lips, some kindly hand may "turn us down," not "underblown"—by all means not "overblown"—some loving hand may turn us down, that we may perhaps be cast in a better mould.

At the Banquet of the American Institute of Mining Engineers, held in Pittsburgh on the following evening, one of the speakers, after alluding to the above-mentioned testimonial, and expressing the heart-felt sympathy of the Institute with its spirit and purpose, although the members as a body had had no knowledge of the testimonial and had not been privileged to take part in it, except as spectators, read the following lines:

> O noblest war of earth or time,
>   Conquest unstained with blood or tears,
> Thy bells of joy melodious chime,
>   And make no victim groan that hears!
>
> Along the sky thy banner streams;
>   Its vapory white, its smoky hue
> Transfused with fire, it glows and gleams
>   Against the background of the blue.

But underneath its waving folds
  No wasted field, no ruined home
Mute, cursing hands to heaven upholds,
  Proving such glory is but gloom !

The prisoned giants of the deep,
  Surprised, o'ercome and rescued, yield ;
Break glad from silence and from sleep,
  To serve their victor in the field.

They whirl his wheels; they fan his fire;
  They flash his thoughts o'er land and sea,
Outrunning, in their fierce desire,
  What boldest dreamers dreamed might be.

"Behold," they cry, "our willing hands!
  "Behold our swift and tireless feet!
"Let him but come who understands :
  "Our service shall be strong and fleet !"

Thus Nature's voices call for Man :
  Thrice worthy he, who, born to rule,
Perceives the call, creates the plan,
  Inspires with life the lifeless tool.

The Macedonian wept with rage
  For other worlds to overrun ;
The hero of a nobler age
  Has found and claimed them, one by one.

Realm after realm of fruitful thought
  Has hailed our ALEXANDER king;
But crowns of conquest all are naught
  To those our loyal hearts would bring.

For weakness at the victor's feet,
  Or reason, may reluctant bend ;
But love's surrender is complete—
  The utter gift of friend to friend.

O brother, known in many lands,
  And master called in many arts !
Behold, we stretch to you our hands
  With nothing in them, save our hearts !

XIII.

SPEECH AT THE DE LESSEPS BANQUET.

As a specimen of Mr. Holley's graceful "after-dinner oratory," the following remarks are presented. They were made at a banquet, given in honor of Count Ferdinand de Lesseps, at New York, March 1st, 1880. Mr. Holley responded as follows to the sentiment,

ENGINEERING, THE INTERMEDIATE POWER BETWEEN NATURE AND CIVILIZATION.

MR. CHAIRMAN: The sentiment you propose so completely defines the master art of engineering that it needs no historian, no prophet, no defender. It were better, to-night, that we magnify its splendid achievements, as we celebrate the advent of its illustrious apostle. It is such grand conceptions as his, such triumphs over difficulty, such faithful and brilliant execution, that draw the members of our profession to him; but our profession it is that draws the whole world in its triumphal march. The ways and means of transportation, of mining, metallurgy, manufactures, defense, agriculture, architecture—all the round of vital and useful arts—are but phases of engineering effort.

But engineers are not proud; they simply cannot help it that they are the way, the vehicle, the power of civilization. They even acknowledge the incidental value of other professions. Chemistry is a noble art—full of promise—but only complementary to engineering. Engineers are, for this reason, sometimes complimentary to chemists! Commerce, banking, jurisprudence, political economy, government, are more or less useful systems,—for what? For formulating and realizing the potentiality of engineering. And so the noble art—stimulating labor, promoting comfort, founding prosperity, diffusing happiness, establishing knowledge—blends, in its own potency, the aims of the three learned professions of old, and itself leads on to universal health, equity, and virtue.

I do not wish to be understood, sir, as claiming much for engineering; so sensitive is the modesty of my colleagues that they would not tolerate an overstatement of its claims!

Viewed from my own department of the profession, there is but one aspect in which the achievements of our distinguished guest are not supremely beneficent. He delves in rock and earth; alas! he constructs not in iron and steel. Unhappy iron and steel! Could he but restrain his insatiable ambition to reconstruct this planet; could he but intersperse his mighty works with some trifling steel railway from New York to China; some trivial steel bridge from his own beloved shores to Albion, he would be enshrined as little less than a divinity, even in Pennsylvania. But, although not a constructor in steel himself, he is a cause of steel construction in others. The canal breeds ships.

And here I may, perhaps, be permitted to emphasize one engineering condition of a transcontinental canal, common alike to all countries and to all routes. The ship grows from year to year. The early Atlantic steamers were of a thousand tons; the Atlantic steamers now building are of eight thousand tons. This growth is by a law as inevitable as that of the tides. Doubling the linear dimensions of a ship increases her resistance fourfold, but it increases her carrying capacity eightfold. The larger ship can thus transport the greater cargo, at the higher speed, and at the minimum cost. There is but one practical limit to this economy—it is the size and directness of the water-way.

I was not called upon, however, to discuss engineering, but to praise it. Do we ever realize the gigantic difficulties it overcomes— its uncompromising struggle with nature, oft baffled, ever renewed, to ferret out the secrets of her power? Do we ever picture to ourselves the engineer, toilfully planting his colossal works on precipitous mountains, in the open sea, under the river bed, in the bowels of the earth, on bottomless and pestilential swamps, amid perils of miasm and fire-damp, wind and wave, caisson and explosion—with every toppling avalanche, and every subterranean stream, and every pent up freshet just waiting to crack his bones and wipe out his works?

As you hold on to some headland against the hurricane, and feel the breakers shake the masonry of nature, his steamship plows its huge canal through forty thousand tons of that maelstrom in one single minute, with the coal one man can carry. The treasure-house of nature he despoils with his hydraulic engine; he raises from the dead the iron she had burned up through the ages. He disparts her continents to make way for his argosies, and spans her seas for his chariots of fire. Thus is engineering truly the intermediate power between nature and civilization; and from this high plane we recognize the guiding genius of our illustrious guest, and bid him hail!

XIV.

A METALLURGIST'S ODE TO SPRING.

THE following verses were read by Mr. Holley at the dinner of the American Institute of Mining Engineers, at Baltimore, on the evening of February 21st, 1879.

Hail, coming Spring, the metallurgist's boon!
Relaxing mines and streams closed all too soon
By cold unchemic, which alike defeats
Reactions, fusions, malleable heats!

Refractory winter to the solving sun
Yields its cold gangue while fluid offerings run,
And nature's furnace, scaffolded within,
By coming Spring is once again blown in.

Now draws the pump upon the river shore,
Now o'er the wheel the new-freed waters pour;
The frost shall burst hydraulic pipes no more,
Nor Pat slow pick the ice-bound piles of ore.

No more shall piston-heads on water pound
From steam condensed in pipes meandering round;
The supple belt shall to the pulley bend,
The oil-cup to the shaft its unguent send.

The furnace charged with coal and ore sans snow,
The gas-producer and the "cupalo—"
These now their functions normal shall perform,
As summer zephyrs keep their bottoms warm.

Thus while the sun these chiefest blessings sends,
It spares some heat to secondary ends;
The seed-time to the husbandman it grants,
His sisters and his cousins and his aunts.

The bursting buds of nature's gasogene,
Her sand-bath and the sprouting seeds within,
The exuding slag from maple saccharine,
The "spiegel" concentrating in the vine.

The flowers resplendent to the visual sense
As all the spectra of the elements,
And their reactions all, by Spring begun,
Shall be wash-heated by the August sun.

The verdant foliage in a blooming-train,
Where the Spring sun doth roll his beams again,
O'erspreads the fields wet down by tempering rain
From clouds hydraulic lifted from the main.

Anon the direct process nature takes,
And o'er and o'er her spongy products makes
Her open-hearth with blasts reverberates,
And casts in mineral molds her various shapes.

And now the cock doth sound his liquid lay;
The bulldog seize the ox hide in his play;
The bear within his silex cell shall dig,
And in the puddle roll the sow and pig.

So genial Spring doth all things put in gear;
Eccentric there, with fly-wheel action here.
Producers thrive, the merchant rolls in wealth;
And here's a ladle to our miners' health !

XV.

THE NOMENCLATURE OF IRON AND STEEL.

THE following paper, read by Mr. Holley, before the American Institute of Mining Engineers, at Cleveland, in October, 1875, was called forth by a series of articles on the same subject, contributed by Mr. H. M. Howe to the *Engineering and Mining Journal.* These articles may be found in the numbers of that journal for August 28th, September 4th, September 11th, and September 18th, 1875. As is well known to the earlier members of the Institute, the discussion thus inaugurated acquired an absorbing interest, and was continued in many papers and speeches (see *Transactions*, iv., 138, 328; v., 10, 309, 311, 355, 515), involving the appointment of an International Committee, and a lively debate over its report. The present purpose being, not to present both sides of the question, but to illustrate Mr. Holley's style in controversy, only the paper with which he opened it is given in this place.

WHAT IS STEEL?

The general usage of engineers, manufacturers, and merchants, is gradually, but surely, fixing the answer to this question. In every country, rails, boiler-plates, and machinery bars, whether hard or soft, are almost universally called steel, when they are made from *cast ingots.* Other names for the softer steels, such as "homogeneous metal," "Bessemer iron," "Martin iron," and the like, have failed to obtain general recognition.

The meaning of the term steel, before it was enlarged to cover newly developing varieties, has been traced, by a recent writer, down through Percy, Shakespeare and the Bible, in a most interesting manner, from an archæological point of view. Undoubtedly it did characterize hardness and other qualities imparted by carbon. It is within the memory of most of us, that all steels were tool-steels, and that the soft, structural varieties were introduced—varieties which harden but little, which bend cold, and which, in many physical properties, are akin rather to wrought-iron than to tool-steel.

But, since both the hard and the soft steels are made by the same processes, and have their great distinguishing structural feature in common, viz., homogeneity resulting from fluidity, it has come to pass, despite every other proposed nomenclature, that all the compounds of iron which have been cast in malleable masses, are called steel, the term wrought-iron being still confined to malleable iron made from pasty masses, and hence laminated in structure.

No inconvenience has been found, so far, in distinguishing between the more or less carburized products, in general, by the terms "high-steel," "low-steel," "tool-steel," etc., and, in particular, by prefixing the percentage of carbon and other ingredients, to the term steel. Steels which contain distinguishing ingredients other than carbon, are called "chrome-steel," "titanium-steel," and the like, just as variously compounded bronzes are called "phosphor-bronze," "aluminium-bronze," etc. Thus the combination of several words or symbols, and figures, may completely disclose the characters of the metal, in terms that are subject to no misunderstanding.

But inasmuch as several high metallurgical authorities and clever writers have of late proposed to disturb this natural and somewhat settled nomenclature, it seems important to consider the claims of the various classifications. I shall attempt, in this paper, to show that the existing classification is more scientific and more convenient than any other, and that those others which have been most prominently brought into public notice are radically defective.

The most common objection to the existing enlargement of the term "steel," so as to include the soft steels, is that it "pirates" a time-honored term, and applies it to a thing which is very different in many of its qualities. People who know nothing about steel, except as they use it in cutting instruments, or read about it in classic authors, say that it is brittle, hard, and resilient, and they are much shocked to hear that it may also be soft and ductile; just as any one who knows nothing about india-rubber, except in the form of springs, would be astonished to find that one change in manufacture turns it into water-proof clothing, and another, into hard crystalline instruments and jewelry. The terms "hard-rubber" and "soft-rubber," as used in technical literature and commerce, have not given rise to any serious misunderstandings. People who do not know that the great bulk of the material made by steel-processes, and having every ingredient and structural arrangement of the old steels, is, nevertheless, soft and ductile, and that it would be unsuitable for rails, plates, and the like, if it were not soft and ductile, are not to be considered authorities in this discussion, any more than a decorative artist in coal-tar would for that reason be an authority on aniline colors.

Where a material is gradually developed into new forms and qualities, there must be some general name to cover the various classes of metal; and whether it is better to enlarge the boundaries of the old one, or to arbitrarily make a new one, which new one must, from the nature of the case, merge into the old one, there being no natural dividing line, will be further considered throughout this paper. I venture to assert here that the charge, specially brought by the inventors of new definitions, against the existing use of the term "steel"—the charge of upsetting the recognized order of things—is wholly without foundation. Nobody *invented* the term "steel," as applied to the soft homogeneous products. There has been no natural or obvious place in the gradual gradation from hard to soft steels, to inject a new definition. As the possibilities of the crucible process were enlarged, the first soft product was hardly more than a variation from standard carburization; the early Bessemer and Martin steels, as produced in a successful commercial way, were hard; and, in fact, it is only quite recently that refractory materials have been adopted, by means of which the slowly receding standard of carbon in cheap steels has reached a tenth of one per cent. The same general name has been thus necessarily preserved for the products of the same process; but its boundaries have been enlarged to admit new varieties, and a gradual growth of subclassification. So that whatever the merits of any arbitrarily devised nomenclature may be, it must bear the demerit, whatever that is, of upsetting existing order and development.

A more common form of this objection is that a blacksmith would not recognize the soft metal as steel. "A blacksmith," it is said, "calls that steel which will harden and temper, and blacksmiths ought to know what steel is." There are various answers to this objection:

If familiarity with soft coking coal teaches a blacksmith how to burn highly carburized anthracite in his smithy, then his knowledge of highly carburized tool-steel ought to teach him what soft steel is. Hard coal is none the less coal because it does not respond, like soft coal, to a blacksmith's coking process, nor is soft steel any the less steel, because it does not respond, like tool-steel, to his hardening process. Anthracite coal was introduced long after bituminous coal was in general use, and the "pirating" of the time-

honored name "coal," to describe this material which is so different
in many of its qualities, has not led to any vast inconveniences. It
may be said that the parallel is incomplete, because both hard and
soft coals are really the same thing only changed in composition and
structure by natural processes, and that they both respond to the
practical test—the influences of heat and oxygen. So are hard and
soft steel the same thing, only changed in composition and structure
by natural laws; and so do they both respond to the influences of
heat and oxygen. Coals are, in fact, more diverse than steels in their
carburization, structure, and strength, and in their requirements of
treatment. If old nomenclature is to be held as a final criterion,
then the modern condensing steam-engine should be a " low-pressure
engine." The fact is, on the contrary, that it is as often " high-
pressure" as any non-condensing engine.

The determination of previously unknown intermediate forms and
functions is constantly enlarging the boundaries of all general classifications, and introducing subdivisions; hence the criterion of old
classifications is inadequate and worthless.

If hardening in water is the determining characteristic of steel,
who is to define " hardening ?" As a matter of fact, all products
of the crucible, Bessemer vessel, open-hearth furnace, and puddling
furnace, containing about a quarter of one per cent. of carbon, will
perceptibly harden in water, just in proportion to the carbon contained; and every one of them, however little carbon it contains,
will harden in some degree, as far as existing tests can determine.
" If the product will make a tool, it is steel," says the blacksmith.
What kind of a tool ?   Is an agricultural tool iron, and a cold-chisel
steel ; or does steel begin between cold-chisels and razors, and if so,
where ?   A water-hardened tool perfectly adapted to certain uses
may be made of Bessemer steel containing a half per cent. of carbon.
The same Bessemer ingot may make a good rail. If one-half the
ingot is steel, why is the other half iron ? The line must be so
defined that people will agree upon it. Does it lie between thirty
hundredths and thirty-one hundredths of carbon, or between ninety-
nine hundredths and one per cent.?   \

Obviously, no two men can agree on the amount of any hardening
element which may constitute steel. And if they could agree, it
would only be after a quantitative analysis had been made in all
close cases.

A recent writer in the *Engineering and Mining Journal* (August
28th to September 18th, 1875) makes a number of ingenious objec-

tions to the use of the word "steel" for all compounds of iron which are cast into malleable masses.

I. The term "steel" is said to be so vague that some words must be added to it to indicate the very dissimilar classes of steel, and the necessity for this explanation is deemed objectionable.

This objection is best answered by its author, who says, in the same column, that it is desirable to discriminate between the different classes of iron, and proposes the following brief and convenient nomenclature : "Cast steel, welded steel, homogeneous wrought-iron, homogeneous iron, welded wrought-iron, puddled steel, puddled iron, blistered steel, Bessemer steel, Bessemer wrought-iron, open-hearth wrought-iron, Uchatius steel, Uchatius wrought-iron, crucible steel, crucible homogeneous iron, etc." This classification, he says, shows whether the metal "has the properties given by carbon." Now, every one of these metals has properties given by carbon. The percentage of carbon must be mentioned anyhow ; so why not briefly say twenty-carbon steel or forty-carbon steel, and so denote both its carbon-value and its homogeneity ?

The objection, in its common form, is that the one word "steel" does not, without farther explanation, define the various classes of metal referred to. Neither do the words "oil," "coal," "rock," "brass," or great numbers of general names express the sub-classes referred to ; nor can any word or any simple sentence define them all. The objection holds equally against all possible general classifications ; and the only way to avoid it here is not to have any general classification in the iron-business.

II. The writer referred to objects to calling the soft homogeneous compounds "steel," because it is sometimes difficult to tell whether they were made from cast or from pasty masses. It is true that a well-worked puddled iron, rather high in carbon, and a low steel with about the same carbon, cannot be distinguished very easily by means of ordinary observation and simple tests.

I will in answer to this objection quote the same writer, who admits the impossibility of any perfectly adequate definition by saying that "classifications are based on important differences between the classes they separate, and not on the facility of distinguishing those classes sharply." Now there are important structural differences between puddled irons and cast steels which look alike—differences which will make themselves known after sufficient stress and wear ; but is the difference between two steels varying only by a hundredth of one per cent. of carbon, one of these "important differences," upon which an adequate classification may be based ?

The real answer to the objection, however, is this : Admitting for the sake of argument, that a considerable range of wrought-irons and low steels cannot be distinguished by the observation of their fracture, nor by bending, nor by the usual quick mechanical tests— people do not largely purchase iron and steel by sampling individual pieces, as they would cigars ; they purchase by specification of *manufacture*, for instance, the Pennsylvania Railroad Company specifies 0.35 carbon steel for its rails, meaning by "steel," that it shall be homogeneous or cast ; and from 0.30 to 0.40 carbon is recognized by makers and users generally as the proper percentage for rails. I note this fact here, to correct the writer whose objection I am quoting. In trying to explain away the fact that such rails are recognized as steel, he says : " Railway managers do not care much about the degree of carburization of rails said to be steel, provided they are absolutely weldless."

The practical usefulness of a name does not, therefore, lie so much in its discrimination between metals after they are made, as in specifying the method and quality of their manufacture. Rails, plates, bars, and iron and steel generally, are ordered on the understanding that they shall be fabricated by processes and of ingredients which are known to have yielded certain endurances to long-continued stress and wear. If purchasers do not themselves specify the ingredient and processes they want, they specify a name and grade of metal, such as " 0.60 carbon Martin steel," which refers the manufacturer to such ingredients and process ; so that the name completely meets the requirements of the case.

Supposing even that it should be, not difficult, but impossible to distinguish between certain grades of steel and wrought-iron by the most searching mechanical and chemical analyses—it can probably be determined in all cases from synthesis. Lawsuits arise as to the composition of material substances about which we have no synthetical record, such as a late suit about a certain paving-stone, based on the question as to whether it was trap-rock, or a sandstone altered by the trap-rock that flowed over it. But there are almost always sufficient records of manufacture to determine whether a metal has been cast or welded. This, however, is an extreme case ; perhaps it is one that could never occur. Destructive tests can, I believe, determine in every case whether a metal was cast or welded. In the great majority of cases the most simple tests can distinguish iron from steel, as at present defined, so that practically the existing classification is entirely adequate.

III. The writer we are quoting misinterprets the current definition of steel, as calling for a product which is *better* than wrought iron; and then he attacks the definition by saying: "Who would call cold-short Bessemer ingots, on the whole, superior to the best Swedish iron?" Now, as cold-short ingots are altogether *nil* until they have been reconstructed, we must admit that "a living dog is better than a dead lion." The bearings of his observation do not lie in its application.

IV. Another objection from the same source, that the current definition excludes certain classes of iron heretofore called steel, such as "blistered steel," "puddled steel," etc.,—is at first sight a valid one. But should not the same objection also be valid against the old and limited meaning of the term "steel?" Does the mere fact that "puddled steel," so called, is carburized more than the usual products of the puddling furnace, although less than tool-steels— does this mere fact of a little more carburization really define steel, according to the old restrictions of the term, despite the fact that the product, so called, has a totally different structure which renders it unfit for tools and for most other things that steel is used for? If then the term "puddled steel" should be excluded under the old classification, surely the classification now current must not be held responsible for its exclusion.

V. Again, classing homogeneous irons high in carbon and those low in carbon, under the same name—"steel"—is objected to, because the range of properties and uses due to variations in carbon, are much greater than those due to variations in homogeneity. Hence the classification, it is said, should be based on carbon and not on homogeneity. Every malleable iron, whatever it is called, contains carbon in some proportions, from a trace to the highest attainable solution; and since these combinations and the properties they impart, form a regular series of variations, running into each other, there can be no general carbon-classification, except by drawing an arbitrary line at some carbon-percentage. Now, 1st, as the irons for some distance on both sides of this line cannot be thus distinguished, except by minute analysis in every instance; 2d, since synthesis, which is the practical matter, cannot be based on a carbon specification alone, because it would omit the vital feature of homogeneity, upon which depend, for instance, the advantages of steel rails over iron rails; and 3d, since a classification based on homogeneity fur-

nishes means for distinguishing between products, while it also
affords, with the addition of the carbon-percentage, a perfect basis
for synthesis—for these reasons, I fail to see why a carbon-basis,
which must be arbitrary and revolutionary, could be useful or desirable. 4th. No less prominent an authority than Whitworth has
proposed to divide wrought-iron from steel at the point of twenty-
eight tons tensile strength. This classification is open to all the
objections we have urged against the equally unnatural and arbitrary carbon-classification. How would Mr. Whitworth like to
order gun-steel by this definition? Any steel-maker can produce a
metal so full of phosphorus and silicon that it will fly into pieces
under a sudden blow, and yet it will stand over twenty-eight tons
statical pull. A steel made with very small proportions of carbon
and manganese, to the almost entire exclusion of phosphorus and
silicon, would safely stand the severest blows, and stretch perhaps
thirty per cent. before breaking; but still it might barely reach
twenty-eight tons tensile strength. A puddled iron totally unfit for
guns, plates, and rails, might stand twenty-eight tons statical tension,
while the most pure and costly product of the crucible might fall under
it. The former, according to this classification, would be steel—the
latter wrought-iron. 5th. It has been stated that what is known as
"malleable iron" will confuse the existing classification. Seeing
that iron is remanufactured into malleable iron by a subsequent process, and not cast while in a fluid state into a malleable mass, as our
specification demands, this objection is absurd.

Without answering the more trivial objections, let us consider
what we are to do if we give up the existing classification.

a. The old and restricted term "steel" indicated certain properties, such as resilience, hardness, etc., in an indefinite degree, which
were imparted by that indefinite amount of carbon which gave hardening and tempering qualities. Now what shall we call the structural steels? We cannot call them wrought-iron, because they have
all the enumerated features, even hardening and tempering in a
gradually lessening degree, as carbon is diminished; and these features
are not characteristic of wrought-iron. Besides, wrought-iron totally
differs in the feature of homogeneity, and is rapidly going out of
use to make room for the homogeneous compound.

b. We may call these compounds "homogeneous iron," but we
must then add the percentage of carbon, and designate them as "ten
carbon homogeneous iron," up to say, "fifty carbon homogeneous
iron," for there is a vast range of grades and uses between these car-

burizations. Now, is it not easier to say "ten carbon steel" up to "one hundred and fifty carbon steel," thus including all the varieties of ingot-metal? And is the general public likely to agree that "homogeneous iron" means metals made from ingots, up to a certain arbitrary point of carbon, which nobody can determine without analysis, when beyond this point, ingot-metal, made in exactly the same way and by the same furnaces and processes, is "steel?" The inconvenience of such a nomenclature is illustrated by certain streets in London, which are called by one name up to a certain number, and by another name the rest of the way—a very inadequate illustration, for one can sometimes find a label on a street, without making a quantitative analysis.

VI. As the author referred to, whose objections I have endeavored to answer, has offered, not dogmatically, but for discussion, a new definition of steel, and has advocated its claims with much learning and ingenuity, I think we ought to examine it in some detail. He defines steel as "a compound or alloy of iron whose modulus of resilience can be rendered, by proper mechanical treatment, as great as that of a compound of 99.70 per cent. of iron with 0.30 of carbon can be by tempering." This is substantially an arbitrary division at the carbon-point, 0.30 per cent., of all malleable iron-compounds, whether made by wrought-iron processes or by steel processes. The chief reasons appear to be: 1st, That this division somewhat corresponds to the distinction made between wrought-iron and steel at a time when there were no soft steels; 2d, that the carbon-point, 0.30 per cent., is a "somewhat critical point in the curve representing the degrees to which differently carbonized varieties of iron possess the properties which are most affected by carbon;" 3d, that resilience being the chief attribute of steel, it should for this reason form a basis of classification.

1. It is difficult to understand why scientific men should be willing to sacrifice a natural classification, which has grown out of the necessities of the case, for one that is unnatural and arbitrary, on the ground that it embraces species which are unlike the earlier species, although of the same genus. It is hardly necessary to repeat what has been said again and again in the foregoing pages on this subject.

2. If the 0.30 carbon-point is a critical one, which I have not practically noticed, and which, for the purposes of this paper, need not be discussed, it is stated to be a point in a *curve*, which must be

arbitrarily placed, and not the point of an angle, which might distinguish homogeneous from welded masses.

3. As to resilience being the most important quality of steels, and for that reason the proper basis of classification, it is unnecessary to discuss this claim for resilience here. The question is whether the importance of a quality can make existence of that quality a definite basis of classification when it exists in both classes, gradually increasing in one and decreasing in the other, and being practically the same near the dividing line.

To sum up once more the answer to this and to all the cases of arbitrary classification: Exact definitions must be based on differences which always exist in every form and phase of the materials defined, and not on differences which, however great they may be in certain forms and phases of the materials, run together at one point, and there cease to be differences. If we divide steel from wrought-iron by an arbitrary line of percentage of any ingredient or of modification due to any ingredient, there must be some point at which the difference between steel and wrought-iron is infinitely small. If, however, we define steel as a compound made homogeneous by fusion, while wrought-iron, although the same in composition, is heterogeneous from welding, there is always, and at every grade of the respective materials, a large and radical difference. Casting fluid steel and welding pasty iron are always distinct in their characters and results; they do not at any point shade into each other.. The latter classification is therefore exact and complete.

4. A very serious objection to the proposed division is, that it occurs at a point about midway in the range of structural steels. It would be less inconvenient, though not less unscientific, if it divided the general class of structural steels from the more ordinary grades of tool-steels. Of a pair of locomotive-tires, both made by the same process, out of the same materials, and containing as nearly as practicable 0.30 carbon, one might be steel and the other wrought-iron ; or, a pair of locomotive-tires might both be steel, the one having been welded up from scrap, and the other drawn from a cast ingot ; or, one end of the same ingot might be steel, and the other end wrought-iron, the first having been hardened, and the other annealed. The convenience of such a nomenclature is not obvious at first sight.

The author of the proposed definition we are criticising, has so vividly portrayed the disastrous confusion which would arise from changing a settled nomenclature that I can hardly do better than quote him in this connection. He says : " It is a complete change in the meaning of a word that is in every man's mouth—a change in which the interests of the whole civilized world are affected, and in contemplating which, the convenience of all mankind is to be considered. . . . . . The natural conservatism of language would prolong this painful period of change, to a most unpleasant length. Moreover, the confusion would not end, till the change had been well established in the other languages of the civilized world. In meeting the word 'steel,' in specifications, contracts, and indeed all literature, whether technical or not, whether English or foreign, it would be necessary to determine whether it had been written before or after the change had been affected."

In conclusion, it seems hardly necessary to *again* sum up what has been chiefly a reiteration, in different forms, of answers to criticisms on the present enlarged use of the term "steel," and of the one great objection to the nomenclatures, that they are fatally indefinite.

The names of new materials and processes, like the laws of trade, are not fixed by the arbitrary edicts of philosophers, but they are gradually developed, to meet the general convenience.

XVI.

THE MANUFACTURE OF IRON AND STEEL.

THE following address was delivered by Mr. Holley at the opening of the Cleveland meeting, October, 1875, of the American Institute of Mining Engineers. As a specimen of comprehensive and acute criticism, it is not surpassed by any of his works. It recalls the trenchant comments which he visited in earlier days upon American railway practice. But the President of the Institute, speaking with the yet greater authority of a wide experience and a splendid fame, was far more certain of an appreciative hearing than had been the ambitious and comparatively unknown young engineer; and the tone of this address shows that he no longer needed to speak loudly in order to be heard. Mr. Holley entitled this address:

SOME PRESSING NEEDS OF OUR IRON AND STEEL MANUFACTURES.

In selecting for this occasion a subject necessarily connected with the iron and steel industries, I have thought that a review of these manufactures, with reference to some of their more pressing needs for improvement, will be more timely than a general or statistical paper. It is, I am aware, comparatively easy and positively useless, if not a little impertinent, for me to preach in general terms—to tell manufacturers that they should work more economically, and make better products, and utilize waste, and develop labor-saving machinery. I shall endeavor to confine my remarks to a few specific defects of practice and management, and to their equally specific and more or less developed remedies.

That serious defects exist; that they must be remedied; that the manufacture is indeed already on the verge of transition, will be generally admitted. But it cannot be revolutionized all at once, however desirable the technical results might be; for that would bankrupt the business at large. We cannot afford to pull down and rebuild all our blast-furnaces that do not make a ton of pig-iron with 25 cwt. of fuel; nor to replace all our hand-puddling furnaces with revolving ones, even if we could select the best revolver. Although the soft steels promise to supplant iron for most structural purposes, there is neither money nor present market to warrant all at once replacing our iron-works, or half of them, with steel-works.

Since, then, these manufactures can neither stand still nor be suddenly metamorphosed, their managers are saying to one another: "We must feel our way into larger development; we must work *gradually* into better practice; we must improve a little at a time." All very true—but some of us have been saying it so long and so complacently, that it is rather acquiring the flavor of a pretext for doing next to nothing at all.

Whatever economies may be made by little improvements of old tools and processes, the grand results are to come from thorough and radical changes, not necessarily *in all departments at once*, but sweeping when they are introduced. Putting a slightly less wire-drawing cut-off upon an old steam-engine, promoting a little better combustion in a heating-furnace, empirically experimenting with refractory materials and purifying compounds, are all more or less useful, but the "survival of the fittest" is to be decided on larger issues than these.

Among the more important and decided improvements demanded in this critical situation of affairs, are the following:

I. *Cheap Power.*—The cost of coal to drive the machinery of an average American Bessemer plant, when applied through engines requiring, as they generally do, 5 or 6 pounds of it per hour for one horse-power, averages about $1.50 per ton of ingots. Engine-builders are ready to guarantee a duty of $2\frac{1}{2}$ pounds per hour per horse-power, and it is perfectly well known that a large number of engines, stationary and marine, are running at from $2\frac{1}{4}$ to 3 pounds. The saving of one-half the steam-coal in a Bessemer works would pay for a quarter of the total labor in the manufacture of ingots, or for all the refractory materials employed, or for all the royalties. In some works it would not be less than $50,000 per year.

The average cost of coal required to drive a rail and blooming mill is nearly $1.50 per ton of rails. Although mill-engines have the advantage over blowing-engines, of high speed, and are often of good type, yet it is probable that taking all our steel-rail mills together, a third of this cost could be readily saved, and this saving would be an aggregate of $175,000 per year.

The economies effected by better steam-engines are not exceptional —they are of every-day occurrence. They have revolutionized the ocean-service and have completely changed the land-service, especially in New England, where fuel is dear. As one of many examples, I quote the Troy steel-rail mill-engine. This had a cylinder of 54 inches diameter by 3-foot stroke, and required the firing of 5 auxiliary boilers. A 44-inch Corliss cylinder was substituted, 9 per cent. of speed and 30 per cent. of work were added, and yet 3 boilers were thrown off, and the economy in fuel was about $25,000 per year.

It will not be questioned, I think, that regenerative furnaces will, gradually but inevitably, take the place of the ordinary heating, puddling and melting-furnaces, thus preventing the application of unspent furnace-heat to steam-generation. For this reason, economical boilers and engines are all the more important. When every rolling-mill and forge comes to burn coal for steam, the saving of a couple of pounds per hour per horse-power will be something enormous in the aggregate. Again, while many schemes for blast-furnace improvement are speculative, almost any expense to increase the economy of blowing-engines is warranted. Making uniform iron out of raw materials that cannot be uniform, requires reserve of power both in the temperature and the force and volume of blast. As coke and anthracite furnish barely gas enough under the best circumstances, combustion under boilers and the use of steam must be in the highest degree economical to meet the worst circumstances.

The blowing-engines of the country are usually very wasteful of steam, by reason of wire-drawing valve-gear, and especially of slow piston-speed. The latter is perhaps the greatest, and the least recognized, of all steam-engine defects. When steam enters the cylinder at say 75 pounds pressure and 320° temperature, a part of it is condensed into water before it can heat the walls of the cylinder to the same temperature. As the steam then expands from the point of cut-off down to the atmospheric pressure, its temperature falls from 320° to 212°, and as it falls, this water is reëvaporated by the heat in the walls of the cylinder, thus cooling them down to 212°. The steam thus formed passes off with the exhaust into the atmosphere, and is lost. At the next stroke, steam at 320°, impinging against walls at 212°, is condensed, as before, and so this perpetual waste goes on. Now, we can conceive of a piston moving so fast that the walls of the cylinder would not have time to be measurably cooled; and we can imagine a piston moving so slowly that nearly all the steam would be condensed. In practice, the indicator-card, which reveals the real work of the steam in the cylinder, shows a very slight loss from condensation in the high-speed engine, but it shows in engines moving at very slow speeds more heat wasted by condensation than there is utilized.

Many of the rolling-mill-engines of the country are of good type, but most of them will use 6 pounds of coal per horse-power, despite their comparatively high speed. What shall we say of mill-engines without cut-offs or condensation, where coal is dear, and where steam is made by firing under boilers?

Now, why does this general wastefulness of steam go on from year to year? Mill-managers have a ready answer. They want "a strong, simple engine, that will stand the rough attendance it gets in a mill, and that won't break down." The first reason is ridiculous; yet, you can find plenty of mill-engines with leaky pistons, out of line, and wasting their cost every year, to save a dollar a day more pay to an engine-driver. The second reason is perfectly sound. An engine may better waste a few thousand tons of coal, if it only makes a regular business of it, than to go to pieces without notice, in the middle of a time-contract. But the inference that an engine which is economical of steam, is, for that reason, more likely to break down, is totally without foundation. The commerce of the Atlantic Ocean is largely done by compound engines, which are just twice as "complicated" as single-cylinder-engines, and which run with $2\frac{1}{2}$ to 3 pounds of coal, and which are subject, at every pitch of the ship —many thousands of times every voyage—to the violent strains of the severe plunging in and out of water—strains which often shake the ship from stem to stern; but we rarely hear of these engines breaking down. I have recently taken time to examine, in detail, the working of eleven specimens of one of the most economical, highly-finished, and delicately-adjusted engines ever built—the Porter-Allen engine—and I find them notably free from breakdowns and abnormal wear. They had been running from $2\frac{1}{2}$ to 6 years, and in some cases the working parts had not been readjusted at all. It is true that some of the earlier Corliss mill-engines were too light, but this had nothing whatever to do with their economical steam-distribution. Probably there are more successful engines of this type than of any other.

The stability and durability of an engine is simply a question of good proportions, materials and workmanship. Of course, a piston that takes the boiler-pressure at the first opening of the valve, receives more force than one which gets only 60 or 70 per cent. of it, and that not till quarter-stroke, of which there are many examples.

13

But on the Porter-Allen demonstration, this force is required to start the very heavy reciprocating parts, which, in turn, give it out to the crank during the decrease of cylinder pressure by expansion, so that the strains on the crank-pin are not necessarily greater with good than with bad steam-admission. If the sudden impact of steam is hard on machinery, what should be the result of a 10-ton hammer-head, falling 6 or 8 feet upon an 80-ton anvil? And yet, steam-hammers are made to run for years. Some of the most economical valve-gears are not complex; the complex ones a boy can work by hand, so that they are not under dangerous strains, and rarely break down. Finally, the mill-engine, by means of the interposed fly-wheel, is relieved from all violent shocks, while the marine-engine has no such protection.

The objection, therefore, that engines are liable to breakdowns and delays, because they are economical of steam, will not hold. If the builders of such engines do not make them strong enough, the engineer of an iron or steel-works ought to know it beforehand, and to know what changes to specify. There are numerous examples of sturdy engines which he can study. I will venture the opinion that more breakdowns are caused by accepting the lowest bid for engines, than by all other causes combined.

There is a great temptation to save the heavy cost of radical change, by patching up old engines, attaching condensers, applying cut-off valves, enlarging cylinders to get more expansion, running faster by means of change of gearing or belts. All these things may save fuel, but do they not stand in the way of a greater economy, by constantly adding cost to the old engine, and so giving it a long lease of life? No man ever throws out an engine which he has just re-built, however bad it may be. The way to get the greatest possible profit out of an engine of bad type, is to melt it down in a cupola. The excuse is often made that a new engine cannot be afforded. One would suppose that an establishment which can afford to waste $20,000 a year in steam-coal, might afford to lay up half that sum every year to invest in better engines.

The blowing-engine presents a larger problem than mere perfection of valve gear. The air-piston should not run fast; the steam-piston must not run slow. Gearing a pair of small engines, making, say, 150 revolutions, to a large air-piston making 25, entirely overcomes the objectionable features of gearing, which only works harshly when the small wheel is driven. There is a possibility by this arrange-ment, of saving more steam than can be done even by compounding, which would cost about the same. Compound engines have certainly achieved a very great success for marine, pumping, blowing and other large scale uses. They, however, involve condensation, and either a large water-supply or extensive cooling-ponds, both of which are often very costly, and in some cases impracticable.

The use of the indicator—not the vile instrument made only to sell, but Elliott Bro's. Richards indicator—should be a matter of regular practice. I will venture to say that a high degree of steam-engine economy cannot be maintained without the regular application of the indicator, to show whether or not the condition and functions of the machine are normal and healthy. Beyond a few hundred dollars cost in preparation, the expense of taking cards once a week is absolutely nothing.

There are vast numbers of bad boilers, as any one will conclude who takes pains to observe the innumerable proportions of grate, combustion-chamber and heating-surface in use for the same kind of fuel. Fortunately for mill-owners, great improvements rarely require such sweeping changes in boilers as in engines. The changes, however, should be scientifically devised. Altering the style of a grate when its surface is insufficient, or increasing draft when combustion-room is too small, will not promote much economy. The employment of a commission of experts to ascertain the real nature of the defect would be a paying investment in a great many cases. The diseases of boilers and their setting are often obscure, and the diagnosis of a cheap engine-driver is not infallible. Perfect combustion, while boilers are being fired by hand, is probably impracticable, but bad combustion all the time is entirely unnecessary. Steam-induced air-jets sweeping over the surface of the fire, where there is heat enough to ignite the combustible mixture thus formed, is an effective and cheap arrangement. Mechanical firing, as done at Barrow and other works abroad, promotes almost continuously perfect combustion. I cannot dwell upon this subject; it would require a treatise by itself.

II. *Improved Heating Furnaces.*—The commercial importance of this subject is no less than that of the preceding. The coal-fired reverberatory furnace, however skilfully managed, must be wasteful of both fuel and metal. Much of the coal placed on the grate is lost through the grate; the very irregular volume of air passing unconsumed through the solid fuel is at one time insufficient to unite with the combustible gases over it, and at another time great and undistributed enough to go bodily over the bridge and consume the metal on the hearth; combustion cannot be perfected when firing is done by hand, without an excess of air which will waste the metal, so that the flame must always be smoky. The heat passing out of the furnace may be utilized under boilers, but not as economically as the same quantity of heat can be under coal-fired boilers, nor any better than waste heat can be utilized in regenerators.

Do iron-makers realize the enormous loss due to oxidation? An iron-rail mill making 40,000 tons of product, heating all the material twice, and oxidizing not less than 8 per cent. of it at each heat, would, at present prices, burn up more than $200,000 worth of iron in a year. Upon averaging a number of results, I find the saving in the oxidation of iron in regenerative gas-furnaces, as compared with coal-furnaces, to be over 3 per cent. In one case of first-rate practice with both furnaces, on small iron billets, it is 3.32 per cent.; in another case of good average practice on large iron piles, it is 4.45 per cent. In heating iron piles for plates, the waste in the ordinary furnace has been in some cases as high as 15 per cent., while in Siemens' furnaces, which have been substituted in the same works, it has been as low as 4 per cent. The smaller of these savings would amount, in the rail practice we are considering, to some $70,000 per year, which would pay for half the labor on rails, or it would pay above 20 per cent. on the cost of a rail-mill. The oxidation of steel is somewhat less in either furnace, because the required temperature is lower; but the proportion of loss appears to be about the same, so that the economy of the gas-furnace is also very important in heating steel.

The amounts of fuel used in gas-furnaces are surprisingly various in different works. They run from 350 to 650 pounds per ton of rail-piles and blooms, and steam-coal varies similarly. These figures indicate very bad working of furnaces in some cases; and the absence of all definite data in some other cases, as to steam and gas-fuel used, indicates, at least, that bad working may be going on without the knowledge of the management. The fuel for heating rail-piles and blooms in ordinary coal-furnaces also varies from 700 to 1200 pounds per ton, the differences not being wholly due to plant or management, but to quality of coal. With ordinarily bad boilers and engines, the saving of fuel, including steam-coal, by the use of the gas-furnace, varies from 5 to 25 per cent. A fair comparison of the two furnaces should be based on the best practice in both cases. If coal-furnaces lose heat enough up chimney to make steam for wasteful engines, no economy of fuel is attained by using economical ones. But as regenerative gas-furnaces, which make no steam, are necessary to the minimum oxidation of the metal heated, steam must be generated by firing under boilers, so that good engines in this case have an unlimited opportunity to save fuel. Thus the gas-furnace economizes, first, and chiefly, in oxidation; second, in fuel directly; third, in fuel indirectly; by giving economical engines a chance; and fourth, it also saves largely in quality of fuel, as cheap slack and small coal may, in most cases, be burned in gas-producers, but not in coal-furnaces. To these advantages must be added decreased loss of coal due to burning it in one concentrated nest of producers, rather than all over a rolling-mill, and the general convenience and economy of avoiding the handling and storage of coal in various parts of the works. Still another important advantage of the regenerative gas-furnace is the facility it affords for varying the chemical character of the flame, and more especially for maintaining the neutrality and perfect uniformity of the flame. This furnace seems essential to the production of the high temperatures required in the Martin steel process. The Siemens furnace has, within the last few years, been so highly perfected in its proportions and details, that its adaptation and working are no longer subject to any unusual risk or embarrassments.

The most imperfect feature of the gas-fuel system, at least in the English and American practice, is the gas-producer, which has not been materially improved for years. As it is simply a fire-box with a grate below, and is subject to variation in firing, in stirring, in the caking of the coal, in the holes in the fire through which carbonic acid gas and air may pass up into the chamber, and in air-admission, due to the irregular formation and removal of clinkers, the most careful attendance cannot insure the regular production of good gas, nor prevent the burning of some gas above the coal-bed. The Ponsard producer, on the continent, and in some experimental practice here, promises well. It dispenses with the grate, promotes uniformity of combustion, and furnishes gas to the furnace at a higher temperature. The gazogen of Mr. Tessié du Motay is said to be very successful abroad; fourteen are running at the works of M. de Wendel, in Lorraine. The same producer is employed for the production of illuminating gas at the new works in Buffalo, Troy, and New York. There are many other schemes for the improvement of gas-generation, which I cannot even refer to within the limits of this paper. It thus seems probable that a considerable

economy will be shortly added to the gas-furnace through the improvement of the producer.

There are cases in which the replacement of old furnaces by regenerative gas-furnaces may not be the most economical proceeding,
as in works situated but a few feet above water, and requiring costly
tanks for the whole producer-department, as well as for the regenerators, or else the raising of the whole floor and machinery. But
it by no means follows that the old furnaces should be left as they
are, in any works, whatever its circumstances. Among the various
improvements which may be added to existing furnaces, or at least
applied without the entire removal of the old plants, are those of
Mr. Sweet, of Syracuse, N. Y., and of Mr. Price, of Sunderland,
England. Mr. Sweet has already described his furnace and its
working in a paper before the Institute. It is certainly doing well
at his own establishment. The furnace of Mr. Price and its results
have been made the subject of a recent paper before the Iron and
Steel Institute, by Mr. Lowthian Bell, with which our members are
doubtless familiar. I will not, therefore, occupy your time with
their discussion, but will very briefly state the facts about the Price
furnace. Solid fuel is burned on a grate; but it is heated (the gases
being thus partially distilled), and the air for combustion is also
heated by the waste heat, before it enters the chimney. The inflow
of the gas thus produced, and of solid carbon, to the grate, and of
air under the grate, is thus uniform and at high temperature, so that
combustion is uniform and comparatively complete. It is thus, in
some sense, a regenerative furnace. The saving of fuel is about one-
third in puddling, and one-half in reheating iron, as compared with
the ordinary furnace; but the cost of steam-coal, otherwise completely or partially saved by means of boilers over the common
furnace, must be deducted from the above-mentioned economy. In
respect of fuel, the Price furnace would seem to be nearly the equal
of the gas-furnace, but it cannot compete with the latter in intensity
of temperature. Mr. Bell states that the character of the flame may
be controlled, and that a reducing flame may be maintained. There
must, therefore, be an important saving in oxidation. The pulver-
ized-fuel puddling-furnace of Mr. Crampton may also be mentioned.
There is no doubt as to the excellent working and economy of this
furnace in respect of fuel. Mr. Crampton tells me, however, that
his experiments do not, so far, warrant the belief that he can apply
pulverized fuel successfully to furnaces which do not have a readily

renewable oxide lining. The particles of coal blown into the furnace cut and flux brick fire-chambers.

An adequate discussion of so vast a subject as metallurgical furnaces could hardly be mapped out within the limits of a single paper. My object has been simply to draw the attention of iron and steel-makers to the great waste in fuel and the enormous waste in metals, which are constantly going on in most of our works—losses which draw a respectable dividend every year from the profits, and which may be prevented by thoroughly developed improvements. In view of such serious defects, and such ample and adequate remedies, it seems hardly worth while for our manufacturers to potter with trivial contrivances to add a little heat to the blast, and to check a little smoke, and to save a little fuel, and so eke out the wasteful life of a furnace-system which is radically bad.

III. *Refractory Materials.*—Improvements in this direction are probably the most important that can be considered, and they increase in importance as iron and steel processes become cheapened, and as products become more refined. A better blast-furnace-lining would be desirable; better heating-furnace-walls would be very valuable; better Bessemer vessel-linings would lead to great economy; better open-hearth furnace-roofs are absolutely essential to cheap Martin steel-manufacture, and better refractory materials generally must be provided, before the Siemens direct process, high-pressure furnaces, the cheap compounding of various metals with iron, and many other promising processes, can be carried on at all with commercial success. It is not too much to say that a better and cheaper fire-brick will be the key to the situation.

The cost of maintaining refractory linings and fixtures in the Bessemer process averages nearly $1 per ton of ingots, of which the cost of vessel-bottoms is about one-third. Merely doubling the life of bottoms would save some $6000 per year in a single works. As the life of a bottom frequently exceeds double the average life, it should not seem impossible to raise the average in this proportion. The cost of refractory materials and maintenance in the American Siemens Martin manufacture is not far from $5 per ton of ingots, while in Wales and in France it is about $1. This difference lies largely between bricks, which cost $50 to $60 per 1000 and stand 50 to 70 heats, here, and those which cost $18 to $20 and endure 200 to 2.0 heats, abroad. Merely equalling the foreign practice would of itself make a good business profit.

Our metal-manufacturers seem less serious and methodical in their

attempts at this than at any other improvement. They can copy the
steam-engine results of others, but the refractory-material problem
is all their own. That it is difficult cannot be denied; but the average attempts to solve it, which consist largely in travelling round
in a circle, are wholly inadequate, and unworthy of the profession.
Bricks, tuyeres, and fire-clay mixtures generally, have not been notably improved for a decade, except here and there, accidentally, by
the discovery of better clays, or, empirically, by trying all sorts of
mixtures hap-hazard. There have, of course, been some attempts at
scientific improvement. Mr. Snelus gives the following facts in his
late valuable paper before the Iron and Steel Institute : The presence of 2 or 3 per cent. of oxide of iron renders bricks unfit for
open-hearth furnace-roofs, and 1 per cent. of alkalies makes them
fusible at high temperatures. There are some apparent anomalies :
lime fluxes ordinary fire-bricks, but 1 per cent. of it used to bind
together pure silica·sand makes the most durable furnace-roofs
known. Alumina by itself, and in the proportion with silica of 30
to 38 per cent., as in some of the best clays, is extremely refractory,
but 3 per cent. of it in a silica brick will flux it at high temperatures. These facts explain the bewilderment and discouragement
that usually attend experimenting on a limited scale ; they also show
the necessity of combining the results of a vast number of experiments and analyses ; and they especially show that the direction of
these experiments should be in accordance with chemical probabilities. Merely varying mixtures, even with a knowledge of their con-
stituent parts, might never lead to improvement, if the laws of
chemical affinity were misunderstood or ignored.

The same conclusions may be drawn from another group of facts,
viz.: the very different behavior of refractory linings in contact
with different metals, slags, and ores, such as the cutting of sand
bottom in the pig-and-ore open-hearth process. The best furnace-
roof brick we know of—as nearly pure silica as possible—is the
worst brick to stand the manganese-reactions in a spiegel-cupola.
In the first case, it might endure 250 charges at an excessively high
temperature ; in the second, it would hardly stand 25 heats at a low
temperature.

In view of these complications, and of the obvious necessity for
prolonged and searching chemical work of the highest class, and for
a systematic series of experiments—also, in view of the extremely
limited progress which has been made by present methods, it really
seems that the time has come for a new departure. No individual

works can, or should, afford the cost of such an investigation, which would be for the general benefit. A clay-bank owner, or a brick-maker, can hardly be expected to do more than develop his own products, since complete experiments might prove them inferior. Why should not the iron and steel-makers of the country unite in carrying out a series of investigations which, if properly managed, would inevitably lead to important savings in the old processes, and to revolutionary economies in the new and developing ones? It has been objected to this kind of effort, that " what is everybody's business is nobody's," and that valuable results rarely follow mixing up the interests of independent companies. If these remarks are ever true, they do not apply to this case. In general, the history of associated effort is the history of civilization; and, in particular, the association of individuals, through governmental and private organizations, to test the strength of metals, to inspect boilers, to analyze ores, to collect facts, and to do numerous things of general and of special interest, is often the foundation of success in commerce and the arts. The proposed investigation would be entirely relieved from those uncertainties which embarrass combinations to sell products under certain limitations of price and quantity. It would be simply a search after physical facts, by a corps of experts in whose ability and integrity all parties would have confidence. However difficult the problem may be, the manner of its solution is plain, and the means of experiment are numerous.

Not to anticipate the proceedings of such a commission, but merely to observe how large and hopeful is the field for investigation, let us for a moment consider the situation and probabilities.

1. The comparative failure of previous attempts to improve refractory materials has been due to the varying presence of unknown elements. Three materials each make a good fire-brick; mixing the first with the second makes a better one; but mixing the first with the third makes an inferior one,—and the experimenter is all adrift. The more alumina, between 40 and 60 per cent., we mix with silica, the better the result; but, the more alumina, between 3 and 10 per cent., we mix with silica, the worse the result. Repeating apparently the same mixture sometimes gives different results. But there are no anomalies in nature; apparent contradictions are merely want of knowledge. Therefore, one important step in this inquiry would be to variously compound pure silica, alumina, and other substances, to imitate nature in their mixing, and then to try their refractory qualities, rather than to confine experiments to variable natural

mixtures. Even if we must use materials as we find them compounded in nature, it is better to know, first, exactly what we want, by means of artificial mixtures of pure materials, and then to come as near it as we can.

It is not certain, however, that we shall be confined to natural mixtures, just as we find them. The chief ingredients of that remarkable refractory material bauxite (which is somewhat rare and expensive), alumina and oxide of iron, can be obtained more free from other substances than bauxite is. Why cannot artificial bauxite be made? The intimacy of mixture, indeed, has much to do with the character of the product. We know that 5 per cent. of alumina, incorporated by nature with siliceous sand, gives more adhesiveness, both wet and glazed, than three times that amount as ordinarily mixed by hand. The artificial distribution of manganese ore with iron-ore in a furnace makes iron pigs and manganiferous slag, while, if the manganese-ore had been rubbed into the iron-ore by nature, the result would have been spiegeleisen. More than intimacy of mixture may be necessary in some cases. Dr. Sterry Hunt has suggested that the difference in the behavior of silica in furnaces may be somewhat due to the manner of its formation—either as an animal secretion, or as found in igneous rocks, or in rocks stratified from their débris. The shape of sand-grains has also much to do with their binding qualities, angular fragments being better than rounded ones. There is, however, a strong probability that refractory materials may be artificially compounded out of pure, or nearly pure, substances, more uniformly than they are compounded by nature. So that the synthetical method we are considering should be useful, not only in showing what we want, but in enabling us to produce it.

2. Other substances than silica and alumina are extremely refractory, indeed indestructible by mere heat, such as lime, magnesia, and carbon. The great difficulty has been to form them into compact bricks without adding such binding substances as will flux them and so impair their refractory qualities. But as pulverized silica—a rope of sand—is sufficiently held together by $1\frac{1}{2}$ per cent. of lime, to make the best heat-resisting brick we know of, the other incoherent refractories should offer a promising field for experiment.

We may learn much on this subject from the experience with crucibles. The two required qualities to be chiefly considered are, 1st, resistance to softening, or to melting by contact with neutral flame —by mere heat; 2d, resistance to the chemical action of metallic

oxides, slags, and free oxide.   Both these qualities are attained by
lining a crucible that will resist fire well with one that will resist
chemical action well.   For instance, a carbon crucible wastes more
rapidly than an earthen one in the fire, but, by lining an earthen
crucible with carbon, it perfectly resists the action of manganese
oxide, which would soon destroy any vessel containing much silica.
Carbon mixtures, however, are affected by oxygen in a surprisingly
small degree.   The endurance of graphite crucibles in a fire of coke
driven by a powerful blast, and graphite Bessemer tuyeres in contact with air-blast and oxide under intense heat, are examples.   The
use of carbon, even in the form of wood, is already on trial by Mr.
Siemens, and, in another form, by one of our members.

Lime is extremely refractory, never having been fused by mere
heat.   Crucibles cut from blocks of well-burned, slightly hydrated lime
are used to melt platinum.   Magnesia is also infusible at the highest
attainable temperatures.   Mr. Tessié du Motay, of Paris, has made
some remarkable magnesia bricks, of which I have specimens.   They
are, certainly, expensive, but they are said to resist not only heat
but the dissolving effect of manganese oxide and various corroding
slags.   There is a prospect of this manufacture being started in this
country.   Dr. Percy says of this material, in his new *Metallurgy*:
" Reverberatory furnaces for melting steel may be lined with a
paste formed of the prepared magnesia and water, which will un-
dergo the necessary drying and firing after the furnace is lighted,
without any special precautions being required."   He also gives
directions for preparing magnesia for use in crucibles and bricks.
This material is also used at Creusot in Bessemer vessel-linings.   The
only difficulty is to make it sufficiently coherent.

Still another requirement of Bessemer vessel-lining and revolving
open-hearth linings, is hardness, to resist the mechanical erosion of
the contained metal.   All the foregoing considerations, indeed, point
to the importance of making refractory materials hard and dense,
without running into the other extreme of increasing their liability
to crack and crumble on the exposed surfaces.   But even this tendency may be prevented by proper treatment.   Silica bricks require
slow heating.   In some Bessemer vessel-linings, made of natural
siliceous stones trimmed like bricks to make a wall, which are now
in successful use, the "spalling off" was permanently stopped by
glazing the wall at its first heat by blowing a charge of metal
within it.

3. It is, further, possible that refractory linings must, in many

cases, be made where they are used.   This is already the case with
the silica bricks we have mentioned, as at Landore and Terrenoire.
They are too tender to bear transportation, but are remarkably refractory when once set in a wall.   The apparatus for making them
is not very costly nor elaborate.   The quartz is crushed to fine sand,
wetted down with lime-cream ($1\frac{1}{2}$ to 2 per cent. of lime), and moulded
by hand into bricks.   These are dried and burned in kilns, containing 32,000 each, for seven days.   Bessemer vessel-linings are also
necessarily made where they are used, and it seems reasonable to
believe that the use of monolithic linings will become more general
in all kinds of furnaces.   It is very obvious that the cost of a furnace roof and sides, rammed up like a Bessemer vessel, dried out
and glazed, would be much less than that of bricks individually
moulded, pressed, dried, burned, trimmed, and set.   And if the material is equally good, the continuous wall should stand much longer,
because it has no joints, which are always the first parts to fail. .We
know that such linings in Bessemer vessels will outlast a dozen linings made of any fire-bricks yet tried.   The vessel-lining is, indeed,
a continuous arch of small radius, while the furnace roof is nearly
flat, and, consequently, more liable to fall by shrinkage due to variation of temperature.   But could not a flat arch be sustained by a
lathing of water-pipes, either in tension or in compression, which
would also cool it, and thus increase its endurance ?   This subject
will be further considered under the following head.

   4. It has been a matter of surprise to me, that the cooling of
refractory linings by means of water-jackets has not been developed
in heating and open-hearth furnaces, when it has been so remarkably
successful in blast furnaces, puddling furnaces, and, especially, in
Seller's and in Crampton's revolving puddlers.   I have seen the
fettling of the Crampton furnace purposely knocked off for more
than a square foot of the shell and front ring, during the boiling of
the metal.   The naked iron plates were thus exposed to the molten
iron and slag on one side, and to water on the other ; in a very few
moments the lining was completely renewed by the chilling action
of the jacket.   Some jacketed cupolas are running with success, but
where increased durability is most needed, as in Bessemer cupolas,
the attempt has not been carried out, although it has been frequently planned.

   If a firebox-sheet of naked iron, in immediate contact with a
white-hot anthracite-fire, will remain sound for years, it is probable
that it would be nearly indestructible under a four-inch coating of

fire-brick. Of course, the cooler the bricks are kept, the more heat will go into the water; but, as we can melt down a gas furnace-roof in an hour or two, there is, evidently, reserved power enough to furnish the necessary units of heat to the bath, while passing as many other units, at the same temperature, through the roof. Nor would water-jacketing, say, an open-hearth furnace, be comparatively wasteful. Even if a quarter more fuel were thus required, half a dollar per ton of ingots (at average rates of fuel) would pay for it, while even doubling the endurance of furnace-bricks would save four or five times this sum.

Water-jacketing should protect the bricks not only from destruction by mere heat, but from chemical dissolution, as this is generally a question of temperature.

The effects of heat are notably lessened as walls become thinner, so as to conduct heat more rapidly to the atmosphere. The thickness at which a lining will remain in the Crampton revolving furnace, for instance, is exactly regulated by the amount of cooling. Where the lining is knocked off, the fluid slag quickly sets up to a certain thickness, but beyond this thickness the water cannot chill it, and it cannot, therefore, accumulate. The amount of cooling by water can be perfectly regulated. The two features requiring experiment are, 1st, decreasing the water supply in such a regular manner, when the furnace has to be stopped, that the lining shall be neither overheated nor rapidly cooled; 2d, how to sustain very thin linings. Water-jacketing a furnace roof a foot thick would not do the maximum good until it was nearly burned out—and then it would fall in. As before mentioned, I believe that a roof composed of groups of wrought-iron water-pipes, either in tension for a drooping one, or in arch form for a convex one, each group having its separate water-connections, the whole to be filled in and rammed with a ganister mixture, like that of a Bessemer vessel, or with a natural or artificial bauxite, would be very durable. Certainly, there might be some very promising experimenting in this direction.

In concluding these observations on refractory linings, I must again call attention to the importance—the necessity, I believe—of putting this whole subject into the hands of a commission of chemists who are familiar with the requirements of metallurgical processes. It really ranks in importance with government-tests of metals and boilers; but, as governments can with difficulty be got to sustain experiments which seem to be of greater public interest, the expenses of refractory-material tests would have to be borne chiefly by

iron and steel-makers. They can well afford to do it; and some
important results can doubtless be determined without a very large
expenditure. But such a commission should be nothing if not
thorough. Immature conclusions would do more harm than good,
as they have done heretofore in iron and steel tests.

IV. *Enlarging the Range of Manufacture and Utilizing Waste
Products.*—The wrought-iron manufacture, by reason of its long
period of development, and the ease with which old and defective
materials and scrap can be reworked, has adapted its products, in a
remarkable degree, to every branch of construction, very largely
crowding out cast-iron from such important works as large columns
and long-span bridges. The following remarks will, therefore,
apply chiefly to the steel-manufacture, which has within it the elements of superseding wrought-iron in a still more remarkable degree.

The rapid adaptation of steel to large structural uses, other than
rails, in foreign countries, should be more seriously considered by
our steel-makers. For instance, three French men-of-war, built
mostly out of Bessemer and Martin steels, were so successfully constructed in 1873, that three more large ships were ordered in 1874,
to be built from the same materials. Notwithstanding the objections so strongly urged against steel ship-plates in England, partly
from the conservatism of "practical" men, and more largely from
their improper treatment of this material in heating, shaping and
applying it, the English government has recently ordered three
vessels to be built wholly of steel, and many private shipbuilders
are working in more or less of this better material. Several Bessemer works in England are running exclusively on a general merchant product, having a large range of grades and uses, and taking
the place of both crucible-steel and wrought-iron. The Continental
Works are turning, probably, a third of their Bessemer product, and
nearly all their Martin product, into other forms than rails. All
the late locomotives—many hundreds—on the London and North-
western Railway are built of Bessemer steel, excepting only the
wheels and necessary castings. Everywhere abroad Bessemer and
Martin steels are more and more satisfactorily employed for plates,
beams, channels and angles for ships, bridges, and other structures,
and for railway tuyeres and axles, general shafting, agricultural implements, and the multitudinous forms of machinery bars and forg-
ings. In the railway and machine-shops, the bridge-works and
shipyards of Europe, and of France especially, the method of treat-
ing steel, of heating and shaping it, and of building it successfully

into machinery and engineering structures, has become, what it must everywhere become before this material can be employed to the best advantage, a distinct and highly developed art.

We learn the following facts from Mr. Menelaus's recent address before the Iron and Steel Institute: Krupp, after successfully making thousands of steel cannon, large and small, is now fabricating 14-inch guns, of fifty-seven tons weight, to carry nine hundred-weight shot nine miles, and is about to build others of double this weight ; Mr. Reid, late Naval Constructor, believes that there will henceforth be no obstruction to the large development of steel for shipbuilding, and that the special arrangements required for steel shipbuilding present no real difficulties to a careful builder ; steel bridges of large span are successfully constructed in Holland, and elsewhere on the continent, and steel bridgebuilding in England is hampered chiefly by the Board of Trade regulation, that the material shall not be loaded above five tons in tension, and four tons in compression. The Bolton Bessemer Works have produced between nine and ten thousand tons of steel plates, three-fourths of which have been used in boilers. Mr. Adamson, the eminent engineer, has built between 600 and 700 boilers out of Bessemer steel, and uses no other material for this purpose.

What, on the contrary, is the condition of the manufacture at home? Out of a Bessemer product of some 350,000 tons per year, probably less than 6000 tons are used for other purposes than rails. Very few Bessemer works have any machinery for producing the various constructive shapes required, or any experience in making steel of high or low grades. Bessemer manufacturers are talking about reducing product, in the fear that rail orders will fall below the capacity of their works. Martin steel is now made in American works, regularly and successfully, of all grades, from springs down to boiler-plates, thus furnishing every constructive grade required. Engineers and machinists are generally asking for just such material as steel has proved to be abroad, but are yet hesitating about the use of steel, because our Bessemer manufacturers have not got much into the way of making other grades than rail steel, and Martin manufacturers have not, until quite recently, begun to adopt those improvements in plant and practice which will make steel sell cheaply, and, also, because our artisans have not, in most cases, made any study of the art of working steel, and are, therefore, afraid of it. Experts say that the use of wood, not only in ocean-vessels, but in river and lake-boats and barges, must soon give way to the

use of metal, as it has done abroad, and is beginning to do here; and
there are thousands of wooden bridges on our railways and high-
ways which must soon be replaced by metal ; so that for these two
large uses, not to speak of general machine-construction, there is
growing up a vast market for a better material than iron. Excellent pig, for the production of cheap steel, is obtainable in all parts
of the country, and ferro-manganese, upon which important qualities of constructive steel depend, is now cheap enough to warrant its
general use. In short, with every facility for making the product
so largely needed here and so largely used abroad, with the best
steel works in the world, and working organizations in them which
have increased product and decreased cost in a remarkable degree,
we are devoting more concentrated action to schemes for preventing
over-production, than we are to adapting grades and shapes of product to the various constructive uses, and to teaching artisans how
to heat, shape, and apply them.

The remedies for this state of things are various and obvious, and
are indicated in the foregoing statement of the case.

1. It is, undoubtedly, the policy of every Bessemer works, whether
it has the machinery for rolling merchant-steel or not, to make, from
time to time, experimental charges of high-quality steel, both hard and
soft, so as to learn the proper ingredients and treatment. As such
steel should be better than the average make, it can be disposed of for
rails, if it is of the right grade, and if of softer or harder grades, what
little would be made experimentally could be sold in one place or
another. There might be no immediate profit in it, but it would give
the maker knowledge of his resources, facts about cost, experience in
treatment, and confidence in his ability; in short, it would put him
in a position to take and execute orders. Steel-makers cannot expect a very brisk demand for materials which they do not know
whether they can make or not, nor what they will cost, or be like
when they are made. An equally great advantage of this experimental steel-making would be an opportunity to test the exact value
of their new products in tension, compression, and elasticity. I have
seen Bessemer plate made and tested at Terrenoire, out of common
Bessemer pig and ferro-manganese, which stretched 19 per cent.,
and had but 0.16 per cent. of carbon. Some crude Bessemer plate,
that I saw made and had analyzed, stood every mechanical test, and
had 0.21 carbon, 0.029 silicon, and 0.054 phosphorus, which shows
what may be done by selecting good materials. If our present pigs
are not sufficiently siliconized to blow hot, the addition of manga-

nese in the vessel, in the shape of good spiegel, will answer the same purpose, and help rather than harm the product. The reason why our Bessemer men do not make soft steels and those adapted to a larger range of uses, is because they do not try. But they must try and succeed, and know what they can guarantee, before they can get orders.

2. It is, also, obvious that Bessemer steel makers should increase their facilities for turning out the various *shapes* required, and for putting rail-ends and bloom-ends into marketable forms. Probably, a stand of billeting-rolls attached to the rail-train, a 14-inch train and direct engine and a 9-inch train belted from the same engine would best cover all up to rail-sizes. Judging from what the one or two works are doing, which have these facilities, one or the other of these small trains should very soon be kept busy on special steels and reworking rail-ends. Probably, the best means of re-rolling old steel rails and rail-ends is the very ingenious device of Edwards & Rogers, of Cleveland,—placing the grooves at an angle with the axes of the rolls. The whole rail-end can thus be utilized, while slitting off the flange and stem makes pieces that are too short for economical use. Re-rolling old steel rails and long ends into smaller rails is done successfully abroad. Even small pieces may be utilized better than by remelting, if they are of proper grade and soundness. The Troy Works, for instance, are making steel cut-nails, which will drive through an oak plank and clinch.

The large use of steel for structural purposes, however, will be in bars, which will require a 21 to 24-inch train, such as angles and small channels, I-beams and deck-beams, and large flats, rounds and squares. To change the rolls of a rail-train to fill orders, which would necessarily be small at first, for this kind of work, would be very expensive. But a couple of stands of rolls on the end of a rail-train could be changed as often as necessary, without interfering with the regular rail-production. The same stands would take the billeting-rolls before mentioned. It is probable that boiler-plates can be made cheaper and better in the long run by the Martin or by the crucible processes, but ship, bridge and tank-plates are successfully made by the Bessemer process. The existing blooming-trains can, I believe, be changed from time to time into excellent and fast-working plate-trains by the mere substitution of suitable rolls and fixtures. This feature was considered in the original design of the mill.

3. It will also be necessary for steel-makers to take the initiative

14

in practicing, perfecting and disseminating the new art of working
steel for structural purposes. The high degree of success which
attended the treatment and use of steel in the French ships referred
to, was due to an elaborate series of experiments, before and during
their construction, on the injury done to plates, bars and beams by
hardening, and the remedies—hardening, not by cooling only, but
by pressure, as by punching, shearing and cold hammering. It has
not, probably, occurred to many boiler-makers, who could do nothing with these grades of steel, and so have condemned steel altogether,
that shearing and locally hammering plates puts them in a condition
similar to that produced by cold-punching, which reduces the
strength of the parts above 20 per cent. These injuries, however,
are entirely local, although their effects, if not remedied, may become general. It has been demonstrated at the Barrow Works (as
set forth by the manager, Mr. Josiah T. Smith, in a late paper before the Institute of Civil Engineers), and most completely proved
by these French experiments, that the injury done to steels of rail-
grade and below, by cold-punching, is confined to the skin of the
hole ($\frac{4}{100}$ inch thick in the French test), and that this injury is only
hardening by pressure, which may be completely removed by tempering or annealing, or by reaming out this thin ring of hardened
metal. The same is true of shearing; the hardened skin may be removed by planing, or restored by annealing. The Bessemer and
Martin steels employed were not the softest grades; they had at
least 0.25 carbon, and stood 30 tons tensile strain. They were easily
hardened, and readily acquired dangerous internal strains; yet, they
were made so completely tractable by proper treatment, that they
did not fail in manufacture as often as iron did, and gave promise
of vastly longer endurance in service. With proper appliances,
these necessary additions to ordinary iron-working processes need
add but little to the cost of construction. There are still other features of the treatment of steel, especially the effects of heat, which
form an important feature of this new art. I will omit its further
consideration at this time, from the fact that we are to have a valuable paper, at another session, which will present this subject in
detail.

The adaptability of steel to constructive purposes was specially
shown in stamped work, such as pieces shaped like a low-crowned
hat, of which seven hundred were produced, without losing one,
while not one good piece could be stamped out of iron. The fact
that steel crystallizes less than iron, by heating without working, and

that steel plates have practically the same strength with and across the "grain," were also demonstrated. The conduct and result of these experiments have been published by M. Barba, and are republished by Van Nostrand in New York.

4. But the advantages of steel as a constructive material, and of its improved treatment, cannot be monopolized by the present steelmakers. There are many iron, merchant and rail-mills, now short of work, and likely to lose business every year, as steel is developed, which have nearly all the appliances for working up steel into shapes for implements and structural uses. Such works, abroad, and, to some extent, here, are insuring the utilization of all this machinery and the permanence of their business by working their way into the steel manufacture by means of the open-hearth furnace. The Siemens-Martin process has, in such cases, the advantage of working economically on a small scale. Where it is best carried out, the product is cheap enough to warrant its substitution for iron in a large number of uses, and it is particularly economical in that the raw material employed may be largely scrap-iron and steel, of good quality, if rich ferro-manganese is used instead of spiegeleisen. Martin steel rails, in successful service in France and Russia, contain 0.38 of phosphorus, neutralized by 0.75 to 1.00 of manganese, which replaces the usual carbon. Of carbon, there is but 0.12 per cent.

5. Finally, one of the most obvious and important methods by which steel-makers can promote, not only the adaptation of better materials to structural uses, but the increased use of iron and steel structures, is to aid in the government-tests of metals, which have recently been inaugurated. Many thousands of tons of iron are annually put into bridges and ship-frames, for instance, when bridge and shipbuilders know and admit that steel is stronger and probably better in every way; but they are afraid to use it because they do not know just what the strength, elasticity and ductility of the various grades are. In default of such knowledge, they will take no risks. Now, this is just the knowledge which this government commission will supply. If steel-makers will take hold of the matter heartily and make it their business to supply specimens of various grades, and to contribute in all ways to the thoroughness of the investigations, they will benefit themselves even more than they will serve the public. This commission intends to avoid the mistake which has made similar attempts, heretofore, of partial and limited value—the mistake of ascertaining only the physical qualities of

metals, the chemical constituents of which are practically unknown. They intend to determine what it is, not only in composition, but in treatment, that makes iron and steel good or bad, or well or ill-adapted to uses in building and in the arts. This information must be of the greatest value to both iron and steel-makers. And the final result must inevitably be, not only the adaptation of better materials to current uses, but the vastly increased employment of both iron and steel for new uses.

In conclusion, while it cannot be denied that the foregoing criticisms are applicable in more than a majority of cases, it would be not only ungracious, but unfair, to put forward their objects as representative and characteristic of American practice and management. Our economies, in some departments, have been remarkable, while our general steel works and rolling-mill practice is, on the whole, superior to that abroad. While the introduction of economical mill-engines is making slow but measurable headway here, the increasing use of reversing-engines in England is a step to the rear. The gas-furnace and the utilization of waste heat are quite as generally employed at home as in other countries.

In this connection, I cannot close these remarks without bearing testimony to the gallant manner in which the commercial promoters of our early Bessemer works poured out money and encouragement to us, who were so long floundering in the slough of technical uncertainties. I refer especially, but by no means exclusively, to the three establishments which first resisted the upper and nether mill-stones of inadequate professional knowledge and popular prejudice against steel,—the works at Troy, Cleveland, and Harrisburg. And it is with a feeling equally of pleasure and of justice that I also refer to the remarkable production of steel, and to the notable economies in its manufacture, which have been accomplished by the technical knowledge, the workfulness and the common-sense of the superintendents of our various steel-works. Let shareholders and directors, remembering the outcome of the troublous past, bear in mind what results the future should bring forth, when technical management of this quality is reinforced by that system of improvements which this paper has but too inadequately set forth.

XVII.

TECHNICAL EDUCATION.

As abundantly appears in the preceding pages from the testimony of numerous engineers, Mr. Holley felt a profound interest and exercised an important influence in the progress of technical education in this country. Not only his faithful work as an instructor, but numerous public expressions of his views, bear witness to his zeal and wisdom in this field. As one of the most impressive of these utterances, the following address delivered at Washington, D. C., February 22, 1876, before the American Institute of Mining Engineers, of which Mr. Holley was at that time President, is here reproduced. It is, at the same time, a good example of the eloquence and logical force with which he handled themes of this character.

THE INADEQUATE UNION OF ENGINEERING SCIENCE AND ART.

The application of scientific methods to the investigation of natural laws and to the conduct of the useful arts which are founded upon them, is year by year mitigating the asperity and enlarging the outcome of human endeavor. More notably, perhaps, are these the facts in that system of productive and constructive arts of which Engineering is the general name. In metallurgical engineering especially, within the period of our own recollection, how rapid has been the rate and how wide the scope of progress—the scientific discovery and mining of metalliferous veins; the economical separation and reduction of ores of every grade; the production and regulation of high temperatures; the varied improvements in the manufacture of iron, in saved heat and work, in uniformity and range of products; and most important of all, the creation and the utilization, to be counted by the million tons a year, of the cheap constructive steels !.

Wonderful as this range and degree of development may appear to the public eye, the close and thoughtful observer must nevertheless conclude that neither the profession nor the craft of engineering may congratulate themselves too complaisantly, but that they should rather acknowledge to each other the embarrassing incompleteness of the union between Engineering Science and Art.

There is a small but most truly scientific and most truly practical school of philosophers whom we may designate as original investigators—men who come close to nature, who search into first principles, and who follow in all things that scientific, and therefore fruitful, method by which the relations of matter and force are discovered, classified, and brought within the reach of practice. These wonderful men do not indeed create the laws of nature, as they sometimes almost seem to, but they go up into the trembling mountain and the thick darkness, and bring down the tables upon which they are written.

There is a large class of men whom we may designate as the schoolmen, a class popularly, and, to a great extent, correctly recognized as the scientific element of human progress; men who are learned in the researches and conclusions of others, and skilled in reasoning or speculating from these or from abstract data upon the certain or probable results of physical and chemical combinations.

And there is the great army of practicians, almost infinite in its degrees of quality, ranging from the mere human mechanism by which mind lays hold of matter and force, through all the grades of practical judgment and power—an indispensable link between nature's forces, as the philosopher thinks they are, and nature's materials, as the practician knows they are.

As the art precedes the science (however the science may afterwards revolutionize the art), let us first consider the matter from the artisan's—the "practical" man's standpoint. While every day's experience could teach him a more helpful lesson, it could hardly teach him one of greater general importance than that the men who speculate, from second-hand data, upon the probable results of combinations of forces and materials, are not the men who can best make these combinations in practice, who intuitively know all the concealed pitfalls, such as friction—that trick of nature, which, like the thousandth part of phosphorus, alters all the conditions of use in iron—nor are they the men who can determine the completeness of these combinations, or read the record of their results, as in the character of a flame, in the feeling of a refractory mixture, in the behavior of a metal under treatment; nor are they the men who, by familiarity with objects and phenomena, are best fitted to pursue that original investigation which is the foundation of even theoretical progress. The expert who delights to call himself "practical," is honestly

amazed at the attempts of experts of school-graduation who have not
been graduated in works, to solve the engineering problems of the
day. And from his stand-point there are numerous and conspicuous
illustrations. While metallurgists are still disputing over the nature
and sequence of reactions in combustion and reduction, the practical
iron-smelter has felt his way from the barbarous practice of a century
ago, to the vast and economical production of to-day. The attainment of powerful and sufficiently hot blast by means of waste heat,
the adaptation of shape and proportion of stack to different fuels and
ores, labor-saving appliances and arrangements—all these have grown
out of the constant handling, not of books, but of furnaces.

Proceeding upon a chemical knowledge little superior to that of
the average schoolboy, Bessemer developed his revolutionary process.
Not knowing for years that the combustion of silicon or of manganese
are the chief sources of the necessary heat, ignoring the fact that not
alone the reaction but the presence of manganese is a cause of soundness and malleability in steel, magnifying the hypothesis that silicon
should promote soundness, instructing his licensees to avoid all irons
containing above 0.02 per cent. of phosphorus, and sharing the ignorance of the whole metallurgical profession as to the sequence of reactions in the converter, and the probability of changing their character, Bessemer and his followers, during the first 15 years of their
practice, nevertheless brought this difficult art, which the metallurgical schools call a chemical art, to a high degree of commercial success, and this in the absence of any metallurgical change or chemical
improvement whatever, in the treatment of the metal. During all
this time, there was almost no literature of the Bessemer manufacture, and no instructor save that grim sphynx the converter, and the
well-nigh inscrutable process. It was a hand-to-hand fight, involving mechanical details, refractory linings, celerity of operations, reg-
ularity of melting and conversion, and economy of labor. With
every fact written in his book, the closeted scientist could no more
adequately prescribe the practical conditions of improvement, than
could the student in optics specify in words and formulæ the glory
of an Italian sunset.

Here is a cupola-furnace, an old and exceedingly simple device;
but one may know all the laws of combustion and fluxing that are
written in the encyclopædias, and yet fail to change its working at
will, or fail to detect the coming change, until by long familiarity
the phenomena reveal themselves as it were instinctively. One may
have learned every law of the reaction of oxides and fluxes upon a

refractory material, yet until his practiced hand and eye and ear can nicely detect its physical qualities and measure the results of new ingredients and temperatures, he may wander for years in a maze of uncertainties. Notwithstanding all our previous knowledge about the inevitable combustion of carbon and oxygen in the presence of heat enough to ignite them, the Siemens-Martin process, both in its calorific and in its metallurgical aspects, was as purely unpractical as the direct utilization of sun-heat is to-day, until after years of patient observation, not chiefly by scientists, but by men unacquainted with books, and knowing nothing at second-hand, innumerable small increments of improvement at last produced a sufficient temperature in a durable furnace.

In the development of machinery, the same history is repeated. The proportions of parts, in fact, the modern formulæ themselves are derived from the study of innumerable experiments. The adaptation of machinery can only be perfected by him who, as it were, enters into it, making it an incarnation of himself. This enlargement of a man's organism is most strikingly illustrated in the locomotive. Oliver Wendell Holmes has happily described this putting of his life into his "shell" boat, his every volition extending as perfectly into his oars as if his spinal cord ran down the centre of its keel, and the nerves of his arms tingled in the oar-blades. The thoughtful locomotive-driver is clothed upon, not with the mere machinery of a larger organism, but with all the attributes of a *power* superior to his own, except volition. Every faculty is stimulated and every sense exalted. An unusual sound amid the roaring exhaust and the clattering wheels, tells him instantly the place and degree of danger, as would a pain in his own flesh. The consciousness of a certain jarring of the foot-plate, a chattering of a valve stem, a halt in the exhaust, a peculiar smell of burning, a sudden pounding of the piston, an ominous wheeze of the blast, a hissing of a water-guage—warning him respectively of a broken spring-hanger, a cutting valve, a slipped eccentric, a hot journal, the priming of the boiler, high water, low water or failing steam—these sensations, as it were, of his outer body, become so intermingled with the sensations of his inner body, that this wheeled and fire-feeding man feels rather than perceives the varying stresses upon his mighty organism.

Mere familiarity with steam-engines is not, indeed, a *cause* of improved steam-engineering, but it is a *condition*. The mechanical laws of heat were not developed in an engine-house, yet without the mechanism which the knowledge derived *through this familiarity* has created and adapted, the study of heat would have been an ornamental rather than a useful pursuit. So in other departments: when one can feel the completion of a Bessemer "blow" without looking at the flame, or number the remaining minutes of a Martin steel charge from the bubbling of the bath, or foretell the changes in the working of a blast-furnace by watching the colors and structure of the slag, or note the carburization of steel by examining its fracture, or say what an ore will yield from its appearance and weight in the hand, or predict the lifetime of a machine by feeling its pulse; when one in any art can make a diagnosis by looking the patient in the face rather than by reading about similar cases in a book, then only may he hope to practically apply such improvements as theory may suggest, or to lead in those original investigations upon which successful theories shall be founded.

These are the conclusions of the "practical" man, and they are none the less true because they are not the whole truth. That they are too little considered by the schoolmen and the graduates of schools is also true, but, happily, less conspicuously so as the years advance.

The evil consequences of this mistake develop themselves in various ways. The recent graduates of schools do not, indeed, expect immediate positions of responsibility and authority, but they often demand them after too short a term of object-teaching. Perhaps the greatest advantage of their scientific training is that they can learn from objects and phenomena faster than can the mere workman, who, although full of the elements of new and useful conclusions, lacks, if I may so say, the scientific reagent which precipitates the rubbish and leaves a clear solution of the problem. It is, however, true—in the iron-manufacture, perhaps, especially true—that men of wide learning and of great mental dexterity, unless they have studied at least as many years in the works as they have in the school, do not successfully compete for the desirable places with the men that have come up from the ranks. Narrow, unsystematic, and fruitless of new results as his knowledge may be, he who has grown up steadily from the position even of puddler's helper, will be selected to take the manager's post in preference to him whose reputation is founded solely on the school.

Nor does this prove, as the schoolmen too often believe, that the owners and directors of metallurgical enterprises are always unappreciative of scientific culture. It rather proves that the lowest functions, as in the case of pure humanity, must first be considered—that the conditions of maintenance and regular working, which constant familiarity with objects and phenomena alone can provide, are earliest in order. Conservation first and improvement afterwards.

Another consideration in this connection, is that scientific aid appears to be more readily provided for the " practical " man, than practical aid for the " scientific " man. The trained scholar can the more readily adapt himself to the situation. He should suggest many more improvements than would ever crystallize in an equally good, but undisciplined mind. Yet his attempt, with mere scholastic aids, to carry these improvements out, might disorganize a whole establishment. As there must be one final authority, judgment founded on experience almost universally ranks the wider and more fruitful culture of the school. And if we ask those great masters whose experimental knowledge is as wide as their scientific culture, they will tell us, that as the inert and clumsy fly-wheel, that typical conservator, is more helpful to a steam-engine in the long run, than a valve-gear so highly organized that it seems to know what it ought to do—so in their own undertakings, plodding, practical economics must sit in judgment upon Theory and limit the reaches of Imagination.

Another evil growing out of the inadequate regard of mere schoolmen for practice, is the frequent failure of their works or their inability to complete them. Inventions and constructions designed after a scientific method and under the light of organized facts and detailed history as laid down in books, may fail simply in default of a practical knowledge of how far the capital at hand will reach, or what the means at hand will do, or what the materials at hand will stand, or what the labor and assistance at hand can be relied on to accomplish. A vast number of facts about the operation of forces in materials are so subtle, or so incompletely revealed or disentangled from groups of phenomena, that they cannot be defined in words, nor understood if they could be formulated. But after long familiarity with the general behavior of materials under stress, a practical expert can, by a process more like instinct than reason, judge how far and in what directions he may safely push his new combinations. Thus while the unschooled practician usually wastes his energies in unscientific methods and on impossible combinations, but generally carries into successful use his comparatively few well-founded attempts, the student merely of principles and abstract facts usually originates the ideas upon which progress is founded, and rarely clothes them with practical bodies. In this chasm between science and art, how much effort and treasure, and even life, are swallowed up year by year!

These are not theoretical considerations. The blast-furnace, the converter and the open-hearth have already been referred to; let us observe some other illustrations. A bridge-builder will tell us that few structures in his department of engineering fail by reason of mistakes in calculating the strain-sheet, but that the majority of failures arise from vibrations, buckling, rapid wear of important parts, shapes that weaken the material inequalities in the material, and similar causes which are not stated in books, which assume different aspects under every change of proportions and dimensions, and which can only be inferred by means of a long familiarity with the behavior of similar structures during varying periods of service, and with the processes by which materials and members are fabricated. The builder of a machine like a marine-engine, or a locomotive, or a roll-train, or a steam-hammer will tell us that, in designing new adaptations, after every stress that can be distinctly analyzed is provided for, mass to resist vibration, changes of shape to insure sound casting, and various modifications which cannot be formulated for the want of even approximately complete knowledge of their conditions, must still be supplied, simply by judgment founded on long observation of phenomena under similar conditions. And he will thus explain nine-tenths of the failures. Who can imagine the volume of a book, or of an author which should adequately teach the principles of construction as affected by the chiefest of all practical considerations— the economics of the foundry, the forge, and the machine-shop? With the tools and facilities at hand, what divisions of a particular structure, what shapes and sizes and methods of joining will be cheap as well as strong and efficient, in all the infinite forms of mechanism? Obtaining such facts from any other source than personal practice, would be like an oarsman studying a book to know when and how in the race he must husband his power, or like a wrestler looking out in a cyclopædia the probable feints of his antagonist.

The successful constructor will assure us that no possible training in the school nor any genius in invention can build economically without such a knowledge of the shop as the athlete has of the possibilities of muscular strength and agility.

These arts have been selected as examples, not because they chiefly depend on skill, but because they so largely involve the highest, formulated mathematical knowledge. How much more important,

then, is practical training in those departments where physical laws
are very incompletely understood and formulated.   How far short
of practical success will abstract science stop in sinking pneumatic
piles through wrecks and boulders, in tunneling rocks traversed by
subterranean streams and beds of quicksand, in cheaply applying
hoisting, ventilating, and draining machinery to mines where the
scene and conditions of operation are constantly shifting, in firmly
founding heavy and vibrating machinery on treacherous ground, in
handling and casting melted steel, in constructing refractory metallurgical vessels, in delivering bars red-hot and crooked in infinite
directions to a roll-train, in fabricating durable breech-loading cannon, in building boilers that shall provide for vaporization, circulation, separation, cleaning, and durability, in designing enginery
like the horse-shoe machine to shape metals, in proportioning gas-
furnaces, in submarine warfare, in aerial navigation, in machine-
tools, in traction-engines, in scaffolding and erection, in railway run-
ning-gear, in forming artificial stone under water, in permanent way,
in coal-cutting, in dredging-machinery, in moulding and casting, in
brick-machinery, in tube-drawing, in coal-burning, in pavements?
Limited or impossible as would be the progress of engineering arts
in the absence of that knowledge and those methods which are imparted in schools, delay and failure would hardly be less conspicuous
if the schoolmen should stay in the schools and thence attempt the
application of abstract science, or expect mere workmen to apply it
by hearkening to their directions.

I hope it may not seem that the dignity of abstract scientific investigation is undervalued by the utilizers of nature's powers and
materials, or that any considerations of profit obscure even in the
average commercial mind, the splendor of those achievements made
in the mere love of truth, with thought of neither commercial application nor pecuniary reward—achievements which distinguish such
names as Faraday, Bunsen, Leverrier, Mayer, Joule, Henry, Darwin,
and Tyndall.   Do not their successes rather encourage us, in our
lower sphere, to more persistently pursue the method of those great
discoverers—the original investigation of Nature's truths?   Not less
literally than in the poet's fancy,

> "To him who in the love of Nature holds
> Communion with her visible forms, she speaks
> A various language."

To the skilled artisan she reveals herself as truly, though not as widely, as to the philosopher. In the aphorism of Goethe,

"Mankind dwells in her and she in them.
With all men she plays a game for love,
And rejoices the more they win."

But the undervaluation of the study of objects and phenomena by schoolmen, is not the principal hindrance to the complete union of science and art. A greater obstacle is the combined misapprehension and ignorance on the part of a large class of "practical" men, of what they are pleased to call "theory," meaning by theory, something which is likely to be discordant with fact—or possibly with the interests of the craft. We can hardly complain that their objection is ill-grounded, in so far as it is grounded upon the practice of theoretical men, but the world has a right to complain of their narrowness of observation, of their stolid incomprehension of the results of science, of that pride of ignorance, of that bigotry, of that positive fear of the diffusion of knowledge, the normal condition of those who range only within the sphere of their own practice, and to whom analysis and generalization, in their business affairs, as well as in morals and politics, are an unknown thing. It is unfortunately true that a large number of managers in metallurgical enterprises—men who are deemed indispensable, and who, probably, *are* indispensable, in the average state of practical science, are thus not incorrectly characterized. Conscious of their power as conservators, ignorant of the elements of improvement, and not unfrequently jealous and blindly fearful for the interests of their craft, they sit triumphant on an eminence (the steady undermining of which they cannot observe), and sneer at the too frequently condescending magniloquence of recent graduates and bookmen. The best of this class are the workful and painstaking men who come up from the ranks—men who are plucky in emergencies and regulative of labor—men whose unconscious reasoning or intuition covers the ordinary exigencies, and who, perhaps for this very reason, never inform themselves outside of their own range of observation, nor observe in a methodical or fruitful manner.

There is also a class of practicians who do secretly and abstractly respect the labors of the scientific investigator, and are unwillingly governed, more or less, by his conclusions; but their minds are so barren of general facts and so untrained in the scientific methods of utilizing facts, and, hence, so distrustful of any ideas which reach beyond their own practice, that they, also, are impediments rather than helpers in the union of Science and Art.

It is often said, I am aware, that there is never any real antagonism between Science and Art, and that all men respect, even if they do not promote, the efforts of both scientists and practicians, to forward the useful arts. What then shall we say of that phase of trades-unionism, which not only tends to repress improvement but which, often, violently defeats the works of progressive thinkers, and some-times destroys their authors? Let us also observe an extreme, but not isolated, case of the executive treatment of science. Long before the professional career of most of us began, the Erie Railway Com-pany commenced a series of experiments in civil and mechanical engineering, sometimes elaborate, like those of Zerah Colburn on traction, and always useful; many of them incorporated with and improving the practice of the road for a quarter of a century. The voluminous drawings and records of this experimental practice, always preserved by the engineers of the road, were just beginning to be remembered by young and inquiring engineers, as a mine of professional information, when it was discovered—you will hardly believe me—that the engineer of the Erie road having been turned out, the whole of this priceless accumulation of reports and drawings was dragged off by the cartload to a paper mill, and destroyed by James Fisk, Jr. In reviewing the railway history of the country, many of you will remember that this act of vandalism has been by no means the worst blow which engineering has received from so-called " practical " men.

I have referred to these exceptional cases, merely to correct a modern idea that engineering progress, especially by scientific methods, is, as yet, the creature of popular favor. It is refreshing to turn from such considerations to the still exceptional but happily growing appreciation and helpful respect of practitioners and scientists for each other, as sometimes exemplified in the various departments of mining engineering. When we see recent graduates patiently leading the untrained, confused, but determined mind of the workman, pain-fully wrestling with hard names and occult processes, into methodical habits of thought and the rudiments of organized knowledge; when we see the grimy workman, not standing aloof for fear of his craft or of his trades-master, but dragging the recent graduate into mines and furnaces, and patiently teaching him how to recognize that matter, in mass and under mighty forces, which he had heretofore contemplated in cabinet specimens, and chiefly in ideas; when we see the commercial manager of metallurgical enterprises opening his works to the graduates of schools, and giving them a chance, not only to complete their education, but, by judicious application of their efforts, to earn a living, meanwhile; when we see such things, as happily we may, here and there in metallurgical works, we may assure ourselves that *one* way has been discovered to promote the union of Science and Art.

In the enlargement of this method of mutual respect and instruction, to a certain extent, lies the solution of the problem under consideration; but it is a complex method, only actively operative under several important conditions, such as:

1st. A *public opinion* among schoolmen that a course of object and phenomena-study in works is not to be reckoned a matter of mere business sequence, but a large and equal feature of that curriculum which is essential to a degree of professional graduation.

2d. A diffusion, among the class which we have termed the "practical" class, of a real appreciation of an organized system of information and of the scientific method of making this information useful to all classes of men, and noxious or unimportant to none; such a general explanation to that vast, preponderating class of workmen, and of foremen and managers who are foremen and managers simply because they have been efficient workmen, as will ever prevent their indiscriminate and contemptuous application of the term "theory" to whatever a schoolman proposes.

3d. An understanding among the owners, directors, and commercial managers of engineering enterprises, that it is not a matter of favor, but a matter of as much interest to themselves as to any class, that young men of suitable ability, and of suitable preliminary culture, however acquired, should have opportunity and encouragement to master the practical feature of technical education in works, not as mere apprentices, but under reasonable facilities for economy of time and completeness of research.

But these conditions do not largely exist, and are only growing with general civilization. They must be hastened and magnified by some better means than merely stating the case again and again, as some of us, I confess, are too fond of doing, perpetually repeating, in a manner more sentimental than efficient, that scientists should appreciate practice, and practicians should appreciate science, and capital should join the hands of science and practice, saying, "Bless you, my children," in the expectation that this will prove a fruitful union. Let us rather inquire if some new order of procedure in *technical education*, some revolutionary innovation, if need be, will not put the coming race of engineers on a plane which is lifted above the embarrassments from which we are slowly emerging.

1st. In order that the technical school should be in the highest degree useful, fruitful, and economical, it must instruct not *men* of good general education, but *artisans* of good general education. The art must precede the science. The man must first feel the necessity, and know the directions of a larger knowledge, and then he will master it through and through. Mark how rapidly the more capable and ambitious of practical men advance in knowledge derivable from books, as compared with the progress of bookmen either in books or in practice. Many men have acquired a more useful knowledge of chemistry, in the spare evenings of a year, than the average graduate has compassed during his whole course. These men realized that success was hanging on their better knowledge. Familiar with every changing look of objects and phenomena, they detected the constant play of the unknown forces which underlie them, and longed for a guide to their operation, as a mariner longs for a beacon light. Their practical familiarity and judgment at once revealed the importance of scientific facts and methods, promoted their acquisition and guided their application. Under what comparative facilities does the mere recitation-room student, or even the mere analyst of the hundred bottles, study applied chemistry? It is to these, a matter of routine duty, without a soul; they are neither stimulated nor directed by a previously created want. Beginning with theoretical and abstract knowledge, is no less an inverted process in the useful arts than in the fine arts—as it would be to take a course of Ruskin within brick walls, as preparatory to opening a studio, and then climbing the mountains to square nature with the book.

Undoubtedly, there may be extremes in any form of educational method. For a youth to begin the special business of technical education by any method, practical or otherwise, before he has acquired not only a common school education, but, at least, such a knowledge of polite literature and general science, including, of course, mathematics, as would fit him to enter one of the classical universities, should be strongly discouraged, for various reasons. It is useless to disguise the fact that the want, not of high scholarship, but of liberal and general education, is to-day the greatest of all the embarrassments which the majority of existing engineering experts and managers encounter. This statement cannot be deemed uncomplimentary to the class, seeing that they have risen to power despite the embarrassment. At the present day, the high-school systems founded by States and by private enterprise, bring such an education within the reach of every one; and it seems of the first importance to promote, if not almost to create, a public opinion that liberal and general culture is as high an element of success in engineering, as it is in any profession or calling.

But this is not all. Professional and business success are not, even in America, the chief end of life. All the social and political relations and even personal happiness are governed, not by the specialties, but by the balance of mental culture. What then shall we say of the policy of wealthy parents—not indeed general, but too frequent—of placing an uncultured boy in a technical school, and then in works and business, without giving him one chance to acquire a general and polite culture?

Many young men display a liking, and others a marked talent in some special direction. There is no danger that these will be crowded out of existence by the culture necessary to make a well-balanced mind; and the nearer the talent approaches genius, the less imminent will be any such danger.

The proposition then is, not that mere common school-boys shall go into works and then into technical schools, but that young men of more advanced general culture, when they do begin the business of technical education, shall apply to nature first and to the schoolmaster afterwards.

It may be urged in favor of beginning in the technical school rather than in the works, that mental capacity for the after acquisition and application of facts and principles, is thus developed. But mental training is not the product of the technical school alone. Habits of logical thinking and power of analysis and generalization may be acquired in any school. And a positive objection to beginning with the technical school, is that it cannot stop at logical methods and sciences which are essentially abstract. It also attempts to teach about objects and phenomena, the first knowledge of which, if it is to be broad and genuine, must come from the fountain-head.

These considerations may be farther illustrated by the course of the inexpert graduate, when he enters works as a matter of business or of study. We have seen that the practical man can, at least, keep the wheels running and the fires burning, and that when he is of a certain grade of ability and ambition, he will most rapidly acquire the scientific knowledge and culture which, joined to his practical

15

judgment, make him a master. The unpracticed graduate, however, can keep neither wheels turning nor fires burning—he has not even the capacity of a conservator. Nor can he for a long time recognize in the whirl and heat of full-sized practice, the course and movement of those forces about which his abstract knowledge may be profound. The youngest apprentices are more useful in an emergency. He must begin with the lowest manual processes, not indeed to become simply dexterous, but, as it were, to learn the alphabet of a new language. He has started in the middle of his course instead of at the beginning. He must go back before he can advance, while the practician goes straight on. The knowledge of the schoolman about physical science, however often he may have visited works and mines and engines, during school excursions, is essentially abstract; it no more stimulates desire and power of practical research, than the calculus creates a passion or a capacity for studying the actual work of steam in an engine, or the actual endurance of a truss in a bridge.

The disappointment of inexpert graduates at finding themselves so far from being experts, their inability ofttimes to pay for farther schooling, the necessity that they should now begin to earn money, as they had persuaded themselves they could so readily do upon graduation, discourage many from pursuing engineering, and what is worse, send many out into practice, who never do complete their technical education, but who, by the character of their work, lower the professional standard.

It can hardly be urged against the precedence of practical culture, that the student will get " out of practice" while he is in the school. He may indeed lose dexterity, but not the better fruits of experience. In fact, those who begin as practicians, almost instinctively keep up their intimacy with the current practice.

A most signal advantage of beginning technical education in the works, is that the mind is brought into early and intimate consideration of those great elements of success which cannot be imparted in any other way—the management of labor and the general principles of economy in construction, maintenance, and working. An early knowledge of these subjects moulds the whole character of subsequent education and practice. There seems to be no corresponding advantage in beginning with the technical school. The fundamental mathematics and general information on physical science may be acquired in the preliminary school.

There is little doubt that the managers of technical schools will favor this order of study. They want to graduate not half educated men, but experts. They desire of all qualifications in the student, that enthusiasm which can only spring from a well-defined want of specific knowledge.

2d. But the *order* of education is not the only desirable change. Whether before or after their course in the school, the hundreds of young men who are every year entering engineering pursuits, are wasting their time in bad methods of practical study, or if after the school course, they are more frequently doing bad work as engineers, when they should still be only students. While the teaching of general facts and principles and of scientific method is highly developed, there is no organized system for guiding students to direct knowledge of objects and phenomena. This statement requires two explanations; I. Apprenticeship is a school of skill in a specialty rather than a school of liberal art. It is intended for a class of men who propose to remain mere workmen, and not for the class who intend to improve and direct engineering enterprises. It imparts a degree of dexterity far beyond the requirements of the general expert, while it would hardly impart in a lifetime his required range of practical knowledge. II. A school of engineering practice, such as that of research in zoology which was established by Agassiz, at Penekeese Island, would be wholly impracticable, because it could be nothing less than a vast and successful establishment for construction and operation in nearly all the departments of engineering. If such a school were not commercially successful, and if its range were not comprehensive, it would be unsuitable and inadequate. Hardly two engineers acquire any part of their practical knowledge in the same curriculum. They pick it up as best they may, usually in a manner that is wasteful of time or damaging to the public.

Now, if there can be a *system* of instruction in the one school, there can be in the other. The same discipline and responsibility, the same guidance as to precedence of study, quality of evidence, and correctness of conclusion should hold good in both cases. To say otherwise would be to say that *all* knowledge should come from un- aided original research, and that every investigator should begin, not where a former investigator left off, but where he began. It, there- fore, appears that there can be a school of practical engineering, but that it cannot be mere apprenticeship in engineering practice, nor a system of engineering construction and operation maintained merely for the purposes of a school.

The only alternative is to establish organized schools in the various existing engineering works. At first, this idea would seem subversive of all discipline and economy, but I am assured, by experts in several branches of engineering, that such would not be the case. . Let us take, for example, a Bessemer works. A score of students under the discipline, as well as under the technical guidance of a master, could be distributed among its various departments, not only without detriment, but with some immediate advantage to the owner, for while receiving no pay, they would become skillful, at least as soon as the common laborers who form the usual reinforcement. Students should, of course, be expected not to work when and in what manner they might choose, but to do good and full work during specific hours. This responsibility, as workmen, would rapidly impart not only the knowledge sought in the works, but a desire for higher knowledge and culture.

These considerations are not merely theoretical. Several students at a time, subjected to no discipline, sometimes working hard, and sometimes not at all, may often be found in a Bessemer works, and I have yet to hear of their embarrassing the management in any way. The laborer has no cause for interference, as the students are not under pay, and whatever they accomplish is clear gain to three parties concerned—the owner, the student, and the operative. A large number of young men may be found studying in machine shops, and sometimes earning small pay, besides having opportunity to work in all departments.

The proposition is to enlarge and systematize the existing desultory study in works—to increase its usefulness to the student, and, at the same time, to make the granting of such facilities to students an object immediately as well as remotely, to the owners of works. To this end, the schoolmaster should be not only well read in the professional literature, but a practical expert who could take charge of the works himself, so that whilst best aiding the students, he could prevent their interference with the regular and economical operations. His functions would be, not those of an instructor, nor, to any great extent, of a clinical lecturer, but those of a disciplinarian. The students should acquire skill, in order that they might acquire judgment of skill, and original knowledge of materials and forces, and the master should see that they did acquire them all. He might do some service by stated examination and current criticism and suggestion, but his chief office would be to promote honest work, and to provide opportunity for work in all departments with reference to the economy of the student's time, and the owner's interests.

It should thus appear that these somewhat radical changes in the curriculum of engineering study—first, a hand-to-hand knowledge, acquired not desultorily, but by an organized system, and afterwards the investigation of abstract and general facts, and their relations, would largely economize the student's time, and better the quality of his knowledge. The novice is nearly as valuable a student in works as the graduate, but he is a vastly less apt scholar in the school. My own belief, founded on the study of many typical cases, is, that this order of procedure would produce a better class of experts in little more than half the time required by the reverse order; that it would always make *experts;* that it would discourage none from finishing an engineering education which would be complete in its parts, even if insufficient time were taken to fully develop it. A well-balanced culture will naturally grow in scope and in fruitfulness.

In this connection it seems proper to say a word about the royal road to learning, which a few ill-advised students attempt to pursue. I do not refer to their availing themselves of professional data and drawings on file in engineering offices, but I do refer to their asking engineers and managers to furnish them special reports on subjects regarding which their own observation would be vastly more useful to the applicants, and quite as convenient to the respondents—reports on the number and duties of workmen in each department, and the particulars of operation and relative cost, which can only be profitably investigated by a student, when not only the facts but the reasons are ferreted out by himself, rather than transmitted to the academic grove through the post office.

In conclusion, if it should appear, upon larger observation, to the profession in general, as it does appear to many of its members, that this want of coalescence, ranging from indifference to antagonism between its scientific and practical branches, is a real and substantial fact, a larger effort would, undoubtedly, be made to change a condition so damaging to the profession and to the public. This inappreciation of one department by the other is not unnatural—neither side has taken sufficient pains to observe what the other side has done. The mere scientist instinctively believes that the achievements of the profession are so far due to the deductions of scientists that all other causes fade into insignificance; and the practician knows that just as far as animal life is from the disembodied spirit, so far is utilization of nature from the formulæ of heat, chemical affinity, and mathematics itself.

The first step is to recognize the fact, and I beg engineers, especially those who, from their scholastic habits, see least of the every-day embarrassments which are encountered by the executive departments of the profession, to take into account, not only the pride of class power, which the artisan feels as keenly as the scientist, but those baser elements of disunion, ranging from trades-unionism to counting-room dictation in technical affairs.

Having recognized the grave and comprehensive character of the evil, the next step should be, not, I think, to attempt any violent alteration in the existing conduct of engineering by the men who are now in active service, but to change, if I may so say, the environment of the young men who are so soon to take our places, in order that their development may be larger, higher and in better balance. Two coöperative methods have been suggested—reversing the order of study, and organizing the practical school.

Whatever the course of improvement may be, it becomes us to leave some heritage of unity to the coming race. How shall we more fitly crown a century of engineering—a century in which our noble profession has risen from comparative potentiality to living energy. And as its force is multiplied by the general advance of science, it becomes the momentum which evermore shall actuate the enginery of civilization.

INDEX.

www.ingramcontent.com/pod-product-compliance
Lightning Source LLC
Chambersburg PA
CBHW030124030726
47498CB00007B/2543